THE CHRISTMAS CRACKER KILLER

THE
CHRISTMAS
CRACKER
KILLER

ALEXANDRA
BENEDICT

**SIMON &
SCHUSTER**

London · New York · Amsterdam/Antwerp · Sydney/Melbourne · Toronto · New Delhi

First published in Great Britain by Simon & Schuster UK Ltd, 2025

Copyright © Alexandra Benedict, 2025

The right of Alexandra Benedict to be identified as author of this work has been asserted in accordance with the Copyright, Designs and Patents Act, 1988.

1 3 5 7 9 10 8 6 4 2

Simon & Schuster UK Ltd, 1st Floor
222 Gray's Inn Road, London WC1X 8HB

Simon & Schuster Australia, Sydney
Simon & Schuster India, New Delhi

www.simonandschuster.co.uk
www.simonandschuster.com.au
www.simonandschuster.co.in

The authorised representative in the EEA is Simon & Schuster Netherlands BV, Herculesplein 96, 3584 AA Utrecht, Netherlands. info@simonandschuster.nl

Simon & Schuster strongly believes in freedom of expression and stands against censorship in all its forms. For more information, visit BooksBelong.com

A CIP catalogue record for this book is available from the British Library

Hardback ISBN: 978-1-3985-3221-2
eBook ISBN: 978-1-3985-3222-9
Audio ISBN: 978-1-3985-3223-6

Typeset by Palimpsest Book Production Ltd, Falkirk, Stirlingshire
Printed and Bound in the UK using 100% Renewable Electricity
at CPI Group (UK) Ltd

MIX
Paper | Supporting
responsible forestry
FSC
www.fsc.org
FSC® C013604

Dedicated to my agent, Diana Beaumont –
always on the Nice List

Puzzles and Games

Game 1 – PRIZE TIME!

At the top of each chapter, including the prologue and epilogue, is one letter from the title of a festive film – rearrange the letters and tag me on Bluesky @alexandra kbenedict.bsky.social or Instagram @a.k.benedict with the answer. The first person to give the correct answer from 12.01am, UK time, on the day of publication will win a prize hand chosen by me. Good luck!

Game 2

Find ten of Edie's (and my) favourite punk songs hidden in the text of the prologue and chapters 2, 4, 8, 12, 21 and 25.

(Hint: they're by X-Ray Spex, Buzzcocks, The Slits, Gang of Four, the Sex Pistols, The Damned, The Clash, Patti Smith, Siouxsie and the Banshees and Television.)

Game 3

Find anagrams of the following Christmas films nestled like baubles in chapters 2, 3, 7, 10, 12, 23, 28, 29 and 33:

1. *It's a Wonderful Life*
2. *Arthur Christmas*
3. *Santa Claus: The Movie*
4. *White Christmas*
5. *Scrooged*
6. *Violent Night*
7. *Last Christmas*
8. *The Holdovers*
9. *Bad Santa*
10. *The Polar Express*

Game 4

Ten of my favourite books and films set in hotels are resident in this book – can you find them in chapters 1, 3, 9, 13, 15, 17, 27 and the epilogue?

Game 5

Ten 'Ghost Stories for Christmas', from both the Seventies and the 2005–present television runs, haunt the text, lurking within the words. Can you bust them in chapters 3, 5, 9, 11, 14, 20, 22, 23 and 25?

The answers to Games 2 to 5 can be found at the back of the book!

Silent Night! Holy Night!
All is calm, all is bright
Round yon virgin mother and child!
Holy infant, so tender and mild,
Sleep in heavenly peace!
Sleep in heavenly peace!

From 'Silent Night', John Freeman Young's
1859 translation of 'Stille Nacht, heilige Nacht'

No man is an Iland, *intire of itself; every man is*
a peece of the Continent, *a part of the maine, if*
a Clod *be washed away by the* Sea, Europe *is the*
lesse, as well as if a Promontorie *were, as well as*
if a Mannor *of thy* friends *or of* thine owne *were;*
any mans death *diminishes* me, *because I am*
involved in Mankinde; *And therefore never send*
to know for whom the bell *tolls; It tolls for* thee.

From 'Devotions upon Emergent Occasions',
John Donne, 1624

List of characters

Staff at the Aster Castle Hotel

Tarn Bayard – head butler/head of housekeeping
Izzie Collier – waiting staff/housekeeping/chambermaid/
room service
Ryan Dreith – head chef
Swindon Marr – caretaker/boatman
Felicity Morecombe-Clark – owner
Ivan Morecombe-Clark – owner
Mara Morecombe-Clark – manager and front of house;
Felicity and Ivan's eldest daughter
Owain Spencer – butler/room service/waiting staff
Kimberley Unwin – sous chef/pastry chef

Guests at the Aster Castle Hotel

Celine Allard – travel influencer
Sean Brand-O'Sullivan – Detective Inspector in Dorset
Police; Riga's guest
Robert Cole-Mortelli – banker
George Delt – local mayor
Anna Malone – travel website owner
Riga Novack – prize winner

Edie O'Sullivan – crossword setter; Sean's great-aunt and adoptive mother; Riga's partner
Henry Palmer – travel critic, journalist and television personality
Lucy Palmer – retired civil servant and investor; Henry's wife

Prologue

December 21st

No nights were truly silent. Listen carefully and sound was always found. Right then, at three in the morning in a remote location, the killer could make out a far-off siren, a mourning owl, the keen of someone weeping. Loudest of all was the insistent tick of their grandmother's alarm clock. Each time the big hand stuttered past twelve, the brass bell at the top shivered, reminding them that time, like the lives they were about to take, was short.

The killer made a pot of strong tea and sat at the table by the window. It was the darkest day of the year, so dark that the window was a mirror reflecting what seemed a merry scene: homemade Christmas crackers in the process of being filled. Carefully chosen tiny gifts were added alongside the usual paper hats and snaps. Next to go in were the riddles, brimming with hints and significance.

Wrapping a blanket around their shoulders, the killer leafed through their notes, checking the details for the second time. Each guest had a dossier, for and against.

The crimes they'd committed, the lies they'd told; the good they'd done, the souls they'd consoled. Time to decide who went on which list.

The killer placed their riddles inside the cracker tubes. Each was for a specific guest, but they wouldn't get that – not to start with. The fortune fish were the last to go in, ready to flex and twist on the guests' palms. At first glance, they looked exactly like the usual ones, but the instructions differed:

Moving Tail – INNOCENT
Moving Head – GUILTY
Moving Head and Tail – HUNG JURY
Curling Sides – SCALES ARE BALANCED
Turns Over – IN DENIAL
Motionless – PASSIVE GUILT
Curling into a Ball – SENSIBLE UNDER THE
    CIRCUMSTANCES

The killer placed a fortune fish on their open hand. Both head and tail moved. At least they weren't in denial, unlike most of those due at Aster Castle Hotel. Unless they confessed, before Boxing Day was unboxed at least four would be dead, others doxxed. The killer would have fled, leaving nothing behind but truth and coal dust.

Unless they were stopped.

Their heart tolled in their ears and shivered in their chest at the thought of being caught. Bringing *her* to Holly Island was the biggest risk the killer had ever taken, and could bring about their downfall. But it had to be done. She was a liar. The old woman must face her past, or potential death: her fortune was in her hands.

The killer had seen to that.

One

December 24th – Christmas Eve

Edie O'Sullivan rested her head against the train window. Everything seemed idyllic, the start to a perfect Christmas. She'd slept surprisingly well in her Caledonian Sleeper cabin; was on a once-in-a-lifetime holiday with two of her favourite people; and had a stunning club lounge view of dawn-lit lochs and heather-faced mountains. Everything *was* idyllic, bar one thing: bruise-grey clouds were blooming on the skin of the sky.

'It's going to snow,' Edie said, in a tone that would more easily fit a death sentence.

'I hope so,' the waiter said as he placed their breakfast plates on the table. 'I've got a twenty-to-one bet on a white Christmas.'

'Well, I hope I'm wrong, and that the nimbostratus clouds nip off *without* shedding crystalline water.' Edie placed a napkin on her lap and nodded with approval at her smoked salmon and scrambled eggs. 'But I'm rarely mistaken.'

'Mum's not keen on snow,' Sean explained from the seat opposite as he tucked into pancakes. His usual breakfast before a shift as Detective Inspector involved protein powder and acai berries. Carbs were a rare treat.

The waiter's eyebrows raised the question before he asked it, looking from Edie to Sean: 'She's your *Mum*? But she's—' He wisely stopped right there, though it was clear what he meant. At eighty-something, Edie was statistically unlikely to be mother to Sean, in his thirties.

'It's a long story,' Sean said. 'Biologically, Mum's my great-aunt, but she adopted me when I was young.' He paused. 'My parents died in a car crash.'

'Oh,' the waiter said, glancing towards the bar, probably wondering when he could get back to work and out of the conversation. Or when he could have a drink to forget it.

Ninety-two-year-old Riga speared a sausage from her plate and presented it to her pug, Nicholas, who was snuffling under the table. 'That, and other traumatic events, took place over a stormy Christmas. Which is why my Edie loathes snow. Although she's less suspicious of Christmas these days.' Riga turned to Edie and kissed her on the lips.

'It's a love story,' Edie explained to the wide-eyed waiter, taking Riga's hand. 'We've been together two years.'

The waiter grinned, perhaps with relief at the swerve from death to devotion. 'There's hope for my gran, then. She's been a widow for twenty years.'

'Love is like losing the remote control,' Riga said, picking at the black pudding. 'Keep hunting and eventually you'll find the one whose buttons you press.'

'She's making it sound like she found me down the

back of the sofa!' Edie said to the waiter. 'We live next door. I'd advise your grandmother to check out her neighbours to see if any of them are hot. Saves on petrol.'

'I'll tell Gran that,' he replied, 'though I might wait till she's merry on sherry after Christmas dinner.' The waiter was still smiling as he headed back to the bar.

Riga was *partially* right about Edie's feelings for snow. It *did* have bad associations, but there was something else, too. Like glitter, snow made her wonder what was hidden beneath; just like Tippex, nothing *really* vanished. And though Edie's enmity for the festive season may have diminished, she remained suspicious.

Still, it *was* Christmas Eve. If the world couldn't be dressed like her, in Vivienne Westwood, Edie supposed it could be clothed in snow. Briefly.

As the train neared their stop, Sean went to fetch the luggage from their cabins.

'We made it without being murdered!' Riga was referring to last night's excited club lounge chatter about the infamous sleeper train murder on this very track a few Christmases ago.

'Ever the optimist,' Edie replied. 'Say that again when we're off the train.'

Sean appeared at the door just as the train approached Crianlarich station. He and Edie helped Riga into the vestibule where he'd placed all their luggage and Riga's wheelchair.

As they stepped onto the platform, snow started to fall.

'You were right,' Riga said as Nicholas bit at snowflakes. 'As usual.'

Edie was going to say that being correct didn't bring her any satisfaction, but it did, so she didn't.

'I hope our taxi shows up soon,' Sean said, dragging the cases into the little covered area. 'We don't want to be late for the ferryman.'

'Could you rephrase that?' Edie asked. 'Makes it sound like we're waiting for death.'

Riga gazed with serenity at the cloud-hatted mountains. 'We're always waiting for death,' she said.

In Oban, Edie, Sean and Riga sat in a café, looking out over the harbour through windows framed by red tinsel. Ship masts jostled and jousted. Not far across the wind-whipped sound, the Isle of Kerrera was being whited-out by snow.

Bruce Springsteen's take on 'Santa Claus is Coming to Town' rasped through the speakers.

'I hate this song,' Edie said, shuddering.

'I *love* it,' Sean replied.

'You know how *I* feel about Bruce.' Riga sighed as if recalling a secret Springsteen tryst which, given Riga's rich history, was entirely possible.

'It's not Springsteen I've got an issue with, it's *Santa*. Listen to him in this song, laughing like a maniac, the smug, beardy cu—' Edie caught Sean's raised eyebrows and eye gestures towards the approaching server, indicating that her vernacular wasn't workplace appropriate. 'Smug beardy *carbuncle* that he is. Why does *Santa* get to determine who's naughty and who's nice? What makes *him* the arbiter of our souls?'

The server stared at her, eyes shock-wide, making Edie realise that she may have been misunderstood.

'*Our souls*,' she enunciated. 'Although the other homophone works too. Anyway, I'll have a hot chocolate, please.'

'Same for me,' said Sean. 'All the trimmings, please, and a slice of that Dundee cake.'

'Cappuccino for me, please.' Riga turned from the server to Edie. '*And* he creeps into kids' bedrooms at night,' Riga backed Edie up, 'but instead of popping him on a wanted list, we celebrate him. The only saint around is right next to me.'

'Thank you,' Edie said.

'I meant Nicholas, and you know it,' Riga replied with a smile.

On the adjacent seat, Nicholas the pug blinked as if to acknowledge the compliment.

'Father Christmas is harmless,' Sean said. 'A heart-warming legend.'

'You put a very positive spin on the world for a police detective,' Edie replied.

Sean grinned. 'My cynicism has been locked in the station till next week. Until then, I've got a free, posh holiday with my wonderful family, and not one crime in sight. Thanks to Riga.'

'I'm just glad my competition obsession has paid off at last,' Riga replied.

Each month, Riga entered dozens of contests – some

online, but mainly in magazines. She'd won various prizes: an air fryer before they were *The One Show* fodder; a frisbee; a year's supply of Chewitts – but none compared with this two-night stay over Christmas at the only hotel, the only residence, on Holly Island. Originally, the prize had been for a couple and two children, but Riga had worked her considerable charm and snagged a huge two-bedroom suite: Edie and Riga in one room; Sean and his husband, Liam – who would be joining them on Christmas morning, along with their adopted children, Juniper and Rose – in the other.

As Edie looked towards the loaded sky, worries flurried. Snow was falling like down from a slashed pillow. The harbour was already iced in white.

'Maybe you should tell Liam to bring the kids tonight?' she suggested to Sean. 'In case it's too dangerous to travel tomorrow.' Edie pictured the kids opening their stockings in the suite with her on Christmas morning. For someone who'd loathed the festive season for so long, she was beginning to love its rituals. Some of them, anyway.

'They can't, I've told you,' Sean replied. 'Liam is staying at his parents' house in Glasgow overnight so they can see the kids on Christmas Day, too. The hotel owner agreed to send the boat to pick them up from here tomorrow morning and bring them to the island.'

'What if we get snowed in without them? What if they get snowed *out*?' Edie's heart was thumping too fast. Being separated from the kids for any length of time triggered old traumas.

'What if we stop worrying about things we can't affect?' Riga countered.

'I'm sure everything will be fine,' Sean added.

'Don't be too sure,' the server said, breezily, as she brought over a wodge of cake. 'This is only a skifter, the heavy stuff's coming later on. Latest weather report has got the snowstorm coming to the islands instead of inland, arriving late tonight.'

Panic surged. 'We could go to Liam's parents' for Christmas? Just in case we get cut off from the kids.' Life could change so quickly. Just under two years ago, after a long and heart-rending process, Liam and Sean had adopted Juniper, and then, six months later, her baby sister Rose. Now, Edie's grandchildren were essential to her life. She'd give up crosswords – her obsession as well as her vocation – jigsaws, *tea*, even, for those kids. Christmas without them was *not* an option.

'Please, love,' Riga said. 'It's my present to all of you. Besides, I've always wanted to come back here. My mum was working in a hotel in the Hebrides when she met my dad, then they moved to Poland, had me and came back in the Thirties. Some of my earliest memories are of Scotland. And, let's be honest, I'm marvellously old. I may never get up here again.'

Edie stroked the petal-thin skin of Riga's hand. 'Sorry. You know me, a lifetime of hyper-vigilance doesn't relent easily.'

'Don't forget that Christmas has been an ordeal for you,' Sean added, his voice soft. 'It's hard to let that go, but maybe see it for what is – part of the past.'

'I wish it were that easy,' Edie replied. 'I know logically that those events aren't intrinsically linked to Christmas, but it's as if my body goes into brace position as soon as tinsel slinks into Sainsbury's.'

'Juniper's counsellor told me about intergenerational trauma, especially in adoptive families. If not addressed, our reactions to adverse experiences can be passed down, and up, generations.'

Guilt pinned Edie to her seat. 'You think I could make things worse for Juniper by the way I act?'

Sean took Edie's hand. 'Mum, I'm just saying that we should all be aware of what we carry with us. Christmas is a time capsule that we open each year, like bringing heirlooms down from the attic. The past collides with the present, preventing us from looking to the future with clarity and openness.'

Edie thought of the Victorian glass baubles she'd inherited from her own grandmother. Kept in an egg box, they were beautiful and delicate. Most were now broken, with slivers that sliced at her skin. She couldn't discard them, yet she wouldn't want Juniper and Rose to be hurt by them.

She looked at Riga, her wonderful partner. Looking to the future was also part of Christmas. 'You're right, Sean. I'll do all I can to unpack the capsule carefully. For now, I intend to have a wonderful Christmas.' She was smiling but, whether from PTSD, habit or intuition, she still couldn't bury the conviction that something was about to go very, very wrong.

Two

Mara Morecombe-Clark was afraid of many things. Blood. The dark. Failure. Bad omens. Bananas. Lifts, though, were the worst. Lifts combined her fear of mirrors, Muzak and human intimacy in one confined space. *You're going to have to use it at some point,* Mara told herself, heartbeat ascending as she pressed for the elevator of the Aster Castle Hotel. *You're the manager, what if a guest has an emergency?*

As the lift came for her, lit numbers decreasing beneath a real holly wreath, something screeched from within its workings. She added 'WD40 lift' to her list of things to sort before the guests were due for the special Christmas opening in, she checked her watch, seventy-three minutes. While it was a 'soft launch', with only six suites occupied and no paying customers, when guests included local dignitaries, travel critics and influencers, the stakes were high. If she got this wrong, then the hotel's launch could have a very hard landing. And as her parents, Ivan and Felicity Morecombe-Clark, had put every penny of their retirement savings into buying the hotel, *they* were the ones who'd suffer.

But all *would* go well. It had to. Besides, she'd seen a

peacock butterfly in the dining room that morning. A good omen if ever there was one.

The lift's doors scraped open. Made in the nineteen twenties, it resembled an ornate brass birdcage surrounded by mirrors. Tchaikovsky's 'The Nutcracker' plinked from Bose speakers. Mara imagined being trapped inside, turning like a ballerina in a music box. Or, worse still, being stuck with other people, their eyeballs on her. Like being sealed in a tin of lychees.

Mara gripped her chest, reaching for breath as she turned away. She *would* learn to use the lift, just not today. And if she *had* to use the staircase, at least it was magnificent. Starting in the lobby, it corkscrewed around the twenty-five-foot Christmas tree, through the centre of the hotel, up to the top floor. The shallow, barely noticeable slow coil of an ascent left her feeling sick and yet always surprised to have reached the top. Some staircases swept; this one crept.

As she got to the top floor, she replayed the irate voice message from Ryan Dreith, Aster Castle's executive chef: 'Mara, mate, I'm in the gym and two spotlights above me are literally on the blink. They're fucking annoying. Sort it, would you? They're flashing like an Eighties entertainer.'

Always two tweets from cancellation, Ryan had been sacked from almost more restaurants than he'd cooked hot dinners in. When hiring, she'd had to weigh the PR benefits of having a controversial, Michelin-awarded chef against the likelihood of him storming out during a service. She'd decided against taking him on, but then the chef she *had* chosen pulled out with only a month to go to the launch. After being assured by Celine Allard – industry insider, friend and guest this week – that Dreith had calmed down, Mara had given him a temporary contract for this event, on the understanding that, if he behaved himself and performed well, he'd have a permanent role. He'd only been in the hotel for five days, though, and while she adored his food, she hated the man. No way was he was getting another contract.

Ryan was lying on the bench press when Mara approached the new glass wall of the gym. Arms shaking, face Santa-red, he strained to lift the barbell back onto the rack.

'That looked heavy,' Mara said when she joined him. 'Should you be doing that by yourself? Isn't there anyone who can spot you?' She knew, of course, that everyone else was frantically getting the hotel ready for the festive VIPs. Ryan, it seemed, was prioritising his pecs over their guests. Maybe he'd get the hint from classic passive aggression. 'Or perhaps they're all busy.'

'I'm ready. If they're not, that's on them.' Ryan swiped a towel right across his sweaty chest. 'It's not like there's a surplus of people here. I asked Owain if he wanted to join me, but he said he had to go on the boat with Swindon.'

Mara felt a shiver of panic and a stab of concern at the lack of staff. As a yet-to-become established business, it'd been hard to get temps over Christmas. They'd already been understaffed, and then this morning two housekeepers, a kitchen porter and a server had pulled out, citing illness. She was heading into the most important period of her career unprepared.

'I told him,' Ryan continued, 'that Swindon could cope without him, and my safety was at stake, but he wouldn't listen. Then I asked Kimberley, but she's busy getting the afternoon teas ready.' He shrugged. 'What can you do? You try to help people, and they throw your advice back in your face. And not just the younger ones. Tarn just rolled her eyes when I told her she'd be perfect as a spotter since she's as strong as me. I mean, she's not. Obvs. I was just being nice.'

The man was oblivious. Perhaps *aggressive* aggression was the only way to get through to him, but that wasn't very Mara. 'When you've finished here,' she said, 'we need your expertise. It's all hands on deck to get ready for the guests' arrival.'

'I know, which is why I told you about the electrics.' Ryan pointed to the ceiling. As if on cue, the lights flickered across the gym, as though the escalating wind outside was trying to blow out the bulbs.

Something shifted in Mara's peripheral vision. Izzie from housekeeping was in the corridor, staring with intensity through the glass at Ryan. Mara couldn't tell whether it was with passion or malevolence.

Just then, her phone rang, and Izzie scampered away, her head lowered towards the stack of pillows she was carrying.

'Everything all right, Swindon?' Mara answered the call. Swindon Marr was the hotel caretaker, and the only staff member insured to sail the hotel's small cruiser. He'd said he'd phone when he reached Oban.

'Depends on what you mean by all right. It was choppy

getting here, Miss Morecombe-Clark, I'm not gonna lie to you. Storm's come in early. The journey back could get tricky.'

Swindon had once rung in sick, apologising profusely for having 'a dicky tummy'. Mara had later found out that he'd been in hospital with severe gastritis, vomiting blood and passing out. If Swindon, a former fisherman and lifeboat volunteer, was describing the sea as 'choppy', things were serious.

Mara hurried down the corridor to the picture window that overlooked the island's tiny marina. The sky was storm grey. Waves crashed against the harbour wall. The holly bushes that had once covered the whole island and now formed a curtain wall to the castle were draped in snow. The pine trees on the castle lawns bent in the wind, bowing towards the sea.

'You're right,' Mara said. 'I've been too busy inside to realise what was going on outside.' She'd have to do better, *be* better. A good hotel manager should be able to see everything, be the overseer. The one beyond the storm clouds.

'Don't beat yourself up, Miss,' Swindon said. 'No harm done.'

It was a shame, though. She'd wanted guests to have a luxury trip to the island – room to relax, enjoying drinks, nibbles and stunning views of Lismore, Western Ardnamurchan and the Isles of Mull and Coll but, in this weather, drinks would be spilled, nibble bowls toppled and sights obscured.

'Right, Miss Morecombe-Clark. Better go, someone's

coming over,' Swindon continued. 'Looks like we've got our first guests. And one of them has a dog.' He hung up, leaving Mara's heart beating as fast as a puppy's. She didn't know what was making her more afraid, the incoming dog or the guests accompanying it to judge the hotel.

Time to pop to her room to get ready and bring down her big surprise. Mara looked towards the lift, then hurried back to the stairs. Above, the lights in the huge chandelier flickered. The storm was probably the cause, and it would soon pass, leaving the hotel in a winter wonderland – Insta ready. She hoped so, anyway.

Mara's room was in the staff quarters, in the basement. She'd chosen the smallest, dingiest room to show she was a team player, albeit the only one of the team who could hire and fire the others.

Turning on the big light, she sat cross-legged on her single bed, dabbing concealer on her rosacea and redoing her lipstick. Her face was ready to meet the public, even if she wasn't. Through the compact mirror she could see behind her to the wheelie bins outside her slit of a window. The bin lids were capped with two inches of snow, with the top layer constantly wind-whipped away.

The view in front of her was better: a dolls' house replica of the hotel. She'd commissioned it from a local craftsperson, and they'd ensured it was identical, right down to the annoying crack in the white plaster above the entrance that kept coming back no matter how many times they tried to cover it. Of course, the real castle was now smothered in snow. She'd have to take some of the fake snow scattered at the base of the real Christmas tree and add it to the dolls' house roof.

The interior was even more impressive. The staircase, the suspended clock in the lobby, the Art Deco reception desk, the rounded glass bay windows of the tower rooms . . . everything had been perfectly miniaturised, including the humans. Mara had commissioned doll versions of all the staff, and she loved placing her own mini-me in different situations – helping prep in the kitchen, standing at reception, lying in her bed when the real Mara hadn't had time for sleep.

Going over, Mara opened the front of the dolls' house. She blinked, pulse rising. The doll of her father should've been sitting in the bar where she'd left it reading a news-paper, a very large Scotch on the table next to it. Instead, he was lying on the floor of her parents' miniaturised bedroom. Her mother sat on the bed, wooden hands covering wooden face. A new doll in blue scrubs loomed above Dad with pretty vacant eyes. Its hands rested on a teeny gurney with an empty body bag on top. Dad's doll eyes were fixed on the ceiling.

Mara's own hand shook as she detached the tiny clip-board from the trolley. Fear squalled through her as she read what was printed on a small rectangular piece of paper:

Mr Ivan Morecombe-Clark, 66. Pronounced dead: 5.45pm, 25th December. Cause of death: unknown poison. No antidote was given.

Three

Below deck on the hotel's cruiser, Edie settled into a plush window seat between Riga and Sean. The lobster pots on the harbour wall bobbed in and out of view.

'This is amazing.' Sean was looking around the cabin in awe. He'd always liked boats. As a child, he'd sit all day with Edie on Weymouth beach and, instead of building sandcastles, he'd count the ferries and ships as they sailed by. And this was a *very* fancy boat. Mahogany-panelled walls, a corner bar of polished marble, optics that reflected the crystals on the chandelier – 'It's the coolest place I've ever been.'

'A little too cool,' Riga said, rubbing her arms. 'It's freezing.'

As she spoke, Swindon Marr was walking down the steps from the deck. With his yellow-smoked beard, skin the tinge of brown rockfish, Glasgow accent chaining words together like fish on a stringer and black waterproof cape down to his wellies, he so much embodied the Platonic ideal of an old-school fisherman that he could've been hired from an extras' agency. Less Batman, more Boatman.

He pressed one of the panels next to the bar, and a hidden cupboard opened. 'Sorry, my fault. I love the cold.

I think I'm part fish.' His eyes twinkled. 'I'll turn up the heating but till it warms up, try these.' Taking several folded blankets out, he brought them over and gave one each to Riga, Edie and Sean.

Edie flounced her blanket over Riga's lap. It was light blue and black with a white overlay. 'Which tartan is this?' she asked.

'Clark Ancient,' Swindon replied. 'Felicity, one of the owners, is from the Clark clan.'

'It's so soft,' Riga said with surprise as she stroked the throw.

'Mara, the manager, calls it "happy cashmere",' Swindon explained. 'Handmade in the Highlands for the hotel, from Black Isle sheep's wool. I told her guests will happily stuff them in their suitcases, but she just said I think too much *about* people and not enough *of* them. I said talk to me when *you're* in your late seventies.'

'Ha! You're still a baby!' Riga said.

Swindon inclined his head. 'I suppose one is always a baby to someone, no matter how old one gets.'

'When you get to your nineties, you'll be thinking the best of people,' Riga said.

'Let's hope they give me cause to do so,' Swindon replied, staring intently out to sea.

Above their heads, something was dragged across the deck.

'You all right there, laddie?' Swindon called up.

Owain, the young man in his twenties who'd helped them onto the boat, appeared at the hatch at the top of the stairs. 'I'm securing the luggage in the cockpit. The tarpaulin keeps billowing, and I don't want the suitcases getting wet.'

Before Swindon could answer, slow footsteps rang on the marina's metal walkway and then stopped by the boat. 'If you'll excuse me, that's either another guest or the signalman,' he said, jumping up and heading for the steps onto the deck.

'I like him,' Riga said. Nicholas the pug watched Swindon go up top and whined. 'Nicholas likes him, too. And we all know what a good judge of character he is.' She based this assessment on the time that Nicholas barked at a postman who turned out to be stealing parcels. The fact that he barked at most people didn't matter.

Brown-brogued feet and cherry-red-corduroyed legs started down the ladder. The man to whom they belonged slipped on the bottom step and lurched for the coat hooks on the wall. 'Nearly went arse over tit and I'm not even pissed!' he said, his cheeks as flushed as his trousers.

'Please watch your step,' Swindon said, ticking something, presumably guest names, off a list on the wall.

'It's Henry Palmer,' Riga whispered. 'Off the telly.'

Edie didn't recognise his face, but knew the name. Henry Palmer was a travel writer and journalist in his late sixties whose articles appeared in the same papers as her puzzles.

'Tell them, Lucy,' Henry said, with a broad smile that took in the whole room. Edie could see how he had a career in telly. 'Tell them I haven't touched a drop!'

A woman appeared at his shoulder. She was taller than him and had the look of someone who used bronzer to appear sun-kissed but never left the shade. Her dress (Monsoon, Edie thought) floated around her as if it carried the wind beneath its voluminous skirting. She took his arm in hers and patted it. 'I can vouch that Henry, my dear husband, hasn't so much as sipped an alcoholic beverage.' She paused, head high, eyes twinkling. 'Since breakfast.'

Edie hoped this blustery small talk would disperse with the storm once they'd all got to know each other. If she *had* to be around strangers at Christmas, or any time, let them be fascinating.

'I'm Edie,' she said. 'And this is my partner, Riga, and my son, Sean. His husband and kids will be arriving tomorrow.'

'Splendid!' Henry said. 'And what brings you on this trip? Are you critics, too?'

'I won a competition,' Riga said, with pride. 'Oh, and I'm sorry for remaining seated. I'd stand to greet you properly, but my sea legs have yet to develop.'

Henry sat on a long, squashy sofa made of soft brown leather that was fixed to the back wall. It looked like he was being swallowed by a massive Medjool date. 'Completely understand. As you saw, I'm not that steady myself. Interesting you mention "sea legs". I watched a documentary on axolotls the other night. *Amazing* creatures. Did you know, they can share organs with each other?'

'What's that got to do with sea legs, darling?' Lucy asked, with the patience of someone used to guiding their spouse back on topic.

'Ah yes! Ta, love. I'm a scatterbrained old codger so

she must keep me on track. Axolotls are aquatic creatures who aren't born with sea legs but *grow* them as they mature. They can also regenerate any limbs that are bitten off by cannibalistic siblings.'

'I thought you said we wouldn't mention your family this Christmas, Henry, darling,' Lucy said.

Henry barked with laughter and slapped his ham hock of a thigh.

'I like *her*, too,' Riga whispered. 'And if he's this pissed already, there'll be drama before bedtime. How marvellous.'

'Be careful what you wish for,' Edie replied.

More footsteps outside, swift and soft this time. A long-limbed woman in her mid-thirties or so scampered down the stairs. Emerging from a long dark bob, her cheekbones were as sharp as the creases on her wide-legged trousers. She wore a black-and-white-striped turtleneck jumper, with a bow that matched her ladybird-red lipstick. She looked like a chic and quirky burglar. Or a mime who'd fallen on good times.

Lucy Palmer, though, was regarding the new arrival as if she were a bug under a microscope, before glancing at her husband, her eyes narrowed. Henry, maybe, had an eye for the ladies. Perhaps he liked to share other organs, too.

'I'm Lucy,' she said, striding over and shaking hands with the younger woman. 'This is my husband, Henry; and over here we have Edie, Riga and Sean.'

'I'm Anna,' the other woman replied. 'And I absolutely loathe introductions, so I'll get this over with quickly – I'm in the travel biz. I recently sold my online agency, and now

I'm setting up an aggregate of romantic destination breaks. Boutique places that are both saucy and luxurious – you know, if you're looking for Jamaica Inn with a touch more sin, or a little death in Venice. *Yes*, I'm thinking of including Holly Island on my list and they're bribing me with this free trip; *yes*, I'm travelling alone; and *no*, I'm not lonely – I find constant company exhausting and I always travel with a vibrator.' She smiled widely and her eyes sparked with intelligence.

'I like *her*,' Edie whispered. Riga nodded vigorously.

Henry roared with laughter and clapped. 'Quite right!'

Lucy, though, took a step back and wiped her hand on her dress.

'Can I get anyone a thermos of tea, coffee, hot chocolate or mulled wine while we wait for the remaining guests?' Swindon asked as he followed Anna down the stairs. 'With or without a jolt of brandy. I was gonna serve you champagne in flutes but, in this storm, they'd be smashed on the floor before you were.'

'Excellent plan!' Henry said. 'Never mind the flutes, we're on a boat. Tankards and thermoses all the way. I'll have coffee with two jiggers of brandy, please. Same for you, love?'

Lucy nodded, still watching Anna, who'd settled on the banquette on the other side of the cabin.

'Nothing for me, thanks.' Edie would have a proper cup of tea when they got to their room. She'd already sent an email to the hotel explaining that she'd bring her own tea preparations. In her suitcase she'd packed a canister of her own blend of loose-leaf, her trusted tea pot, bone china teacups and, most importantly, her own kettle. She'd heard what people did in hotel kettles.

Swindon took everyone's order then disappeared into the tiny galley at the back of the cabin, singing Chris Rea's 'Driving Home for Christmas' but replacing the mode of travel with 'Sailing'. It made Riga smile, which was all Edie really wanted.

A set of heavy footsteps clanged down the walkway, accompanied by a low, rolling laugh. 'Anyone on board?' a voice boomed from the deck, somehow smuggling a chuckle in every word. 'Is this the boat to Holly Island?'

Swindon hurried out of the galley and yelled up the steps. 'Owain? We have another guest!' When there was no reply, he climbed up the stairs, muttering.

After a pause in which luggage was stowed and laughs dispensed, a large, middle-aged man in a Homberg descended slowly into the cabin, gripping the banister on each side. He was still laughing, unnervingly, at nothing. As he bent to check his footing, his hat fell to the floor, revealing a hair-free head.

'I'm George Delt,' he announced.

'And why are you here?' Lucy asked.

'Well, isn't that a philosophical question to be asked before noon!' he replied, in a rumbling Borders accent. 'Why are we here indeed? I like to think it's to bring joy and comfort to as many humans as possible.' As his shoulders shook in causeless laughter, he could've been a middle-aged, bald and beardless Santa.

'Mr Delt is Provost of Kintyre and the Islands,' Swindon said, halfway down the steps. 'He's been invited to view

27

Holly Island being inhabited for the first time in many years.'

'And very grateful I am, too.' Delt laughed again.

Another, older, man started down the stairs. Tall and as slender as the banister he didn't seem to need, his tailored pale-yellow-and-black pinstriped suit made him look like a pencil. An expensive one, judging by what Edie suspected was a genuine Hermès tie, and the gold watch glinting under a linked cuff. A Montblanc pencil of a man.

His poise, however, slipped, along with his feet. He slammed into the wall and then righted himself, if not his composure. 'Not my most dignified entrance,' he said, in a voice as posh as Fortnum's plum pudding.

'I don't think anyone noticed, Mr Cole-Mortelli,' George said quietly.

Cole-Mortelli swivelled to face the provost. His pale face reddened; his long fingers curled into fists. 'Provost Delt,' he said. 'I didn't know you'd be here.' A sallow undertone to his words suggested he wouldn't have come if he'd been furnished with the knowledge.

'How do you two know each other?' Anna asked as she pretzelled her legs on the banquette.

'We worked together, if you can call it that, on a housing project,' Cole-Mortelli said. 'I'm a financier.'

Edie couldn't help picturing him as the French patisserie rather than the profession. He had a similar tan and crisp eggshell exterior. She bet he wasn't, however, as fluffy inside.

'It was a long time ago now, Robert.' George's jaw was

clenched, his chuckle muted. 'The proposed development never came to pass.'

An awkward silence docked between them. Robert tacked away and rubbed his shoulder where he'd fallen into the wall.

'You could've hurt yourself,' Lucy said to him, showing an urge to smooth any ruffles in the social pond. 'There really should be grit *everywhere* in this weather, not just on deck. The hotel could end up with a lawsuit before it even opens. Not from me, I hasten to add.' She raised her hands in the air as if innocent of all things. 'I just know what people are like.'

'Are you a lawyer?' George asked, a flicker of feeling crossing his face too quickly for Edie to interpret.

Lucy shook her head. 'God, no. I dealt with claims when I was in the civil service: potholes, paving slabs and wonky cobbles make the public very angry.'

'When someone says they were once in the civil service,' Anna said, voice mischief-spiked, 'I like to imagine them as spies.'

'I assure you I'm *not* a spy.' Lucy's reply was as thin and barbed as her smile.

'An agent would say that, wouldn't they?' her husband added, grinning at Anna. Lucy jabbed his side with her elbow. 'Anyway, Lucy left duty behind her and made her fortune, or should I say "our" fortune, as an investor.'

Swindon came back down into the cabin, frowning at his phone. 'Is everything okay?' Edie asked him.

'It's nothing,' he said, 'don't worry.' His forehead, though, remained furrowed. Swallowing, he placed his phone back in a hidden pocket in his cloak, then headed into the galley. Moments later, he re-emerged with a tray of thermos flasks with named luggage tags tied around the lids with string. He delivered one to each guest apart from Edie, presumably having taken the others' orders out of her earshot.

'Tell us about the island,' Edie said to Swindon when he'd finished, hoping to distract herself from his disquiet and the worsening bobbing of the boat.

Swindon looked around the cabin of expectant faces, then settled into the seating opposite Edie. 'I was going to do my rehearsed spiel on the trip over, but I could give you a flavour now, while we're waiting for Ms Allard.'

'You're all going to love Celine!' Anna said, her face lighting up more than the gleaming lamp above her head.

'You know her?' Lucy asked.

'We're really good friends,' Anna replied. 'We met on an Insta collab, cross-promoting a featured hotel when I had my travel agency. We're *comme deux gouttes d'eau*. Salty ones.'

'Ms Allard is a French travel influencer,' Swindon explained.

'Does she only influence French travel?' Sometimes Edie's pedantry reflex was too strong to stopper.

Anna laughed. 'That's your famous attention to detail in action, Ms O'Sullivan.'

'You know me?' Edie was surprised – she'd been featured in a few national newspapers after solving the jigsaw murders and other crimes, but she was hardly famous.

'Mara told me all about you,' Anna explained.

'Mara?' Edie asked.

'The manager of the Aster Castle Hotel, where we're staying,' Anna continued. 'Celine and I met her at a spa hotel in Switzerland a year or two ago. When she invited me on this trip, she said I'd be among fascinating guests, including you. She's chuffed to have you here – you're her favourite crossword setter. I personally prefer *red* setters. Any dog, really.' She crouched and held out her hand. Nicholas the pug trotted over and licked her palm.

'I didn't realise this was going to be such a cliquey affair,' Lucy said. 'Have you also met these women, Henry?'

Henry looked away, colouring slightly. 'I don't think I've had the pleasure.' Lucy eyed him with suspicion.

'"*These women*"?' Anna repeated.

'*Anyway*,' Swindon said, trying to gut the tension. 'You wanted to hear about where you're staying. So, settle back and listen to my tales of Holly Island, named after the vast holly thicket that enwreathed the isle like a thick, prickly moat, as if the sea wasn't enough. The island was once an unused part of an aristocratic estate on Mull, then was sold on to various owners who tried to tame it.' He paused, eyeballing every guest in the cabin. 'Each one discovered, however, that the island doesn't want to be controlled. It fights back.'

'How?' Sean leant forward, caught on the boatman's storytelling hook.

'Everyone who has tried to turn the island to their advantage,' Swindon continued, 'whether it's a home, a business or a tourist attraction, all have died in mysterious circumstances.'

31

'You don't expect us to believe that?' Lucy scoffed.

'I expect nothing of you, Mrs Palmer,' Swindon replied softly. 'I am simply repeating what has been passed down for centuries. Each time someone tries to cut back the holly and bring the castle to life, disaster befalls them.'

'It's true,' George said, nodding, 'or rather, I've heard the same thing. And that the spirits of those who tried and failed still haunt the castle.'

'Like all local folklore,' Edie said, 'a strand of unhappy truth will have been woven into a skein of fiction.'

'Don't spoil it, love,' Riga said. 'You know how I love a ghost story.'

'Please enjoy the island,' Swindon said, 'but don't underestimate it. After all, its nicknames include "Unholy Island". Once upon the fifteenth century, it was known as "Blood Isle", not only due to the holly berries, but also its small beach. When wet, after the tide has turned, the peach-skin-coloured sand seems red. And at sunset, it looks like blood. Scholars suggest that an early cultivator of the island mixed sand from Red Point Beach with the red of Blackgang Chine. Others say its nature's way of warning you away.'

'What do *you* say?' Riga asked.

Swindon blinked, as if released from his own spell. He was frowning again, as he had earlier when looking at his phone. 'I'm telling a ghost story, as you asked, Ms Novack. But if I were you, I'd pull on that DNA strand of truth and cling on tight. And hope no one dies in the process.' He paused, then assumed a smile. 'I'm joking, of course.'

Four

Tarn Bayard, the hotel's head of housekeeping, crouched by the dolls' house, taking in the macabre tableau. She'd come as soon as Mara had called her, as always. 'I wouldn't worry. It's just a joke.'

'Do you really think so?' Mara asked. 'It's not funny.'

'Pranks never are.' Tarn re-read the tiny note. 'Why, what do *you* think it means?'

'A threat, maybe? But Dad doesn't have enemies. Everyone loves him.'

Tarn nodded slowly. 'Your dad *can be* a marshmallow in corduroy. It's hard to imagine anyone being vindictive towards him.' Tarn had been part of the Morecombe-Clark family's ether for decades. She'd been Mara's nanny – one of Mara's earliest memories was of Tarn arriving at the house in a brown VW Beetle, with a green pixie cut and a one-sided smile from bouts of Bell's Palsy. The two had bonded over both being adopted and a mutual suspicion of the Spice Girls. After Mara and her siblings had grown up, Tarn had stayed on as Felicity's P.A. and housekeeper.

Mara's smart watch showed that her pulse was slowing, but a whisper of suspicion remained. Tarn might not be concerned, but then Tarn was unflappable. An electrical fire had broken out one night when she had been looking after Mara, her sister and her older brother, and she'd calmly turned the power off, removed the children from the house, phoned 999, collected a class-C fire extinguisher from the 'emergencies bag' in the boot of her Beetle and returned to the house to douse the conflagration. Mum and Dad had returned to a fire engine parked outside, and Tarn on the lawn with Mara falling asleep on her lap. She was nothing if not stoic in a crisis.

'Have you shown this to anyone other than me?' Tarn asked now.

'Only you and Swindon know.' Mara had sent him a text after phoning Tarn, in case he knew something. He'd responded with a shocked face emoji. 'Mum and Dad don't even know about the dolls' house, let alone this. It's supposed to be a surprise,' she said. 'I was going to present it to them before everyone arrived. I came here to fetch it.' Mara's parents were hippies at heart – hippies with heart conditions. She was already risking their retirement cash on the hotel; she wasn't going to put their arteries under more stress by revealing a threat that could be a misunderstanding. 'I wanted to talk to you before I said anything.'

Tarn sat on the edge of the bed, smoothing the duvet cover. 'Very wise.'

'Who do you think would do this as a joke? It must be one of the staff, as I told them about the dolls' house last week, and this happened sometime in the last few days.'

She tried to imagine Swindon, Izzie, Kimberly, Ryan or Owain breaking into her room and laying out that death scene. But how well did she know them beyond their LinkedIns, CVs and staff room gossip?

'I wouldn't put it past Owain,' Tarn said. 'He's the epitome of young, dumb and full of—'

'You don't have to spell it out,' Mara interrupted.

'I was going to say "full of shit",' Tarn said. 'He thinks far too much of himself. And he *does* like to play tricks – yesterday, he threw a real spider in Izzie's face.'

'That's horrible.' Mara imagined a spider climbing her cheek. Her skin itched at the thought, and she had to scratch it away. 'You should've told me.'

'My job is to run the staff, yours to run the hotel, Mara, love,' Tarn said, gently but firmly. 'I reprimanded Owain and gave him a first warning.'

'What about Ryan?'

Tarn paused to think, then shook her head. 'He strikes me as too self-absorbed to bother.'

'When I was talking to Izzie and Kimberley about the dolls' house last night,' Mara said, 'Izzie was fascinated, wanting to know about the dolls I've had made for the guests this week.'

'It's *possible* she did it,' Tarn mused. 'But she could just have been exaggerating her interest, as you're her boss, and you do love a dolls' house.'

Mara's therapist had suggested that Mara's love of miniaturised domestic settings was a way of controlling her own life for once.

'Whoever it is, though, broke into your room, and that's

unacceptable, joke or not. Everyone knows that spare keys are kept in your office, so any of them could've taken the one for your room or taken yours from your handbag. When I have time, I'll check the CCTV that covers your corridor, find out who came in and give them a final warning. Or sack them if you prefer.'

Then they'd be down another member of staff when they were already on a skeleton team. 'A warning is fine. Unless . . .'

'Unless what?'

'Unless it's *not* a joke.'

'I really think it is,' Tarn said, putting her arm around Mara. 'But if you're worried it's a real death threat, there are other options.'

'And they are?'

'We could call the police. Or even cancel the event.'

Mara's heart fell like a disconnected lift. An image flashed back of her dad, grey-faced in his hospital bed. Still smiling, even though his chest had been crustacean-cracked and his heart handled by strangers, he'd taken Mara's hand and said, 'As the anaesthetist counted down, I had an epiphany. You've been so frustrated at work, and your mum and I need something to focus on in retirement: I think we should go into business together!'

And then came the memory of his face when they got the literal keys to the castle. He'd jumped up and down like a kid at Christmas. And he *really* loved Christmas. He was so looking forward to standing behind the bar before dinner, making cocktails for the guests.

A message pinged through from Swindon. 'Last guest

has arrived and we're on our way. Just left the harbour. See you in a few hours.'

She *could* phone Swindon, get him to turn the boat around. Then she imagined walking into the hotel lounge and the smile fading from Dad's face when she told him their big Christmas event was cancelled. And all her hard work in preparing everything, and her parents' money, would be wasted.

'What do *you* think we should do?' Mara asked, feeling like she had as a teenager, seeking Tarn's advice.

'Go back to your original plan. Put your dad's doll back where it was, take away all the weird extra bits and we'll take it down to present to your parents now. I'll handle the prankster, and we'll get on with creating a great event that will set the hotel up for a stellar future.'

Tarn was right. Tarn was *always* right. She'd been spot on when she'd warned Mara about her last boyfriend, and dead on the money when she'd told her dad to go to his GP to investigate his dizziness as it might suggest cardiac problems. She was most likely correct now. Maybe Ryan or Owain or both had conspired to play a prank. Or Izzie, or even Swindon. The message was written on paper the same shape as a Christmas cracker joke. That's all it was. A silly joke.

'Thanks,' Mara said. 'That helps. This is just a stupid trick. If it *is* more sinister, and I'm sure it's not, then we have a decorated police detective as a guest, and a renowned puzzle-solver.'

'Very true,' Tarn replied. 'But they're here to relax, so

it's a good job they won't be needed. Now, shall we take this downstairs?'

Nodding, Mara moved over to the dolls' house and was about to move her dad's doll when Tarn called out, 'But make sure you take a picture of the mini crime scene. Just in case.'

Five

Swindon's voice came through the cabin's speakers, giving the eerie impression that he was everywhere. 'We're off, heading into Oban Bay on our journey to Holly Island for your exclusive festive stay at the Aster Castle Hotel.'

George cheered, Anna whooped, Lucy rolled her eyes, Henry checked his watch, Robert crossed his stick insect legs and the last guest to arrive, Celine Allard, tapped her thumbs and forefingers together.

Celine, in her late twenties at most, had a soft French accent and long brown hair in a plait over her left shoulder. Her pink, belted trench coat was speckled with melted snow. When she'd shaken Edie's hand, she'd given intense eye contact with her startling violet gaze. Now she and Anna were rolling a tennis ball to each other across a table.

'The trip will take at least two hours,' Swindon continued. 'The conditions are a little windy, which could affect the timings. Once we're properly underway, I'll be pointing out highlights of the scenery and wildlife as we pass. Visibility may be poor in places, so when I say there's a minke whale to your left you may have to just trust me!'

Robert harrumphed. Believing in Swindon, or perhaps anyone, was clearly beyond his means.

'Hopefully, though, you'll see the beauty that the western isles of Scotland have to offer. As we get closer, I'll give you a little more background to the hotel and the island but, for now, sit back and enjoy the journey.' As Swindon finished his spiel, the engine surged and the boat sped away from the harbour.

Edie closed her eyes at a wave of motion sickness, then opened them again. It'd made it worse. She distracted herself by trying to think of anagrams – 'Swindon Marr' should have something hidden inside. She imagined the letters of the name rearranging themselves and came up with *narrow minds* and *worm innards*. She didn't think these were ones to mention to him.

Owain jumped from the top of the steps into the cabin, landing on his feet in a crouch. Edie cupped her knees in automatic response. Owain just bounced up, across the room and into the galley. Oh, to be young and not worried about shattering kneecaps. He should watch out, though. If he damaged himself now, he'd pay for it in his future. The past was buried in the body but never forgotten.

'On your left,' Swindon said over the speaker, 'is the Isle of Kerrera, a physical breakwater that protects the centre of Oban and its bay. It's not till we get past Mull, though, that you'll see how the sea is truly feeling today.'

Edie squeezed Riga's hand, but it was her, not Riga, who needed reassurance: Riga's eyes were bright and sparkling.

'We're now passing Rudh-a-Chruidh,' Swindon announced, 'a tidal island connected to Kerrera by causeway.

Not somewhere you'd want to get trapped. But then, no island is ideal in that situation!'

Owain came back out of the galley carrying a platter stacked high with mince pies. As he handed them out (handmade, crumbly, a little too much orange zest), Celine took a ring light and phone stand from her tote bag. Catching Edie and others watching, she said, 'I hope you don't mind if I take some footage during our trip?'

'As long as you don't include me,' Lucy said. 'I can't bear candid shots.'

'Don't worry,' Celine replied. 'My reels only have me, the scenery and a cup of coffee. And, yes, that does make me a little, or a lot, self-centred. If it helps, I don't like it about myself either.' She froze, then, her head inclined, her hand outstretched as if on pause. Like a woman of stone, she didn't even blink.

Nodding suddenly, breaking the spell, she poured coffee from her thermos into its black plastic cup and placed it on the table in front of her. Then she picked up her phone, holding it at a twisted angle.

The boat dipped, and the cup skidded across the surface. Celine quickly took a stream of photos and casually caught the cup before it toppled. Not a drop was spilled.

Swiping a few times at the phone, she showed the screen to George, who was sitting nearest to her.

'How did you do that?' he asked, eyes wide. 'You've captured the steam in a question mark!' He turned the phone round to show those in the cabin. Edie couldn't see the details from the opposite side of the room, but from the others' reactions, it was impressive.

Celine's smile was gummy and charming. 'I calculated the boat would shift the cup towards me, and the steam would drag behind. The rest is digital manipulation.'

'That's all influencers are, after all – manipulators,' Owain said, a sneer on his face. 'But if you lot were called that, it wouldn't be a sought-after Gen Z career option. Then again, if all influencers looked like you, they could call themselves anything they want and still sell the product.'

Edie was about to tell him to 'fuck off', but then Anna said, 'I thought negging had gone out of fashion. But you do it very well, Owain. Well done.' She and Celine then proceeded to ignore him, making Edie want to cheer.

As promised, Swindon pointed out Maiden island, the otters on the Mull coastline, Duart Castle – home of the clan MacLean – and Aros Castle, although all Edie could see of the latter was sea spray caught by the boat's swinging lights and a buoy that kept bashing at her window.

'I'm sending Owain round with binoculars,' Swindon said. 'Visibility is dipping, and I don't want you to miss out.' As he said this, Owain appeared with a load of binoculars hung around his neck and handed a pair to each passenger. 'We're just passing the famous Mull town of Tobermory with its fantastic whisky distillery, and coming up, again on your left, is the Rubha nan Gall lighthouse. Keep an eye out – I saw dolphins playing here earlier.'

Excitement surfed the cabin. With all but one of the pairs of binoculars trained on the lighthouse, it was Riga, looking up into the sky, who spotted something first. 'What's that?' she asked.

As if he could hear her, Swindon said, 'And above, flying ahead as if they're guiding us home, are three white-tailed sea eagles!' His voice was full of excitement. 'I've never seen three together like this. It's incredible!'

Edie watched in awe as the eagles swooped and soared, circled and spiralled.

'I can see a dolphin!' Anna shouted. She'd taken off her shoes and was crouched on the seat, binoculars pressed to the window.

'Me too!' Celine opened a top window, angling her phone out to get footage.

'There are two of them, together! It's like they're dancing.' George's smile was as wide as a dolphin's. 'How lovely would that be, to journey through life's seas with someone special?'

'I for one wholeheartedly recommend it,' Riga replied, leaning into Edie.

As Christmas presents go, this was one of the best.

'Thank you so much for coming with me.' Riga's head was on Edie's shoulder.

'Wouldn't miss it for anything,' Edie said, although the snow on the coastal hills made her worry. If snow had settled in the face of salt, the storm must be strong.

As they passed Corrachadh Mor, the most westerly point of mainland Great Britain, the sea eagles disappeared into the snow-dipped mist, and the sea, as unsettled as Edie's stomach, made itself known. The boat bridled and ducked. Thermoses rolled across the floor.

Edie, clinging to the edge of her seat, leaned forwards and called across to Owain, who was sitting with Anna and Celine. 'The storm will pass, right? And the boat will be able to get my grandchildren in the morning?'

'I'm sure it'll be fine, Miss,' he said, not even looking at her, alleviating her concerns a little.

'See?' Riga said, hugging Nicholas. 'Try and relax, Edie. Stop expecting to find trouble all the time and try to enjoy Christmas!'

Edie's flurry of relief was salted, however, when Swindon said over the speakers, 'Hang on, everybody,' sounding at once worried and excited. 'This is where you'll need those sea legs. It's going to get wild out here.'

Six

Head moving slowly, Mara's mum, Felicity Morecombe-Clark, stood imperiously in reception, taking in every detail of the holly-adorned lobby. She was a tall, red-headed surveillance camera in a green Ghost dress. It took her seconds to spot Mara and Tarn as they carried the dolls' house castle under its blanket towards reception.

'And what's this?!' Felicity said, when they'd placed it on the reception desk.

'I've got a Christmas Eve surprise present for you and Dad.'

'How sweet of you.' She went to lift the cover but, without thinking, Mara stopped her, grabbing her hand.

'I thought we could wait till Daddy got here.' Mara winced, hearing her own childishness.

Mum flinched, retracting her hand. 'Of course, darling. Whatever you want. You keep your little secret for now.' She gestured around the lobby. 'I must say, you've done such a brilliant job. The Christmas tree, the garlands, the holly wreaths you made, ruining your hands in the process, the flower displays . . . everything's come together.'

Mara waited, heart-braced, for one of the usual maternal

45

caveats: 'Of course, you'll have to see to the . . .' or 'With the exception of . . .' When none came, she flushed with startled pride.

'Although you could do with touching up those thread veins.' Felicity held Mara at long, Reformer-toned arm's length, scrutinising her daughter's skin. Taking a pot of Trinny London concealer from her bag, she dabbed some around Mara's nostrils. Mara wanted to pull away but couldn't face the fuss Mum would make, so stayed put, as she always did.

'There are my two favourite girls!' Her dad, Ivan, beamed as he bounded over to them. His jacket flapped open, showing one of his 'jazzy' shirts, covered with holly leaves. He kissed Mara's forehead. 'I'm so proud of you, Pudding! I knew you could do it.'

A giggle came from behind Mara. Turning, she caught Kimberley, the sous chef, frowning and putting her finger on her lips at Izzie. Izzie was smirking, although her eyes looked as if they'd been crying. Mara thought she heard her whisper, 'Pudding!'

'We came to find you for an update,' Kimberley said. 'Has Swindon picked the guests up yet?'

'Sorry, I got distracted by the dolls' house.' Mara paused, but neither Izzie nor Kimberley reacted, though that didn't mean one of them hadn't played the trick. 'Yup, they're on their way, so everything needs to be ready for around half one, in case this wind brings them in early. Could you give the whisky glasses an extra polish, Izzie?' she asked. 'And fill the decanters for the tasting.'

'I'll put the scones in the oven and check the curd has set,' Kimberley said, already on her way. 'And I'll phone Ryan again and get him to help.'

'I'll go and get him,' Izzie said quickly. 'I know where he is.'

'Dad,' Mara said when they'd both gone, Izzie scampering up the stairs and Kimberley to the kitchen. 'Can you not call me "Pudding", not in front of the staff, at least? I'm forty, and their boss.'

'Say no more, love. My lips are sealed,' Dad replied, giving her a hug.

'Aren't they just?' Mum said, stroking his arm.

'Though you'll always be my precious Pudding,' Dad continued. 'Delivered to me on Christmas Day, like the very best of presents.' He and Mum had adopted Mara when she was a few days old, at the time of year you're told not to get a puppy. 'A baby's for life, not just for Christmas,' was one of his favourite sayings.

'Talking of gifts,' Mara said, pointing to the covered miniature castle. 'I've had something made, to celebrate opening the hotel.'

'Is it a massive cake?' Dad asked, rubbing his flat belly.

'No,' Mara laughed, placing her hand on top of the dolls' house. 'It's this.' She whipped the blanket away, revealing the hotel in one-twelfth miniature.

'Oh, Pudding,' Dad said, eyes filling with tears. 'It's beautiful.' He pointed to the door. 'Does it open?'

'Take a look,' Mara replied.

'Do the honours, Dearest,' he said to Mum, standing back so she could get through.

'No, no, I think you should, Sweetheart,' Mum replied, blowing him a kiss.

'Honestly, you two, get a room. We've got enough,' Mara said, unfastening the doors to lay bare the interior. 'There you go. It's all been made to my plans; in fact, it was ready before the hotel was. It was like my lucky charm. If the mini version could be finished, the real one could too.'

'Does that make it a simulacrum?' Tarn asked. She'd been studying postmodernism on her part-time Philosophy Masters. 'A copy without an original?'

'I have no idea,' Mum replied, 'and I'm sure you don't either, Tarn, darling.'

'That's not accurate,' Tarn said, 'I've been reading Jean—'

'It's a shame,' Mum interrupted, pointing to the top of the castle, 'that we couldn't have the welcome reception on the roof terrace. We could have shown off the pool and the view. We had Swindon make those railings in a rush, *and* we bought those patio heaters and fake snow machines. All for nothing.'

'Nothing's ever wasted, love,' Dad said. 'And the pool is covered over for winter anyway, so all we'd have to show is new tarpaulin. As for snow, we have the real thing!' He pointed to the snowdrift against the glass front doors.

'I suppose.'

'Tell you what,' Dad went on, forefinger extended. 'Tomorrow morning, we should have a snowman-making competition! The winner gets to come back this time next year!'

'Have you seen all of the dolls?' Mara asked, knowing her neediness was showing but not how to stop it. 'I've had dolls made of us, the staff and, as a one-off special present, the Christmas guests, too. I'm going to put them around the dinner table, by their place settings.'

'But we already have the brass name plates,' Mum said.

'Oh, let them have both,' Dad said, peering inside. 'Look! We're in the lounge!' He pointed to his little doll, now out of its shroud and back in a replica of one of his Paul Smith suits. 'I've got my paper, and the crossword is half filled in. I'll ask Edie O'Sullivan to help me finish it.'

'My mini-me has a Martini glass,' Mum said, 'which is more than I have right now. She's a little on the short side, though. More like you, Mara. Where is your doll, anyway?'

Mara was about to point to the miniature version of her office, behind the reception, but her doll wasn't in the chair where she'd left it two days ago. 'I don't know,' she said, scanning every room. Ryan's doll was in the kitchen, knife in hand; Kimberley next to him, with a brass pan of custard; Izzie was making the provost's bed; Tarn was by the linen closet, a to-do list in her hand; and Mum and Dad were, as he'd said, by the fire in the lounge.

But Mara's doll was missing in non-action.

'It must have dropped out somewhere,' Mara said, knowing there was no way it could have fallen en route.

'You'd better find it, then, darling,' Mum said. 'We don't want our guests spotting it by a skirting board and thinking we leave voodoo dolls about the place.'

'That's not a term you should use, Mrs Morecombe-

Clark,' Tarn said, gently. 'It's culturally insensitive. Maybe go for "poppets" instead?'

'Maybe *you* should go for a break, Tarn,' Mum suggested. 'See if you can find our Poppet's poppet before the provost does.'

'That's quite the tongue-twister, Mrs Morecombe-Clark,' Tarn replied, eyes flashing. 'Perhaps we should suggest it as a party game tonight.'

'I'll come with you,' Mara said to Tarn. She felt Mum's gaze burn into their backs as they headed for the stairs. When they were out of earshot, she said, 'What does it mean, that they took my doll?'

Tarn put her arm round Mara. 'I don't know. But I don't like it.'

Seven

The sky was storm-dark, and the boat bucked and swayed. Nicholas hid his head behind Riga's back, whining. Edie knew how he felt.

'The Inner Hebridean island of Coll is to your left,' Swindon was saying through the speakers, 'although I doubt even binoculars will give you a glimpse. The snow's thicker than I've seen at sea for years.'

Riga put down her binoculars and petted poor Nicholas' back. 'He's right. Can't see a thing. Shame, because I thought I saw a golden eagle.' She scrutinised Edie's face. 'Feeling *really* queasy now?'

Edie nodded, then stopped. The world was moving enough already.

Riga dug into her handbag and pulled out a bottle of her homemade ginger, lemon, lavender and peppermint pastilles. A bit of a kitchen witch, she was always knocking up herbal remedies and potions. 'Take two of these and see me in the morning. And now, and forever.'

Edie sucked on the sweet tablet, trying to fix her eyes on the slippery horizon through the opposite window. Owain's head kept getting in the way as he tried to impress Celine with another futile joke. George was gamely attempting to engage Henry and Lucy in talk of any size, but Lucy was ignoring him, and Henry was trying to get Owain to give him more brandy. Everyone trying, everyone failing.

'For those of you with dicky tummies,' Swindon said from wherever he was, 'try to hang on to my words as you would a life raft. Focus on facts, that's my suggestion. And I am about to send you a flotilla of facts, along with the odd buoy of legend.'

Edie closed her eyes and concentrated on his voice.

'A while away to your right,' the boatman continued, 'lie the Small Isles, but within twenty minutes we'll be approaching a smaller island still – Holly Island itself.'

'At last!' Robert said, wedged in the corner. His skin was a sickly shade of verdigris. 'There had better be a good welcome party.'

'Equidistant between Coll and Barr islands in the Hebrides,' Swindon continued, 'Holly was bought by Vivian and Alberto Magliani in the mid-nineteen twenties from the estate of a minor royal, intending to create a holiday retreat for their large family. Vivian worked with an unknown architect to merge traditional Scottish castle design with Art Deco style. All smooth lines and curves, it's as elegant as I am scruffy.'

'Then it must be immaculate,' Robert said. Nobody laughed, not even George.

'In the summer of nineteen twenty-nine, halfway through the build,' Swindon continued, 'the Magliani clan visited Holly Island to see the castle's development. They made hand- and footprints in the plaster, marking it as theirs for all time.' Swindon's tone now wore a sombre shade. 'On one of those stunning Hebridean days when the sun is high and the sea blood-warm, their six kids went swimming off Red Cove.'

The cabin was hushed, the atmosphere anticipatory of tragedy.

'Witness accounts varied on the details, but all agreed that the youngest child, ten-year-old Aster, which means "star", swam too far out. Unable to see her in the distance, the eldest, Aurelio, meaning "gold", went after her. He was a strong swimmer, but he, too, disappeared. Another sister tried to swim to help but was held back by the others. Neither of them surfaced. Vivian Magliani sat on that beach for five days, waiting. The bodies of her two beloved children washed onto the dark red sand three weeks later.'

Silence in the cabin. Edie placed her hands over her chest as if that could ward off such a disaster befalling her own grandchildren.

'And a happy Christmas to you, too,' Anna said, breaking some of the tension.

Swindon cleared his throat. 'Following the funeral, Vivian Magliani couldn't bear to return to Holly Island, yet Alberto couldn't bring himself to leave it. He continued to build the castle, in memoriam to his two children, naming it Aster Aurelio Castle. He made the gold star you'll see on the front of the hotel himself. On Christmas Day, a few days after the castle's completion, Alberto also drowned. While it was recorded as an accident, few believe that to be the full story.'

'So sad,' Celine said.

'While the current owners decided to call it the Aster Castle Hotel, they wanted to memorialise both children, which you'll see when you arrive.'

Anna scribbled in her Leuchtturm notebook. Edie wondered whether these tragic details made it more or less likely that the hotel would make it onto her website.

'You can still see the Maglianis' handprints preserved in the plaster,' Swindon continued, 'on the east turret's outside wall.'

'I'll be sure to make a special trip,' Robert interjected with sarcasm.

'Since then,' Swindon continued, 'the island has, in between stretches of abandonment, been a look-out post, a Seventies conference base and a training centre for a big department store. Those who stepped onto its shores underwent difficult or tragic times, reporting strange sightings in the sea and the castle, especially around the festive season. It's thought that something terrible waits in these waters.'

'I'm not surprised,' Henry said. 'The water companies have a lot to answer for these days!' His grin at his own 'joke' faded when it wasn't returned.

'These rumours contributed to the island's dereliction but, in 2023, it was bought by the Morecombe-Clarks,' said Swindon, 'a mother–father–daughter team with a background in art and design, finance and hospitality respectively, who have no interest in superstition and gossip. They've made a real difference to the isle, thanks to investing a fortune. Wildlife's thriving thanks to them removing dead, damaged and diseased wood, and they've restored the castle to its Art Deco glory while giving it a contemporary style. It's – and I promise they didn't script this – really bloody lovely. Although I should leave the judgement to you lot.'

'If you would,' Henry said to the speaker. 'I'm hanging on to my job by a thread. Legacy media is as dead as the unfortunate Magliani family.'

Edie thought of the children washing up on the beach and leaned into Sean's side. He was kneeling on the seat, face pressed to the window, trying to see through the snow. The thought of losing him, or his kids, was an ice-burn to the heart.

Ten queasy minutes later, Sean said, 'I can see lit-up turrets!' Sometimes he didn't act like he was in his mid-thirties. Edie hoped he stayed that way.

'As we approach the island,' Swindon said, 'I'll ask you to remain seated while we dock, and to take care on the deck and pathways. Your luggage will be taken to your rooms during a reception in the lounge, where you can all warm up by the fire. If that doesn't work, later I'll lead a whisky tasting to accompany your afternoon tea.'

Riga's cheers were even louder than Henry's.

While Swindon and Owain moored the boat, Edie clambered onto the seat next to Sean and peered through the steamed-up window. Nicholas put his paws up and jumped in a futile attempt to see out. Edie held the pug to the window. Festoon lights swung along the pier like a lit skipping rope. Beyond, the top half of the castle loomed over its holly bailey and tree sentries. The roof was perimetered with railings.

After Riga had ascended in the chairlift like a queen in a litter, Nicholas on her lap, Edie stepped onto the salt-baked deck. Salined sleet hit her cheeks like hard tears. The boat dipped and she grabbed the railing, gazing into the dark water.

Something seemed to move under the surface. Though she knew it was a trick of pitching light and refraction, Swindon's recent words floated up: 'something terrible waits in these waters.'

Edie shivered. Riga was right. She should stop looking for trouble where there was none and concentrate on having a happy Christmas. Still, she kept staring, into the depths.

Eight

Owain burst through the revolving doors, snowflakes smuggling themselves in behind him. 'They're here. Showtime!'

Adrenaline coursed through Mara, stifling her anxiety, for now. 'Right, everyone,' she said to the staff gathered in the lobby, 'I'm really proud of us as a team for getting everything ready. Let's show our guests a brilliant time and launch the hotel in the best possible way. It's going to be a manic forty-eight hours, but it'll be worth it. And we'll have a big party when they're on their way on Boxing Day!'

Kimberley and Izzie both cheered, although Izzie's was traced with sarcasm. Tarn, standing behind the serving table, bit her lip; Ryan gave a peace sign.

Lucy Palmer was the first guest through the hotel's door. She strode in, eyes darting around the lobby. Her husband followed, brushing snow from his shoulder. Spotting the table of empty glasses ready for the toast, he picked one up. Stared at it with suspicion, as if it contained invisible wine – the emperor's new Claret.

'Welcome, Mr and Mrs Palmer, to Holly Island!' Mara said quickly, pointing towards Tarn's table. 'When everyone is here, I'll crack open the fizz and fill those flutes to celebrate the hotel's official opening. For now, there's mulled wine, white and red wine, tea and coffee over there, as well as ginger tea to appease any queasiness. Canapes will soak it all up, but save some room for the special whisky tasting afternoon tea. And, of course, our gala dinner.'

Henry headed straight over to Tarn; his wife took out her phone and made notes. It was well known in the travel industry that Lucy was the true critic. If Henry went somewhere alone to review, he was often won round by fine wines, food and a big slice of bonhomie. When accompanied by Lucy, however, his reviews were considerably harsher.

No time to dwell on reviews now; Mara would do that in bed later. Celine and Anna had just bundled into the lobby. Their laughter was as welcome as her first glass of fizz would be. Celine flew at Mara, hugging her tight then doing a little dance.

Anna loped over, grinning, with two mugs of mulled wine. She handed one to Celine. 'We made it! The three of us, back together again!' She went to take a photo of their reunion, then said, 'No signal. What's your Wi-Fi, Mara?'

Mara took code cards from her pocket and handed one to each of them. 'We had to install a specialist connection as nothing else would reach the island. We want guests to be secure in the knowledge that they can work from here.'

Anna tapped her phone. 'Good to know. You know what I was like when I couldn't get reception at the spa!'

'I'm surprised, Ms Morecombe-Clark,' Lucy said, lip twitching with apparent disapproval, 'that you've assembled your friends for this venture. I was under the impression this was a press event, not a paid endorsement.'

Celine's hands went to her hips. 'Neither of us is being remunerated. We're friends, yes, but Mara made us promise to treat this like any other review. Therefore, if I enjoy myself, I'll give the hotel an honest plug; if I don't, I'll say nothing.'

Mara hoped above anything that they loved her hotel. Celine had over a hundred thousand followers on Instagram, half a million on TikTok and a knack for going viral. And it would be *huge* to be listed as one of the original recommendations on Anna's new site. Her last online travel company had been bought for an undisclosed but mighty amount of money.

'On the boat, Ms Malone said that she was being bribed with bed and board.' Lucy's tone shrugged with smugness.

'Mate,' Anna said, tone set to wither. 'I'd never put someone on my list without good cause. I was *joking* about being bribed, just as I was about travelling with a vibrator.' She paused and winked. 'As if I'd only bring one! You can borrow my spare, if you like? Enjoy yourself – it's Christmas, after all!'

Celine clapped her thumb and forefingers in her signature gesture of approval. Mara felt a laugh try to wriggle out. Lucy's mouth was wide open in shock, which didn't help. Luckily, Mum swept in and took Lucy away, asking about her charitable work and how she could help.

'*You*, Anna Malone, are very naughty,' Mara said, a

giddy lightness in her chest that almost made her forget her stress.

'Sorry to interrupt,' George Delt, the provost, said, shyly leaning into the conversation. He was taller than she'd imagined and smelled of lime and lavender. His face was soft, as were his eyes and his voice. 'I just wanted to say "hello" and "thank you" for inviting me. It's an honour to be here.'

'You are very welcome,' Mara said. 'I'm glad you didn't have a more important engagement to attend.'

'I was invited to an official function tonight in Argyll but wanted to get away. Plus, it's rather nice to take off the ceremonial robes for once. And the chain is *really* heavy. Especially at a ceilidh.'

Mara had wanted to put on a ceilidh at the Christmas event, but Mum had vetoed the idea. 'No one is going to see me sweat,' she'd said.

'And I was curious about this island and the stories that are told about it. My grandmother was born on Eigg and said Holly was the Hebridean equivalent of the Bermuda Triangle: no one came back alive.'

'So, coming here is a death wish?' Anna asked.

George laughed nervously. 'I hope not,' he said. 'A morbid interest at most!'

'And no plus one?' Celine asked. 'I can see why Mr Cole-Mortelli would wander the world alone, but you . . .'

'I was going to bring my mum, but she died earlier this year.' George looked around the huge lobby, tears in his eyes. 'She'd have loved it here, too. She went to Burgh Island in her youth and never stopped talking about it.'

'So, there's no Mrs or Mr George Delt?' Anna asked innocently.

George stared at his shoes. 'I've been Mum's carer for a long time. Between that and my council duties, it doesn't—' He stopped himself, the present tense of grief catching up with him. '*Didn't* leave much time for anything, or anyone, else.'

'Christmas is very hard when you've lost someone,' Celine said, swirling the wine around her mug. Everyone was quiet for a moment. Mara thought, as she always did this time of year, of her unknown biological mother, and how, on the longest night, she'd left Mara screaming outside a police station.

'I love the smell of mulled wine,' Anna said at last, sniffing the air. 'Makes me think of where we three met.'

'Where was that?' George asked, seemingly relieved to be back in less emotional territory.

'At a spa in Switzerland,' Anna replied. 'One that pampers you while you look at the Alps, eat Zuger Kirschtorte and drink hot chocolate, thankfully not one of the birch twig and bum-purging ones where you leave six kilos and six grand lighter, then stop at the airport Starbucks for the plumpest muffin.'

George roared with laughter. 'I wish I'd been there. Sounds like the best holiday.'

It had been. Mara had visited the spa as part of a research trip, experiencing the details of luxury hotels. She'd booked to stay one night but, after meeting Anna and Celine in the steam room, where pores had opened and emotions poured, had stayed another five. She missed those times already. Was it possible to look back with nostalgia at an event only eighteen months earlier?

Spotting Robert Cole-Mortelli, Mara excused herself and walked over to where he was taking a canape from Izzie's tray. 'A pleasure to meet you, Mr Cole-Mortelli,' she said, holding out her hand. 'I'm Mara Morecombe-Clark, General Manager of the hotel. I'm delighted that you won this lot.'

He shook her hand with some reluctance. 'It's not winning if you *pay* for something. I'd *really* been after the magnum of 2015 Benevolent Neglect Las Madres Whole Cluster Syrah but was outbid. *This* was the only other lot at the raffle that remotely interested me and, as patron of the charity, I had to buy *something*.' His sniffiness was undermined by the pastry crumbs in his moustache.

Behind him, Tarn darted to help Swindon open the access door, which he was struggling with against the wind. Edie O'Sullivan, Mara's favourite crossword setter, came in first, looking grey around the gills. She turned and held out her hand to a tall, elegant woman who must be Riga Novack. A dog followed close behind. Mara tried to control her breathing. She'd been bitten by a small dog when she was five and had never been comfortable with them since. But she could hardly ban them from the hotel. Where would it stop? If she banned all the things she was scared of, there'd be very little left.

'I hope this stay lives up to its five-star promise,' Robert said. 'The lot was a *lot* of money, if you'll forgive the pun.' When he smiled, his teeth were so white they were almost blue.

Edie and Riga moved slowly into the lobby, with Tarn showing them towards the back and the open lounge area. They settled into armchairs by the fireplace, flames kicking up a welcome. The pug snuffled at Riga's feet. Despite its presence, Mara wanted to go and sit with them, and leave Robert to his puns.

Having already brought in Riga's wheelchair, Detective Sean Brand-O'Sullivan was now helping Swindon lug in the cases. Owain should've been doing that; instead, he was standing next to Celine, talking at her. Celine and Anna were sharing knowing looks. He was probably mansplaining the travel industry.

'Dad!' Mara called over to Ivan, who was talking with Henry and Lucy. He made his excuses as charmingly as ever, judging by the way Lucy actually smiled in response, then bounded over. When he'd put his arm around her, Mara asked, 'Could you please talk to Mr Cole-Mortelli about the rarer examples in our wine cellar?'

'Of course!' Dad replied, beaming. 'My specialist subject. Are you a collector, Mr Cole-Mortelli?'

Mara moved away, knowing Dad would win Robert round better than she could. He was a man, for one thing.

Tapping Owain on the shoulder, she gestured for him to follow. When out of any guests' earshot, she said, 'Why are Swindon and a *guest* bringing in the luggage? That's *your* job. One of them, anyway.'

'You said it was important to be friendly to all the guests and give good service.'

Mara didn't like the twinkle in his eyes when he said

'service'. 'Take all the bags up to the suites, then get back quickly. Everyone's here, so I'll be giving my speech, then you'll be in butler mode.'

Owain walked away without acknowledging her, his swagger and the set of his shoulders shouting 'fuck you, boss' even as he checked the luggage tags and began allocating them to trolleys. He had come with such good recommendations from the agency but had yet to show any of the qualities they'd promised. It was like he was a completely different person. Maybe one who'd play stupid jokes on her. She'd complain to the agency when these two days were over and get a new hire for when they opened properly.

Walking round the side of the small crowd, Mara tugged a bottle of Champagne from the vast ice bucket and went several steps up on the staircase. 'Hello, everyone!' she called out. 'I'd like to formally welcome you all to the soft opening of the Aster Castle Hotel. I'm Mara Morecombe-Clark, the General Manager, and I'll be hosting you, along with my wonderful parents, Ivan and Felicity, for this very special Christmas break.'

Celine moved closer, filming; Dad took pictures of Mara with his Leica, the same smile of pride on his face as when she'd ridden her trike for the first time.

'You'll find a welcome hamper on your beds,' Mara continued, 'containing info about the island, goodies and a programme of events. For now, all you need to know is that, after this welcome reception, you'll be shown to your rooms and given a tour of the hotel if you so choose. At three, there's the whisky afternoon tea, with tastings run by our very own Swindon, a former distiller, among other things. If you don't fancy that—'

'Then you're crazy!' Swindon shouted from by the fire-place, where he was rubbing the belly of Riga's dog.

Everyone laughed, especially George.

'Thank you, Swindon,' Mara said. 'But if you'd rather, you can take a tour of the hotel with our housekeeper, Tarn. This would normally include a tour of the grounds, but the storm has rendered the tennis courts, putting green and gardens a little treacherous. Then, at six-thirty, cocktails will be served in the Gold Bar, which is behind this rather grand staircase—'

'With a special Aster Aurelio cocktail of my design!' Dad called out.

'Yes, thanks, Dad,' Mara said, smiling at his shining face – this was exactly what he'd imagined owning a hotel would be like. She'd done the right thing in not mentioning the dolls' house prank. 'And I can assure you that it's *delicious*. If you can bear to leave the bar, though, at seven thirty you'll be treated to the gala dinner in our restaurant. The menu has been designed and personally overseen by our executive chef, Ryan Dreith, who is hoping to bring a Michelin star to The Star.'

'If he can behave himself long enough, the daft bugger!' Henry sounded like he'd already had a couple of drinks.

'After dinner, there'll be port and liqueurs,' Mara continued, 'then, for the brave, there'll be a Christmas ghost story by the fire in the library, read by yours truly.'

'Ooooh!' Anna said in a ghostly manner.

'You should do the sound effects, Anna,' Mara said, laughing.

On cue, the wind ramped up. As if auditioning for ghost story foley, it was everywhere at once: rattling the revolving doors, hissing down the chimney.

'Now, let's launch the Aster Castle Hotel in the traditional way.' Mara held up the bottle of Champagne and popped the cork.

The small crowd cheered.

'Here's to a very merry Christmas!' Holding the bottle as she'd been taught at a sommelier school ('one thumb in its bum, the other on its frenulum') she poured the fizz into flutes and gestured for Izzie to hand them round, carrying two glasses over to Henry and Lucy herself. They'd settled on a sofa within roaring distance of the fire. 'Here you go,' she said. 'Dad chose it himself. He insisted on going to as many vineyards as possible.'

'Poor him,' Lucy said, with not one hint of sarcasm. 'You didn't think to have an English sparkling wine? To keep it British? We've tried some excellent ones in Kent and Sussex.'

'Up here,' Mara said, trying to find a way into civility, 'the south coast of England and the Champagne region feel pretty much as far away as each other. Bearing in mind it takes forever to get anywhere, we might as well get Champagne.'

'On your head be it,' Lucy said.

While she'd only taken a sip, Henry's flute was already half empty. 'That's very good!' he said. 'Rhubarb, rose and loganberry notes, along with—'

'Save it for your article, darling,' Lucy said, patting his arm rather hard. 'You don't want to say something in public that you later change your mind about, then say the opposite in print on Boxing Day.'

'Your article already has a release date?' Mara asked, hoping her heart wasn't beating as loudly as she felt it was.

'It's due first thing on the twenty-sixth,' Henry said, 'and the paper wants it to make a splash on a slow news day.'

'Midlist criticism doesn't do anything these days,' Lucy explained. 'They want something that does the numbers. Hits the stats.'

Henry shrugged and looked sorrowful. 'Basically, I must write up these two nights as either brilliant or terrible. Nothing in between.'

'I know what I'm hoping for,' Lucy said, her eyes glinting.

Mara managed to keep a smile on her face before turning away. With Lucy in the hotel, it was going to be a very long forty-eight hours.

Nine

'I dated a butler once,' Riga said as Tarn pressed the button to summon the lift. Edie grinned: one of Riga's stories was incoming.

'He had very smooth hands,' Riga mused, a slight smile on her lips.

'Do I want to know this?' Edie asked. Something screeched within the lift.

'He made his own hand cream, that's all,' Riga said innocently. 'It was a secret recipe that he developed for a certain member of the royal family.'

'I didn't know butlering was so involved,' Sean replied.

'The course I was sent on,' Tarn said, 'encouraged us to learn as many skills as possible so that we could anticipate a client's every need, whether it was crocheting antimacassars, learning different languages or studying poetry to help write love letters.'

Edie was about to ask which skills Tarn had acquired when the lift door opened, revealing an ornate interior of reflective walls and metallic vines.

About to step inside, Riga hesitated. 'Not sure I want to go voluntarily into a mirror box.'

'What do you mean?' Sean asked.

'Mirror boxes are used to either reflect a person's bad actions back upon them,' Riga said, 'to encourage self-reflection, or to allow people to see someone for who they truly are.'

'It's a witchy thing,' Edie explained.

'Well, it's either get in the mirror box or walk up the staircase, I'm afraid,' Tarn said. A note of impatience had slipped into her voice.

Nicholas the pug trotted into the lift and blinked at Riga.

'Looks like Nicholas has decided for me,' Riga said. 'He doesn't fancy the stairs.'

Not that Riga could've managed them. Edie didn't think she could either, as beautiful as the staircase was.

Their room, 'Suite 1', was at the end of a corridor. Tarn took an old-fashioned brass key from her pinafore pocket, unlocked the door and stood back to let everyone else enter.

'Wait,' Sean said, walking into a large room with plush sofas, a massive telly, a writing desk and a huge, rounded bay window – one of the turrets, presumably. 'This is all for *us*?'

'This is your lounge, shared between the bedrooms,' Tarn said, her hands behind her back. 'Your tea- and coffee-making facilities are here on the cabinet, and the mini fridge is hidden underneath, containing complimentary water, wine, beer and juice. Everything will be replenished tomorrow, so don't hold back. There's also a pillow menu – just ring reception or me for your choice of goose down, hypoallergenic, hard or memory foam, and you can also choose your bath oil.'

'No baths for us,' Edie said. 'Showers all the way. I had a fall in a slippy bath last year that nearly cost me my other hip.'

'The bathroom is fully accessible, so that won't be a problem.' Tarn went across to the window seat. 'This is the suite I'd pick if I were to choose. A room with a view of the harbour and out to sea – I'd sit here using these all day.' She picked up the binoculars on the windowsill. 'You could spot shags, sanderlings, red-breasted mergansers . . . maybe a greylag goose.'

Edie made a mental note to compile a crossword based on coastal birds. It'd mean she could get inventive with the word 'shag'.

Tarn moved back towards Sean. 'Your bedroom, Mr Brand-O'Sullivan, is over here.' She opened a door, behind which Edie spotted a king-size bed with a wicker hamper on top. Sean lifted the lid of the hamper and started digging inside. 'You need to look in *your* hamper, Mum – mine's got shortbread, chocolates, gourmet popcorn . . .' He pulled out two teddies with bowties in Clark tartan. 'And things for the kids!'

The room also had a made-up sofa bed for Juniper and a cot for Rose. Edie imagined reading the kids a bedtime story after an amazing Christmas Day on Holly Island. Jealousy sliced her like a papercut – right now they'd be with their other grandparents. What if the storm made travelling by boat impossible and they couldn't get here?

'Don't worry, the storm is due to die down by midnight,' Tarn called back, as if reading her mind. 'I bet the sea will be mirror-calm by morning. Swindon will pick them up and all shall be well.' Coming through to the lounge, she looked over to Riga who was leaning on the back of the sofa, head down. 'The other bedroom is just here.' She was anticipating all their needs. Butler school had taught her well.

Nicholas ran into Edie and Riga's bedroom and jumped straight into a dog basket by the window.

'We thought you'd want him in your room,' Tarn said, with the fond smile dog-lovers give other owners' hounds.

Nicholas thumped his stubby tail and gnawed his claws.

'If he's trying his bed, I'll give mine a go,' Riga said as she sat down. She bounced gently on the mattress. The hamper at the end of the bed bobbed like a ship on the ocean. 'Not bad.'

'Would you like me to empty your luggage?' Tarn asked. 'I could put your clothes in the wardrobe, press your things for tonight and lay them out?'

'No, thanks.' Riga lay back on the bed, eyes closed. 'Makes me think of being readied for a coffin, my clothes empty of their corpse.'

Tarn laughed. 'Fair enough. I'm here to help, though, so just give me a call on this number if you need anything at all and I'll jump to it.' She placed a card on the bedside table. 'Basically, whistle and I'll come to you. As Mara said, I'll be leading a tour of the hotel at three, once I've settled the other guests in. Let me know if you'd like to join me.'

'I'm afraid I'm all in for the whisky,' Riga replied.

'And I think I'll wander round on my own and skip

afternoon tea,' Sean said, opening a packet of posh-looking crisps, presumably plucked from his hamper. 'Build up an appetite for dinner.'

When both Sean and Tarn had left the suite, Edie lay down next to Riga. 'Are you okay?' she asked softly. 'That was one very long journey.'

Riga turned over, so slowly that Edie could tell how much pain she was in. Now facing each other on the edges of their pillows, the backs of their hands were touching, their noses two inches apart. Riga smiled and Edie's concern subsided, or rather submerged.

'I'm aching, yes, and I'll have a nap before we go down for tea, but I am *so* happy. I'm back in Scotland at last, for one. And how many days involve waking up on a train in the Highlands, then spying dolphins and eagles in the wild? This is already one of my favourite memories, and I'm still living it.'

'*And* you haven't even had a whisky yet.'

Riga kissed Edie on the tip of her nose. 'Exactly, so I'm ecstatic. Now, open that hamper. I want to see our gratis goodies.'

Edie yanked the hamper over. 'I get first dibs.' Opening the lid, she took out the programme of events. 'Do you fancy going to the ghost story tonight?'

'Wouldn't miss it,' Riga said. 'On "Unholy Island", it's only right that we meet some spirits.'

Ten

'You've got to try the curd,' Kimberley said, handing Mara a clean spoon and pointing to a ramekin. They were in the kitchen, putting the final touches to the afternoon tea. Izzie dolloped cod roe onto tiny tattie scones; Owain was arranging finger sandwiches on the bottom tier of a cake stand; Ryan was nowhere to be seen.

Mara dipped into the thick and shiny preserve. It was just the right shade of orange to feel festive. 'What's it made from?'

'Wild sea buckthorn and whisky. I foraged the sea buckthorn within a mile of the distillery on Lewis.' Kimberley was born and raised on the Isle of Lewis, the largest island of the Western Isles. She returned as often as possible to see her parents. Now she gazed at Mara as she tasted.

The curd was delicious, the buckthorn giving the citrus tang, but with a sweetness that contrasted with the whisky's smoke. 'It's amazing. So smooth.'

Kimberley rarely smiled, but now she grinned. 'Wait till you've tried it on the scones.'

Ryan loped in, yawning. 'Someone should've come to get me. I had a nap and overslept.'

'I rang you, texted you and knocked on your door several times.' Kimberley's jaw tensed, her smile long gone. 'No response.'

Ryan shrugged. 'I'm a very deep sleeper. In fact, I'm very deep all round.' He raised his eyebrows as if waiting for them to applaud his apparent witticism.

Izzie sniffed, as if disputing his depth.

Tarn popped her head round the kitchen door. 'They're gathering in the lounge for tea. I've got no takers for the tour, so direct me as you wish.'

'Just chip in where you see a gap,' Ryan said.

Kimberley glared at him. 'As pastry chef, afternoon tea is *my* show. Tarn, if you could deal with the tea and coffee orders, and make sure they've got their timers.' She pointed to the silver tray of tea paraphernalia. Kimberley rivalled Edie in tea specificity. 'Izzie, could you arrange the middle tiers as we discussed, and Ryan, seeing as we've managed without you so far, perhaps you should get on with the rest of your dinner prep?'

Ryan shrugged again. 'Suits me. And it's how it should be. You'd never get the lead singer of the main band playing keyboards for the support act.' He then went over to the walk-in fridge and shut the door as if he was in *The Bear*.

Mara, Kimberley and Izzie shared a glance. Kimberley mouthed the words, 'What a wanker.' Mara didn't disagree.

In the lounge, all the lamps were on, taking over from the last of the midwinter sun. Swindon was behind a long table, pouring a snifter of the first whisky into bevelled shot glasses with the hotel's crest. Edie and Riga were at the little table nearest the fire; George was on a sofa with Celine and Anna; Lucy and Henry were in matching high-backed armchairs, facing and yet not looking at each other; Robert was sitting on his own by the long mirror, correcting his hair. Silver tea and coffee pots with matching timers, strainers and milk jugs gleamed in the firelight.

Mara placed stands on Edie's table and that of George, Celine and Anna, at the same time as Tarn and Izzie delivered the rest. 'Wow,' Riga said, making Mara smile despite Nicholas sniffing her shoes.

Kimberley stepped forward. 'Your afternoon tea today is based on the flavour profiles of our chosen Scottish whiskies. Everything has been handmade, or carefully sourced from local suppliers. The finger sandwiches are wild Scottish smoked salmon with cream cheese and dill; fresh crab caught this morning in Oban; smoked Scottish cheddar with mango pickle; and peppered ham with foraged Western Isles leaves.'

Henry reached for one of the sandwiches, but Lucy slapped his hand away. He glared at her, then stared lovingly at the table of shot glasses.

'On the second tier,' Kimberley continued, 'you have a crustless kedgeree quiche with wild haddock; local cod's roe on mini tattie scones; and Highland Blue Murder cheese on oat cakes. Then we get to the sweet treats, my favourite. On the third tier you'll find Dundee cake; our take on a Tunnock's tea cake with a marshmallow kirsch centre; and scones, both plain and our signature Aster spiced fruit, amped up to a festive level. To go with the scones, we have bramble and Rùm rum jam, clotted cream and sea buckthorn and whisky curd.'

'What if we want a different jam?' Lucy asked. 'Or butter?'

Mara knew what Kimberley would be thinking. When Mara had suggested adding a simple raspberry jam, the pastry chef had said, 'Everything, and I mean everything, has been planned. I have orchestrated every sense. There's no way I'll be serving up raspberry jam.' On this occasion, though, Kimberley simply blinked and replied, 'We have everything you could wish for in our stores. It may not be handmade in-house, but you are welcome to anything that could improve your experience at the Aster.'

Mara wanted to applaud her. She settled for patting Kimberley on the back as she bowed slightly to a few claps, then went back to the kitchen.

'Now it's my turn.' Swindon's low rumble carried around the lounge.

'About time!' Henry shouted.

'Thank you, Mr Palmer – I agree, it's always time for me. Our first whisky is a very famous one, from Skye.' Swindon lifted the bottle of Talisker as Izzie carried round the tray of filled shot glasses. 'It goes perfectly with the sandwiches, bringing out the smoke notes while they accentuate the peat of the whisky.'

Mara watched as everyone took a sip. George looked over to her, raised his glass and smiled. Lucy scrunched the whisky round her mouth then spat it back in the glass. Henry looked at her shot glass as if considering finishing her dregs.

Swindon led them through his list of whiskies, taking them on a journey around the Scottish Isles and Highlands, advising them on the pecan and raisin notes in one glass, the butterscotch blancmange in another. They ate and drank; he talked and talked. By the time he'd reached his parting shot, the whole group seemed happy. Even Lucy's perma-scowl had lifted.

'Any questions?' Swindon asked.

'From what you've told us,' Riga said, 'you've been a sailor, a fisherman, a distiller . . . how did you end up here?'

'I think he meant questions about the whisky!' Tarn said.

'Oh, I'll answer anything,' Swindon said, settling down near to Edie and Riga. After a couple of armchair thrusts towards the fire, he stretched his long legs out and grunted in satisfaction. 'And *to* anything. I've had more names than jobs, and I've had a lot of jobs.'

Tarn backed away, a tight smile fading.

'I heard that the castle was being renovated into a hotel, and that the owners needed a caretaker and boatman. And, as I can take care, and boat, I applied. The Morecombe-Clarks were kind enough to take me on in June and I've been helping out ever since. I've hacked down enough holly to make thousands of wreaths.'

'Do you live here?' Edie asked.

'I do now,' Swindon replied, 'in the staff quarters, thanks to Mara and her parents. Before that? Well, I was in Oban for many years, then lived on Uisce, then a houseboat on Loch Tay. It wasn't much of a boat, though – it was leaking, so I'd have ended up on the bottom of the loch like a brown trout.'

'As fascinating as this is,' Lucy said, standing up and raising her eyebrows at her husband, 'I need to rest before dinner. I don't know how you expect us to eat again after all this food!'

'You didn't have to eat,' Edie snapped. 'You make it sound like they force-fed you.'

Riga's lips pressed together, as if suppressing a laugh. Mara would love to have that with someone.

Henry followed Lucy's clipped steps to the lift, stopping to hoover up leftover shots of eighteen-year-old Glen Ord.

Robert watched them, then wrote something in his pocket-sized Moleskine, refolded his napkin, containing the crumbs, and left without saying a word. At no point had he mentioned anything about the food, or the whisky, or talked to any of the other guests. For the first time, Mara wondered why a man like him would come here, on his own.

When it was just Edie and Riga left of the guests, Mara sat with them and Swindon. His hands shook as he picked Nicholas up and held him on his lap; his skin was grey beneath the all-year tan.

'You look like you need a break,' Riga said with concern.

'I'm okay,' he said, flushing as if unused to people being worried for him. Which, Mara supposed, he probably was. She'd never seen him with anyone, or even speaking on the phone. 'I don't normally talk so much in one day. I've used up a year's supply of consonants.'

Mara was jabbed with guilt. Swindon was nearer eighty than seventy, and she'd had him working since four that morning, sending him out early to get the freshest fish from the market, collecting and looking after the guests, and now the tasting.

'Take the rest of the day off,' she said. 'You've done so much today, and in the run-up, too.'

He looked to the fireplace – one of his duties was to keep all the fires and candles in the hotel burning till midnight. 'I'll look after the flames,' she continued. 'You get some sleep. It's another big day tomorrow.'

'Sure is,' Swindon replied. 'Need to make sure I'm at Oban again at nine am.'

'We're very grateful. I can't wait to see my grandkids,' Edie said, looking from him to Riga, eyebrows furrowed. She was probably worried he'd be too tired to collect them.

Getting up with difficulty, Swindon placed Nicholas on Riga's lap. Mara stepped backwards, away from the dog, hoping no one noticed.

Edie watched Swindon head for the staircase in the Gold Bar, down to the staff quarters. 'He's an interesting man,' she said.

'Sure is,' Riga echoed. 'I admire people who live life *their* way.'

Edie nodded, although she was rolling her lips together as if holding something back. 'How did he say he found out about this place?' she asked Mara.

'I think it was one of the suppliers in Oban,' Mara said, trying to remember Swindon's first email. 'But it could've been anyone. Us buying Holly Island has been the talk of the Western Isles for the last eighteen months. They all think it's a folly.'

'What makes you want to prove them wrong?' Edie's eyes were sharp, piercing, but somehow kind.

'Edie . . .' Riga said with a note of warning.

'No, it's okay,' Mara replied. 'It's a good question. I suppose it's partly to please my dad, who wanted to set up a business with me, to help me in my career in hospitality. I'd been floundering in mid-level management, being too afraid to take the next step or to ask for more.'

'You're afraid of lots of things, aren't you?' Edie said gently, her eyes flicking towards Nicholas.

'Edie, Mara doesn't need the third degree on one of the most important days of her life!' Riga said. 'She needs a break, and a glamour tisane – black tea, cinnamon, nutmeg and milk, stirred seven times, drawing in confidence.'

'If you're so scared of life and, I suspect, love, what made you take the huge leap of faith into trying to tame this apparently cursed island?' Edie asked.

Mara's cheeks heated under Edie's scrutiny. 'I don't know.' How had Edie read her so quickly? How had she given herself away?

'People aren't crosswords to be solved,' Riga chided. 'Leave her alone.'

'I'm just encouraging her to think about it,' Edie said. 'Because I'd say, for a scared person, you're showing a huge amount of courage. And I admire that more than anything.'

Eleven

The killer stood at the back of the Gold Bar, sipping their Aster Aurelio, a take on the Bellini. Grenadine added a sunset stripe to the peach fizz while cinnamon vodka gave it a Christmas-kissed kick. Each glass was rimmed with gold leaf, echoing the counter that took the establishment's name too literally. The star engraved on the glasses was a nice touch, although the killer bet most would be stolen before the first year of trading was out.

Most of the staff and guests were here. Small talking. Sequin wearing. Swaying to Bublé. One scowled, another looked sad; not even free drinks could crack them.

Raising their glass to one of the guests, the killer smiled. All had gone to plan, so far, at least. Even the storm had played into their hands. The snow was a beautiful touch, giving a seasonal frisson to the occasion. If the killer believed in external forces, they'd think an entity was blessing them, but they didn't. Intervention and judgement must come from human hands. Theirs.

The killer walked to the French doors that looked over the back lawn. Not that you'd know the lawn was there – all the Narnia-style lampposts now showed was snow. Deep snow, too, creeping halfway up the legs of the bench.

ALEXANDRA BENEDICT

Next to it, the black twigs of the ash tree shivered in their winter sleep, dropping keys in the snow.

From here, the killer had a good angle to peer through the glass panels of the restaurant doors. They wanted one final look before the evening snapped into place.

Precision was everything, in both hospitality and murder: crisp linen, polished plates, the perfect measures of vermouth and poison. The killer had made sure that the crackers had been put in front of the right name plates – they couldn't count on anyone else doing things right. No one was reliable these days. Not staff, not friends, not family and certainly not narrators.

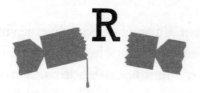

Twelve

Edie pushed her cocktail away after just one sip. It tasted like an M&S festive candle. Why would you put gold leaf on the rim? It was coming off in people's mouths, and that shouldn't happen at the beginning of an evening.

Riga, though, was on her third glass, finishing her own, Sean's and now Edie's. 'It's growing on me,' she said.

'It's *sticking* to you,' Edie replied. 'You'll look like a gold idol before long.'

'I was a make-up artist on *Goldfinger*, you know,' Riga said. 'I helped paint Shirley Eaton. I tried gold leaf instead, but she said it tickled too much.'

'Is there anything you haven't done?' Sean asked.

'A lady never tells,' Riga replied, with a twinkle that suggested there was nothing she hadn't done.

'Well, I'd never have gone to a place as posh as this without you winning that competition,' Sean said, looking around in wonder. 'Thank you *so* much.'

The Gold Bar *was* very swanky – low lighting, flattering mottled mirrors, high booths of plush purple velvet and tasselled oversized lampshades hanging over the tables. Even Riga had glanced around on their arrival and given one slow nod of approval.

The restaurant doors folded back, revealing a small, muscular man in too-tight chef whites standing with his legs wide and his hands on his hips. 'I'm Ryan Dreith,' he said, 'executive chef of The Star restaurant. This special Christmas Eve tasting menu combines the best of my carefully crafted dishes.' He placed his hands in prayer position. 'It means a lot to me that you're sharing such a special moment here this Christmas.' He then bowed, and walked backwards, his arms outstretched.

Edie caught Riga's eye. 'Wanker,' Riga mouthed.

'I'll eat his food, though,' Edie said, standing up. 'As long as he's washed his hands.'

Sean went in first to check where they were sitting. They were on the first of two round tables. Thankfully they hadn't mixed the parties up, although Edie had been placed two seats down from Robert. She turned up her new hearing aid, otherwise she'd struggle to hear Celine and Anna opposite.

At each place setting was a baroque, deep-purple cracker bearing their name, an engraved name plate and a little doll. She held the doll up – it was of her.

'Have you seen this?' Riga thrust her doll towards Edie, laughing. 'I've got my own me!'

'They haven't captured your cheekbones,' Edie said. 'Yours are far higher.'

'Your effigy looks even more astute than you,' Riga said of Edie's doll. 'If that's possible. I wouldn't want to try and hide something from her!'

'I'd hope you'd never need to keep anything from me or her,' Edie replied.

'My life's an open book,' Riga said. 'With so many pages it takes a long time to read.'

Across the table, Celine and Anna were making their little figurines fight – at least, it looked like fighting. Robert was not amused. He didn't touch his Cole-Mortelli doll, just moved it away with his butter knife. Edie wondered what that meant for his ego.

More crackers were piled in cross formations on either side of a holly and gold-sprayed eucalyptus display with a gold candelabra at its centre.

Putting her doll and cracker – handmade by the look of it, and heavy – to one side, Edie picked up her brass name plate and turned it over, watching it glint in the candlelight. Between those, the dolls and the crackers, they'd gone to a lot of trouble for one short break.

'"Tasting menu" means "many tiny courses", right?' Sean said to Celine.

'Yes, that is how it translates into French,' she smiled back. She picked up her own cracker and tugged at one of the thin purple bows. 'Tell me, when do we pull these?'

'Often now, before the meal starts,' Sean said, looking over to Edie, who had only occasionally tolerated Christmas crackers when he was growing up. 'Although I've known people who pull them after the starter or before the pudding. Depends on the tradition in each family. It's like presents – every house has its own opening etiquette and rules. It's unusual to have the crackers on Christmas Eve, but I'm all for it. The more cracks, the merrier. We'll probably have them tomorrow, at Christmas dinner, too.'

'I vote we pull them now,' Edie said, the guilt of past Christmases lingering.

Sean picked up his cracker and, crossing his arms, offered the other end to her. Edie waggled her cracker at Riga. When all six at their table were holding two cracker ends, Anna called out, 'One, two, three, pull!'

The crackers snapped like cap-guns. Gifts, hats and pieces of paper shot across the table. The smoked smell of silver fulminate hung in the air.

'You won!' Sean said to Celine, who was staring at the larger end of the cracker in her hand.

'What does that mean?' she asked.

'You get to keep whatever's inside,' Edie explained. 'Although was that the one with your name on? As, judging by the dolls, they may have gifts specific to each guest.'

Celine showed Edie that her name was written in looped writing on one side, then peered into the tube. Extending her forefinger, she dragged out a thin piece of paper, a paper hat and a fortune fish. 'There's something else in there,' she said. 'Something gold.' She shook the cracker and out fell something heavy. She held it up by a red ribbon loop. 'It's a gold-plated dart! I love darts!'

'Beats a mini pack of cards or a screwdriver,' Edie said.

Robert held up a mini screwdriver, eyebrow raised in irony.

'That looks fancy, though,' Edie said. 'Wooden handle, maybe even silver-plated.'

Robert shrugged and discarded the tool next to his doll. On the other table, more crackers snapped. Ivan and

Felicity were sitting alongside Henry, Lucy and George. They were clearly out to impress the critic.

Edie peered inside her own cracker. Within it, alongside the usual hat etc., was a keyring, but this wasn't the typical cracker crap. It was a gold-plated, Vivienne Westwood tartan keyring. Mara, or whoever had had these made, had done their research. 'This is incredible,' Edie said, turning to Riga. 'I like this five-star life.'

Riga, though, was staring at a black-and-red beaded necklace. 'I don't understand,' she was saying. She started pulling it through her fingers and Edie realised it was a rosary. Riga lifted it to her nose and sniffed. 'It doesn't smell.' She sounded disappointed. Scent was very important to Riga.

'Did you tell them you wanted a rosary or something?' Edie asked. The hotel had sent through a questionnaire asking for their preferences and any requests. Maybe Riga had suggested Midnight Mass, and they'd made the leap?

Riga shook her head. 'No! Still, it's a very nice one. What did you get?' she asked Sean.

Sean was holding up a ping pong ball as reverently as if it were a gemstone. 'It's signed by Andrew Baggaley!'

'And that is . . . ?' Edie asked. Sean had taken up table tennis at the end of last year and become obsessed, joining a team in Weymouth and following the sport nationally.

'Only the youngest ever British Men's Singles Champion,' Sean said. 'He won the title, aged fifteen, in Oban, no less.'

'Oh my God!' George shouted, leaping up from his chair. His laughter came as thick and fast as the snow outside as he held out a large hand to show the room something shining on his palm.

'Give us a clue, old chap,' Henry said,

George ran over to Mara, who'd been standing by the desk, watching him and smiling. 'Thank you so much!'

'I wish I could take the credit,' Mara said, 'but Mum found the maker at a craft market and commissioned bespoke crackers for this occasion. What present did you get?'

'It's a gold-plated carriage that goes with my train set.' He looked shyly again at his shoes.

A look of awe crossed Mara's face. 'What's the scale of your train set?'

'Who cares?' said Robert. 'Where's the food?'

'And drink!' Henry said.

George reached into his jacket pocket and took out his doll. 'This size. One-twelfth. It takes up all of my attic, like Rod Stewart, but with less affection for Farage. I'm going to dress little me up as a driver and put me in the railway cottage opposite the station.'

Mara's mouth opened but no words came out.

'Can someone explain why I've got a gold cookie cutter in the shape of a murder victim?' Anna held it up. It really did have the cliched chalk outline of a crime scene victim.

'It's a ginger-dead man!' George said, laughing.

'But I don't even like baking,' Anna replied. 'Or cooking. Or cookies. Why did I get this when others got things that are specific to their hobbies or interests?'

'I got a gold-plated sewing machine decoration,' Felicity said. 'And I've never sewn anything in my life.

And my Ivan got a gold brush, when he hasn't needed to do more than comb his remaining hairs for years. Sorry, darling.'

'No, you're quite right,' Ivan replied, smiling.

'Whereas my cracker gave me a Charles Dickens two-pound coin with threefold striking errors!' Henry said, slurring his words. 'Do you know how rare they are? Extremely!'

'We all got a present,' Riga said, going through the rosary. 'Can't we all be grateful for that?'

'You're right,' Anna said, lowering her head as if ashamed. 'Got carried away there. Shows me up as an only child.'

There was a pause filled by the young server with pink curls and blue roots arriving with three baskets.

'I'm Izzie,' she said, 'and I'll be looking after your table this evening.' She placed a basket between Edie and Riga, Sean and Robert, and Celine and Anna in turn. 'Today's fresh bread selection is tarragon and sea-salt focaccia, scorched Bannock and caraway rye roll. The three butters on the table are garlic, green olive and pink salt.'

Edie went for a warm hunk of focaccia that stretched like a concertina as she pulled it apart. Celine eased a purple hat with gold trim onto her head, positioning it at just the right angle to be jaunty before taking a picture. Only she could look this charming when taking a paper hat selfie. 'What is this?' She took the red fortune fish from its packet and waved it in the air. 'And what am I to do with it?'

'Pop it on your palm, and it'll divine what kind of person you are,' Riga explained.

'Oh, I love telling people's fortunes. Especially my own.' Laying the fish across her lifeline, Celine watched its edges curve inwards. 'So, what am I?'

'It'll say on the instructions. Usually it's something like being "passionate" or a "dead fish".' Edie didn't believe in stuff like that but always felt a frisson as the fish flipped.

Celine read from the paper that came with the fortune fish:

'*Moving Tail – INNOCENT*

Moving Head – GUILTY

Moving Head and Tail – HUNG JURY

Curling Sides – SCALES ARE BALANCED

Turns Over – IN DENIAL

Motionless – PASSIVE GUILT

Curling into a Ball – SENSIBLE UNDER THE CIRCUMSTANCES.'

'I've never heard of *those* fortunes before,' Edie said.

'So, my "scales are balanced"? What does that mean?'

'I suppose, given the rest of the fortunes,' Anna said, frowning as she read the instructions, 'That you're balanced between guilt and innocence.'

'I could've told it that,' Celine said. 'You try now.' She tipped the now flat fish onto Anna's palm. It didn't move. 'You have "passive guilt".'

'Nonsense,' Anna said in faux indignation. 'I'm never passive!'

'In the old way of doing it,' Edie said, who'd looked

up the traditional instructions, 'you are dead emotionally. Or perhaps it indicates your upcoming death?'

'What?' Anna covered her heart and pretended to die.

'Is that true?' Celine said. 'Have I predicted your death?'

'Relax, prophetess,' Edie said to Celine. 'It's a bit of fun. Cheer us up by telling your joke.'

Celine unrolled the piece of paper, then her brow furrowed. 'It's not a joke. It's some kind of riddle.'

'Oh, marvellous!' Edie said. '*Now* we're talking.' She settled back to concentrate. 'Read it out loud.'

Celine recited:

'*Named a dad with no known child,*
A housebreaker beatified,
I punish those who're on my list,
Yet no one knows my naughtiness.
I've many names, yet posts still find me;
I leave cookie crumbs behind me.
WHO AM I?'

'Too easy,' Edie said. 'Santa Claus. Father Christmas, if you prefer, seeing as it mentions being a dad. Or Père Noël.'

'You're very quick,' Anna said, eyes wide. 'I hadn't even made sense of the first line.'

'No one likes a know-it-all,' Robert said.

'I do,' Riga said, kissing Edie on the lips.

Anna cheered and Celine silently cymballed her fingers. Robert turned away, looking instead at his own piece of paper. 'Try this then:

"*My first another word for 'pack',*

My next another name for 'cat'.
To punish I will use a birch,
But how? You must do your research.
I'm horny and have Schnappsy breath;
I run from my harm, my name means death.
WHO AM I?'''

Robert read through it again silently. 'I don't understand. In what way is this supposed to be fun or festive?'

Edie pressed her lips together to stop the answer coming out. Her brain had already flown through the riddle and landed on the solution, but she should let others play. 'It's definitely Christmas-based. Although less so in this country.'

'Give us a clue,' Anna said.

'There are so many in the riddle. Some don't quite fit, but such is the way with rhymes. I'll go through them – what is another word for "pack"?' Edie asked.

'Wrap?' Riga suggested.

'Load? Box? Parcel?' Sean listed.

'Could be as in the "rat-pack", like "group" or "gang"?' Celine said.

Maybe it wasn't as easy as Edie thought. 'Okay, maybe try another word for "cat".'

'Feline? Moggy?' Robert suggested.

'Pussy?' Riga said, because of course she did. Anna's sudden bark of a laugh made the other table look over.

'Very nearly,' Edie replied.

'Puss!' Sean slammed his hand down on the table, making the gold salt and pepper shakers jump. 'Which means the synonym for "pack" is "cram"!' He turned to

Edie. 'That's what growing up with a teacher and cruci-verbalist can do for you!'

Robert shrugged. 'You're going to have to spell it out for us, son.'

Sean bristled slightly at the 'son', but just said, 'The answer is Krampus!'

'Which explains the "horny" section.' Anna extended her forefingers and stuck her fists on top of her head to make horns.

'Are you doing the riddles?' Lucy called over from the other table. 'Because the one I got has left us flummoxed:

"With one big foot, in a torn cloak,
I oversee the spinning folk.
On twelfth night The Bright One acted,
Shook her head; a Star redacted.
Disobey and touch the treadle:
I'll stitch you up with sweat and pebbles.
WHO AM I?"'

'Whoever she is,' Henry said, 'I wouldn't take her for dinner.'

Lucy rolled her eyes. 'Sure,' she said.

'We've had Santa and Krampus so far, so I suspect it is one of the Christmas visiting figures,' Celine said. 'A German one, perhaps.'

'Well, of course it is,' Robert said. 'That's obviously the theme.' He was rubbing his chest. Probably indigestion – he'd eaten his bread rather quickly.

'Which figure is this one, then?' Edie asked him. 'Seeing as you're so certain.'

Just then, from the kitchen, Ryan Dreith blasted a curse

at the kitchen staff and slammed the door. Robert stood and shook breadcrumbs from his napkin. His paper hat fell from his lap. From a pocket of his jacket, a fortune fish packet poked out like a prognosticating pocket square. 'I'm sure you'll work it out by the time I return.' He strode towards the toilets.

'Do you know who the riddle means?' Riga whispered to Edie.

'It's in my brain but I can't find it,' Edie replied, shaking her head as if that would dislodge the name. She really should remember this: she'd compiled a crossword three Christmases ago that contained many festive bestowers of reward and punishment, and had researched lots more. She knew the answer, she was certain.

Izzie came over, laden with small plates covered with tiny cloches. She laid one in front of each diner, asking them to take off the metal covers in unison to reveal a tiny disc of risotto that smelled like a burning forest floor.

'Your attention, please,' Ryan said, bursting out of the kitchen and jumping onto a spare chair. He held his arms out wide as if he were surfing. 'Your first dish is a truffle risotto bite, slowly cooked over a pine smoker and finished with parmesan snow. I foraged the truffles myself with my own pet pigs, one of which you'll be eating tomorrow. It's been paired by Mara and me with a robust Barolo, overturning the usual rules of starting with white. Enjoy!' He then jumped back off his chair and half ran through the kitchen door.

Izzie was back, pouring out half glasses of brick-orange wine.

'Is he going to do that before every course?' Sean asked. 'And did he say that we are going to be served his *pet*?'

'He's an edgelord eejit, ignore him.' Edie had used 'edgelord' in a recent crossword and was glad of the opportunity to repeat it in real life.

Anna pulled a face as she looked at her plate. 'I don't know whether to eat this truffle out of respect for the pig's last act or refuse on principal.'

'Perhaps its last act is feeding us?' Celine said while taking photos, or maybe a video, of the risotto.

'If the pig's as delicious as this,' Edie said, after the risotto closed her eyes in umami bliss, 'I'll salute it along with the blanket it's buried in.'

'Are we going to do the game, then?' Henry called over.

Robert had arrived back at the table. 'What do you mean?' he replied.

Henry held up his unfurled cracker. 'On the inside of mine there's a question – it says it's a "game", so we should play it, yes? You know I like to play games.'

From Felicity's jump in her seat and roll of her eyes, Edie suspected that Henry had pinched her bottom. God. How were men like him still around?

Edie unfurled her own curled tube, and there it was, printed in big black letters: 'ICE-BREAKER GAME! Question: what's the worst thing you've ever done? Answer honestly or face the consequences!'

'What are the consequences?' Riga asked.

'It doesn't say,' Edie replied.

Sean unwrapped his cracker, and it had the same question, as did Riga's and everyone's else's.

'Looks like they forgot to put in more than one question,' Mara said, frowning.

'That's a bit of a swizz,' Anna said. 'That's like us only having one ice pick between us to break up an iceberg!'

'Are you saying our conversation is frozen?' Celine said, laughing. 'Then I'll start us off. The worst thing I've ever done is . . .' She paused for dramatic effect. From the clear shine in her eyes, Edie suspected that Celine thought she'd done very little wrong in her life. 'I once stole a textbook that I couldn't afford for my university course. But I felt so guilty I took it back the next day.'

'Come on,' Robert said, eyes glinting. 'You can do better than that.'

'No, really. That's it! And you?' she asked him in return.

'There is no worst thing I've done,' Robert said. 'My copy book is clean. I have no guilt.'

'That's either completely untrue or alarming.' Celine turned to Anna. 'What about you?'

'Oh, I don't know,' Anna replied, smiling. 'I once jumped over the barriers on the Northern Line? I used to steal Pick'n'Mix when I was a kid, but I stopped when my mum caught me and laid into me like a warrior in Woolworths.'

'You can do better than that!' Riga said. 'Everyone's got a tale.'

Anna bit her lip. 'I don't think I know everyone well enough to open up that much. Why?' she asked Riga. 'What's the worst thing *you've* done?'

'Far too many to choose from, darling,' Riga replied.

'The *worst* depends on the day. Today . . .' She paused, rubbing the beads of the rosary one after the other as if moving through a string of misdemeanours. 'Today, I'd say the worst thing I did was also necessary at the time. But that's all I want to share.'

'You're right,' George said, thoughtfully, taking a sip of wine. Mara was looking at him intently. 'It's hard to know what the *worst* thing one's ever done is, categorically speaking. The one *I* feel worst about,' he paused, chin quivering, 'is hoping that Mum would die. She was in such pain, and she wanted to go, but I was wishing for me, too. No, not "too". For me. I wanted her to go so I'd be free.'

The dining room went quiet.

'Keep it light, mate!' Henry said, bashing George on the back. 'It's Christmas Eve, for Christ's sake! This is supposed to break the ice, not make us cry!'

'I thought it was a way of making connections,' George said, quietly. 'I do enough small talk as provost. This is a way of being real.'

'You're right,' Mara said. 'Why answer if it's not genuine and heartfelt? I, for example—'

'Remember you're the General Manager, darling,' Felicity said, more than a chip of ice in her voice. 'It's not appropriate for the staff to get involved.'

'But all the staff have crackers,' Mara replied, holding up an unbroken one with her name on from where it lay in a pile with several others. 'I assume they have the same question.'

'And we can answer it in our own time, in the staff quarters,' Ivan said. 'Now, I spy our Chef Ryan at the kitchen door, waiting to announce the next dish. We can play more games later.'

The tasting menu coursed by for the next two hours. Plate after delicious plate was placed down by Izzie, described by Ryan, then replaced. By the time Edie was licking mulled wine soufflé from a chocolate spoon, she'd lost count of the dishes and wines she'd tried. Even Riga, who would usually be describing how everything smelled and tasted, was silent. Awed, perhaps, by the sheer amount of food and its world-class execution.

'Are you all right?' Edie asked, so full she could hardly speak.

'I'm exhausted,' Riga explained, placing her cool hand on Edie's. 'This has been amazing; the whole day has been . . . jaw-dropping. But it's also been long. I need to go to bed.'

'I'll go up with you,' Edie said, beginning to stand.

'No, it's okay,' Riga said quickly. 'You want to hear the ghost story, and I want you to tell me all about it. You're my proxy.'

'I'll make sure she gets up to the room okay,' Tarn said, making both Riga and Edie rear back in surprise. She was crouching between their chairs, having arrived silently, already foreseeing Riga's needs. 'Would you like your wheelchair?' she asked.

Riga nodded, and three minutes later she was kissing Edie on the cheek before being wheeled away. Nicholas looked back at Edie, then ran after Riga.

'I should go with her,' Edie said, watching Riga disappear through the restaurant doors.

'Let her go for now,' Sean said gently. 'She told me earlier that she needs some time on her own.'

'Did she? When?'

'When you went to the toilet between the fifth and sixth course, or was it the sixth and seventh? Anyway, she seemed more quiet than usual, so I asked if she was okay.'

'Why didn't she tell me that's what she needed?' Edie asked. 'I'd've understood.' *But would she?* she wondered. She never wanted to be separated from Riga and thinking that Riga needed time away from her made Edie feel like a cracker, torn apart.

Thirteen

Mara knelt by the library fireplace, flames whispering heat towards her cheeks. She'd left the dinner early, sneaking out to feed the fires and take a minute to breathe while Ryan was singing the praises of meadowsweet. She only had a few minutes; the guests would be here soon, ready to be warmed by the fire and chilled by the ghost story.

Cortisol burned through her. What if no one came? What if she was left to read a ghost story only to the ghosts that haunted the halls? The last time she'd performed, in a play at the Edinburgh Fringe ten years ago, there'd been only two people and one dog in the audience. If no one had turned up, she'd have been able to slope off, find a pub and drink away the shame, but any more than one ticket holder and the show had to go on. So, it had, in front of three snoring mammals. Mara had given up acting not long afterwards. Mum had said it was 'for the best, given your talents'.

But she couldn't think of that now. Placing another chunky log on the fire, she stood and checked her list: decanters on sideboard, tea and coffee urns hot, petits fours laid on trays, candles lit, lamps dimmed, ghost story on her armchair, ready to go.

Voices floated across the lobby. Dinner was over and, from the sound of the laughter, everyone was very drunk.

Mara settled into the red wingback armchair closest to the fire. The story was printed out, now scrolled on her lap. She held her knees to stop them juddering and focused on the lights on the small Christmas tree in the corner.

Henry came in first, face flushed and blotchy. Swaying into his wife, he whispered something that made her face twist as he stumbled over to a bookcase, stroking the spines of books and grey box files as if they were the faces of long-lost loves.

'Help yourself to a drink and pull up an armchair,' Mara said. 'There's sherry, port, whisky or brandy in the decanters, or you could have tea, coffee or mulled wine.'

'How long will this last?' Lucy said as she took the stopper from a decanter and sniffed the sherry, made a face and put it down again. Edie, who had just walked in with Sean and George, made a similar face after seeing Lucy.

'About half an hour,' Mara replied, trying to calm her heartbeat.

'And there's nothing else when this finishes?' Lucy continued. 'When I looked through the programme, I was surprised to find no carol singing or Midnight Mass, because that's what you'd get at a *grand* hotel.'

'Tricky to have a midnight service without a church. Or a vicar,' Edie said drily.

'And it'd be difficult to rustle up carol singers on an otherwise deserted island,' George added. 'Although I can belt out "Good King Wenceslas" after a port or two. Talking of which . . .' George poured himself a heavy slug of Quinta do Noval Nacional 1991. Ivan had been keeping several bottles in the Morecombe-Clark cellar for years and had decided this was the time to unleash them.

Lucy didn't reply, just sat at the back. Henry, however, took a seat in the front row, beaming, placing his hand on Celine's knee. 'I *adore* ghost stories,' he said, 'especially in December. The darkest time of the year should be reflected in the shade of the tales we tell.'

Celine removed Henry's hand and went to sit next to Anna on the sofa. 'Sometimes we don't need to be told the stories to experience darkness,' she said. 'We experience it in others.'

'I think that it's best to relay positive stories at Christmas,' Lucy said. 'After all, that's why we have fairy lights and Yule logs – to remind us that the sun will return before long.'

'I like the Mark Gatiss ghost stories on telly,' Anna said as she shook off her high heels. 'The M. R. James ones especially. I applied to the same college as him just so I could imagine him reading his stories by the fireplace.' She placed her feet on the French woman's lap. Celine automatically began rubbing Anna's soles.

Mara wondered when they'd become so close, and how close they really were. They hadn't said they were together. But Anna was pan and poly, so maybe . . . anyway, she wished she could feel intimate enough with someone to entrust them with her feet, let alone her heart.

'And you can't beat the ones from the Sixties and

Seventies,' George said. 'Although now I can't stay in a hotel room with a spare bed.' It was true – he'd emailed the hotel requesting a single or double room as he couldn't bear a twin. He took a packet of Rennies out of his pocket. 'Don't know about you lot, but indigestion is kicking my chest in. Anyone want one?'

As George dealt out the tablets, Robert walked in and took three.

'I didn't expect this to be your thing,' Henry said.

'Thought I'd see what all the fuss was about,' Robert replied as he poured himself a whisky. He sat in the corner by the tree and held the bevelled glass close to his face, watching everyone through the amber.

When they had all settled, Mara nodded for Izzie and Tarn to turn down the lights bar those on the Christmas tree. She then struck a match and lit the tall candle next to her. The library hushed.

'This story,' Mara said, her voice deepening, cranking up the Banff accent she'd shaken off at drama school, 'is one I was told in the oldest pub in Oban harbour, on a night like this, not long ago.'

She'd added that bit, to add some atmosphere. She wouldn't dare talk to anyone just like that, in a pub, on her own. Her fictional self, though, wasn't afraid.

Robert took a fortune fish and balanced it on his hand. It flipped over. Was that guilty? She couldn't remember. *Focus*, she told herself as Mum and Dad walked into the library and sat down where they could see her. Mara's leg started to shake again. How had she thought she'd be able to do this? Especially in front of Mum.

Tarn gave her a thumbs-up; Celine made a heart shape with her thumbs; Anna blew her a kiss.

'I can't account for whether it all happened,' Mara continued, trying to lasso herself back into character. 'All I know for sure is that the woman this happened to believed every word. And now she is haunted by her own tale.'

The small crowd leaned in, beginning to take the story bait.

Mara felt the power of the expectant hush and harnessed it. 'This is her account,' she said. 'It's called, "Swim, Little Fish, Swim".'

Fourteen

That Christmas Eve began like any other day of my year: steeped tea and a bowl of porridge in my pyjamas. Why are you smirking? Oh, I see the confusion – my modifier was left dangling like lugworm bait. I was in M&S jim jams, supping strong tea (the first of the day is always the best) and waiting for the brown sugar crust atop the porridge to melt. Staring through the window, I saw myself in the dark glass sky and looked away. No one needs to see my face first thing, least of all me.

Half an hour later, I was weaving through the town, avoiding the heavings and leavings of the previous night's Christmas festivities. Revellers slunk past me on their way to bed, real ale and definite regret on their breath. I didn't envy them. I'd always preferred my way of life. Like a fish, I slept away the day, grazed at dawn and dusk and saw things more clearly in the dark. Now, these days I'd give anything for a head beset by a hangover and not ghosts.

Anyway, back then I reached the quayside, stopped for a moment and settled my gaze on the sea. Water always calmed me, absorbing like charcoal my worries and past. That morning, I cast a stone into the sea while I whispered of a dream that had netted and nettled me the night before. The sea swallowed both stone and nightmare.

Feeling lighter, I headed for my mooring. My long-term reliable boat hand, Julia, was off sick, so, as Christmas Eve demanded a bigger catch than normal – traditions of fish and chips and other feasts had to be fed, as did holiday freezers – I'd hired two extra hands.

Oscar, my nephew, was waiting by the Caroline-Louise, my boat. The red glow of his vape as he inhaled was the only way to see him through the dark and fog.

'All right, Auntie Rox.' Oscar had helped me on board since he was a slight ten-year-old. Now he was twenty-five, six foot two, a foreign rights agent in publishing and as strong and reliable as the black bollards on the quayside. He had studied languages at Cambridge and had just come back from working in Italy.

'Thanks so much for stepping in,' I said. 'I appreciate it.' He'd changed so much since graduating; become secretive. Withdrawn. Gaunt. This was a chance for me to catch up with him.

'Mum said you needed the help.' Oscar was my sister Kirsty's eldest, and my godson. I may not have been integral to his religious instruction or spiritual development, but I was very good at remembering his birthday, even if it was usually several weeks after it had happened. Oh, and placing fifty quid in an envelope and calling it a present.

'I'll make it worth your while if we have a good day.'

He gestured into the gloom. 'You call this day?'

'The best time of day. Not only do we have the world to ourselves, but the fish are waking, and they're hungry.'

110

'So am I,' Oscar said, rubbing his concave belly. 'Bella's gonna sneak some pastries from the bakery on her way here.'

Bella was Oscar's longest-lasting girlfriend to date, by which I don't mean that the others have died. You know what I mean. They'd met five years ago in the summer holiday. She was a beautician, but I often saw her in the early hours, helping out at her family's bakery on the high street. Long hair under a net, flour dust on her hands and face, she'd wave through the steamed windows as I walked past. She'd get there at two and be there till twelve. That kind of nocturnal hardworking made her the perfect addition to my little team. I wouldn't normally like this change to my routine, but it was Christmas after all. A time for family and merriment and three people killing fish.

The sound of running echoed over the cobbles. 'Am I late?' Bella said, out of breath.

'Don't worry. You're three and a half minutes early,' I said. 'And I hear you've brought pastries.'

She held up a pleasingly full paper bag.

Oscar, though, was looking at his phone. 'You're spot on with the timing, Auntie Rox. How do you do that without checking your watch?'

'One of my few talents,' I replied, boarding my boat. 'Shall we get on? We've got fish to catch.'

'Oscar showed me the ropes, as it were,' Bella said, 'yesterday afternoon, and took me through what I'd need to do, but is there a ritual or anything, before we set out?' Her face was so smooth and eager.

'Well, I like to sacrifice a young man to Amphitrite,

queen of the sea, then have a cup of tea. It's why Oscar's here.'

Bella blinked at me in clear confusion; Oscar laughed. 'She's joking,' he explained. 'Auntie Rox is the least super-stitious person I know. She doesn't have an illogical fear of the number 13, or Wednesdays. She says, "Superstition is humanity's way of trying to control the uncontrollable."'

'How wise am I?' I replied.

As we chugged out of the harbour, the sky was still blessedly black. Not one slice of dawn gave it flavour. The Caroline-Louise *purred like my sixteen-year-old diabetic cat and peace seeped into my skin. This was where calm lived.*

'You're off tomorrow, aren't you, Rox?' Oscar asked as we dropped anchor at our first fishing stop. There was just enough south-westerly wind for the boat to bob and the fish to bite. The sea shimmied in its black silk nightie.

'And the next day,' I replied. Two whole long days off until the fishery opened again. I hated the waiting. It gave me too long to dwell. The past, like spawning grounds and marine protected areas, should never be dredged.

'The bakery's the same,' Bella said, handing out some of that establishment's finest flaky products. 'Mum's always gagging to get back, though. Says "If the darts is on telly, I should be serving Danish pastries."'

'Sensible woman.' Landed on shore leave, I didn't know how to be or breathe. I gasped for salt air and solitude. 'Now, no talking. If you must talk, then whisper. I don't want to scare off the fish.' Or scare

them. While a frightened fish may freeze in place, making it easier to catch, fear also makes them taste bad. Terrified fish make for jellified flesh – not what you want with your chippy tea. But that's not the only reason I keep quiet. I respect fish, too. Death comes to all, but it needn't be harsh and fear filled. Death can just be an end.

At least that's what I thought as I flung out the nets and watched them envelope this sip of the world's oceans. I wouldn't think that for long.

I was down in the tiny galley when I heard the whispering. Assuming it was Oscar and Bella, I tried not to listen, busying myself with coffee.

Coming up the steps, the whispers coalesced into something like words. They were familiar, yet they slipped through meaning and out the other side. Maybe Oscar and Bella had a language of their own, I thought, trying to ignore a tiny hook of jealousy inside me.

On deck, though, Oscar was checking a net on the port side of the Caroline-Louise, whereas Bella was starboard, cleaning a bucket. Their whispers had stopped – they must have heard me coming and split up to look like they were hard at work. And to be fair, they were convincing. Oscar appeared surprised when I stood next to him, as if he'd been concentrating so fully he hadn't noticed my approach.

'I found this caught in the netting,' he said, holding out a box. Studded with moon-shone barnacles, it resembled a seaweed-wrapped gift from the sea. An early Christmas present.

Something about it, though, made my stomach turn and twist like a fortune fish.

Taking the box from him, I was unnerved by its density. Small, less than the length and width of my hand, it was somehow heavier than Oscar when he was born.

As I turned the box over, something solid rolled around inside, making me feel strangely sickened. Symbols had been stamped on the sides: a birch tree, a cotton reel, a catfish with long whiskers, a door, a horse and a cradle.

Four words were also carved into the underskin of the box: 'Swim, little fish, swim.'

My heart thumped like the tail of a dying fish. It felt like a warning. To the curious mind, it might bring interest and fascination. To my fearful one, it brought revulsion. Nausea rising, I threw the box overboard.

'Why did you do that?' Oscar asked, watching it sink, too slowly, into the water.

A good question. One I couldn't answer. 'It wasn't for us,' I replied, not knowing what else to say.

'You've always told me the only things we throw back are fish that are too young or beyond our quota; anything else is up for grabs.' He shuffled his feet, looking suddenly younger, and as sad as the day I took him to the aquarium when he was six and wouldn't let him smuggle the octopus home, disguised as a backpack. 'I was going to keep it. Dry it out, buff it up,' he said, of the box, not the octopus. He glanced across the boat to Bella.

'Were you going to give it to her?' I whispered.

'I thought it'd be a memento of our first catch together.' His voice was low. He didn't look up from the deck. 'And that it might be nice with a ring in it.'

I patted his shoulder. I've never been good with affection.

Love teems within me but rarely lands. 'I'm so sorry.' There was a catch in my throat.

'Doesn't matter now.' He turned away and started checking lobster pots.

'You should go for it. The closest I've ever come to being romantic was when I once went to a workshop at St Bart's in order to make a Valentine's gift for a boyfriend.'

'But that does sound romantic. Although as it's St Bart's, does that mean it was in the Pathology Museum?'

'Yup. It was a workshop on how to preserve a pig's heart in a jar.'

'Ah. Right.'

'I had to hook the heart and suspend it with surgical thread in a mixture of formaldehyde, vinegar and other preservatives.'

'That does sound more like you. How did that go down?'

'My boyfriend held it at arm's length, which is pretty much how I held my own heart, so I don't blame him. He split up with me the next day.'

'What happened to the heart?'

'I try not to think about it. The point is, be you. Keep your heart open. Don't pickle it.' Feeling a bit too much in my own formaldehyded heart, I left him to it and went over to Bella, who was sharpening my knives.

'Careful you don't cut yourself,' I said as I passed her. She nodded blithely, which didn't reassure me. Last thing I wanted was to send her home hurt. Blood isn't the best for baking. Although if she'd sliced her palm, making us head back to shore right then, she'd have

healed in time, and all would've been fine. Unlike what actually happened.

I busied myself with the crab pots, not expecting much yet, and not getting much, either. As I retied a knot, the water became still. I was so attuned to the constant shifting of the boat that when it stopped, it felt wrong. Looking out, the sea was as if in a child's painting – a flat line, not just on the horizon. The illusion of a solid block beneath us.

Then it started to move, but not as water. It wafted, resembling a sheet shaken out and landing upon some-thing. On a human shape.

It's me, not the sea, I thought, turning away. It's so long since I was with someone that I'm conjuring bodies in the Channel.

'This net is ready,' Oscar called out, surprise in his voice. 'We should haul it in.'

Thinking it too soon, I checked the weight of the net, assuming I'd tell him to leave it – but he was right. If anything, it was too full. The net had never taken on that much before. 'We need you, Bella,' I shouted as Oscar, and I started bringing it in. My stomach felt like a fish-bowl, fluttering as it had once before.

'Woohoo!' Oscar shouted when the net and its contents were on deck. 'I've never seen this many fish! Do you reckon we've got enough already? Can we go back early?'

I was about to reply when I saw Bella, stood statue-still. She was watching the hip-high, squirming heap. Her skin had a grey-green sheen; her mouth was as open as the fishes'.

'Try not to think about it,' I said. 'I concentrate on the people we'll be feeding, rather than—'

'Rather than creatures dying in front of us,' Bella interrupted.

'Well, yeah,' I replied. 'First time Oscar came fishing with me, he was sick over the stern. I told him not to look at the catch for the next few trips – sorry, I should've remembered and said the same to you.'

'It's not your fault. Oscar told me yesterday to stare at the horizon, didn't you, baby?'

Oscar didn't reply. He was gazing at the catch. 'I can't believe it.' He reached into the mass of writhing fish.

I had to look away myself, feeling as if I was going to be sick.

'Aha!' Oscar jumped up and held out the box that I had ten minutes ago, max, lobbed into the sea. 'What are the chances of catching that again?' he said.

Ocean-cold chills crashed against my sternum. 'Such a small chance that it's hardly possible.'

The whispers resurfaced, but I still couldn't make them out. Something like 'wishwishwish'.

'Exactly! How lucky are we!' Oscar was dancing on deck, holding the box above his head. Seaweed ribboned from it, slapping his face.

'That's not luck,' I said. 'Something else is going on. We need to get rid of it. Quick.'

Oscar scoffed. 'That sounds suspiciously like superstition, Rox. I've always thought you were talking bull. You act all no-nonsense, but so much about you doesn't make sense.'

I blinked. He'd never talked to me like that before. 'I

don't know what you mean. All I know is we need to put it back.'

'I think you should listen to your auntie, Oscar,' Bella said. Her right hand covered her mouth, her left her heart. 'I don't like it.'

Oscar brought the box in close to his chest. 'Funny thing is, I was talking bull earlier too. I didn't want to give it away and used that as an excuse.'

'But why?' I asked.

'I don't ask for what I really want. Like when I say I like the raisin Danish Bella makes, when really, I'd prefer anything at all that her mum bakes.'

'What?' Bella said.

'That's just a white lie,' I replied. 'Being nice. At least it would've been if you hadn't just told her.'

Bella was blinking, as if trying to take the information in through her eyeballs.

Oscar's eyes, though, seemed lidless. Wide open, staring. Watering. 'I told you all that I was enjoying my job. Well, I'm not. And it's not what you think. I hate it. I want to bring change and justice. I'm supposed to be a rights agent, but I'm an agent of wrongs.'

As soon as he said those words, he blinked many times. An Inner Seas-wide smile crossed his face. 'That feels much better. I felt like I was going to break unless I said it.' He looked down at the box. 'I know this is ridiculous, but I think the box itself made me spill.'

'If it did,' Bella said, hugging him, 'then I'm glad, cos that must've been a lot to carry without telling anyone. And we'll sort it out, won't we, Rox?'

I nodded. His secret was small fry. You're young, there's time and scope for a new direction. We'll work it out together.'

'Can we throw it away now?' Bella stepped back, staring at the box. 'Just being near it makes me feel weird.'

'As long as one of you two chucks it,' Oscar replied. 'Don't think I can.'

Bella turned to Rox, eyes imploring. 'I don't want to touch it.'

Acid burned in my chest as I lunged for the box. It was heavier now – the weight of Oscar when he was nine, when I could hardly carry him anymore.

Stumbling, I heaved the box over the side. Again, it was too slow to sink. The sea didn't want it either.

'What's that?' Bella's voice quavered. She pointed out to sea.

I saw only the moon-tipped quiffs of waves. 'What can you see?' I asked.

'It's like a . . .' She paused, swallowing several times. 'I don't know what it is.'

'You're lying, love,' Oscar said, taking her hands with such gentleness. 'I can tell.'

A dull, resonant thumping came from the other side of the Caroline-Louise. *Something was hitting her hull. Dashing over, I tugged on a taut and straining crab pot line. 'Come and help,' I called. Whatever was in the pot was too heavy to be a crustacean.*

The whispers grew louder, a shushed tinnitus that never left. Maybe they'd always been there, and I was only hearing them now.

Between the three of us, we hauled the pot over the side and onto the deck. The box was inside.

'How did it get in there?' Bella asked. 'You threw it over the other side.'

'Logic went overboard with it,' Oscar said, crouching down and unlocking the pot.

'What are you doing?' Bella asked, backing away.

He dragged out the box. 'It won't stop returning till it's finished with us.' Oscar's voice was strangely flat.

'How do you know?' Bella asked.

Oscar just smiled. He inclined his head and turned to me. 'We have to say what's beneath the sea. The shapes we've all seen under the water. The ones in our past. We must speak the whispers.'

'Nope,' I said. 'If it won't leave us, we'll leave it.' I ran to crank up the anchor. 'Fuck the rest of the haul, we're going back.' I had to get him, get us, away from whatever this was.

Bella helped me release the nets and bring in the pots. Starting the engine, though, the motor stalled. I tried again. Nothing.

'If you want to ever go home and see your cat, if you want to bring in this record haul, a gift from the sea for your Christmas stocking, you'll have to say what haunts you.' Oscar was swaying; his words sounded like they were up close to my face. 'Look up.'

The sky was cloud free and still full dark. Starless. Sunless.

'It should be dawn by now.' Bella sat down next to Oscar and ducked under his arm. 'I don't understand.'

THE CHRISTMAS CRACKER KILLER

Oscar lifted the box and placed it on her lap. When she tried to push it away, he said, 'Just tell me. Whatever it is, we'll make it okay.'

Tears streamed from Bella's unblinking eyes. Her skin was lined, creased like a stormed sea. 'I can't. You won't love me anymore.'

'Tell me. Find out.'

Bella's chin trembled. 'You know the day I passed my test, and I didn't turn up to meet you for drinks?'

Oscar nodded slowly.

'Well, I drove over a cat. It ran out and I couldn't stop in time.' The words were hurled from her mouth. 'It was still on the road, blood on its head, and I panicked. I should've looked for its owner, picked it up and taken it to the vet's.'

'Say it,' Oscar whispered.

'But I drove away. I didn't even know if it was alive. I'm such a bad person.' Bella rocked backwards and forwards over the box. Her mouth was wide open, gasping for oxygen. But her eyes were closed, and the worry lines on her face had dropped away.

Oscar lifted the box from her lap, huffing with effort, and placed it on the deck. 'I think the box is there to let ours sins out. The misdemeanours. Can't you hear it whisper? About the cotton, the birch, the catfish, the groom, the cradle, the dead man.'

'The dead man?' I replied, my voice shaking.

'You know what this all means, Auntie Rox,' he said. 'It's your turn.'

'I can't,' I said. 'This isn't the time.'

His gaze was soft, his eyes reflecting mine. 'Then when is?'

From the water I caught the whispers: 'Swim, little fish, swim.' The words inscribed on the bottom of the box. Words I remembered saying.

I peered over the side of the boat. Under the sheet of water, the body was still there. Legs, arms, torso, head. The sea was a shroud.

Then the head turned, slowly, showing the outline of a face. Palms stretched at the sea's meniscus. The corpse was moving.

I turned away, holding my lurching stomach. My heart felt like it had been hooked. Above us, the sky was still deep-sea dark and would stay that way, unless I said what I had to say.

Sitting down next to Oscar and Bella, I took a wide, saline breath. I leaned over, placed my hands around the box. I could no longer carry it; it was too heavy. Had to drag it across the planks towards me.

I tried to blink away tears, but nothing happened. I could no longer close my eyes. My lids were hooked to my brows.

Eyeballs burning, stomach churning, I turned to Oscar. 'I haven't talked about this for so many years. I don't even know the words.'

He didn't say anything.

'I've never told you this before, but I got pregnant and, before the baby arrived, I asked for it to be adopted.'

'So, I've got a cousin, somewhere?' Oscar said.

'No,' I replied.

My smart watch bleeped a warning – my heartbeat was 160bpm. It thought I was exercising, not exorcising.

'Oh no,' my nephew said. 'The baby died?'

I shook my head.

'I don't under—' Oscar stopped talking. His face flushed; his hand went to his heart.

'I gave birth to you, Oscar.' My mouth was salted with the tears rolling from my unblinking eyes. 'And your mum, my sister, agreed to adopt you. No, she didn't agree; she salmon-leapt at the chance to be your mum. She and your dad had wanted a child for so long.'

Oscar was the one rocking now. 'Why didn't anyone tell me?'

'We thought it'd be easier this way.'

'Easier for who?' he asked.

'I told myself it'd be better for you. But it was really about us being able to pretend. I wanted to save myself heartache. If I always thought of you as my nephew, I could love you like that.'

'You wanted to keep your love pickled in a jar, suspended in formaldehyde,' he whispered.

I took a deep breath. 'Yes. I am so sorry. I never forgot, though, the feeling of you fluttering in my tummy. When you didn't move, I worried, and said, "Swim, little fish, swim." And you woke up and started swimming within me.'

My eyelids sagged then, my eyes closing as the box opened under my hand. Nothing was inside, but it was still heavy. Nothing was written beneath in, but now all the symbols were of the dead man.

The sobs came, along with a white pain that gripped my torso, travelling down my arm. I pressed my hand against my box of a chest, gasped for air. It was as if I'd dragged away the sandbags I'd placed around my heart, and the tide had come in.

Oscar gently laid me down. The sky was now the colour of a stocking satsuma. Seagulls swooped over me, cawing at the dawn.

'I think she's having a heart attack.' Oscar's weighted words floated over me. 'We need to get back to shore. Now.'

I sank deeper; all pain. Sounds were behind glass. All I could see was the body beneath the sea, breaking the surface. And then nothing but the dark.

I woke in hospital apparently, many hours later. Oscar told me the first thing I said was, 'Where's the box?' But I don't remember. The rest of that day has disappeared into the Mariana Trench of memory, as mercifully out of reach as the box that Oscar locked in a weighted lobster pot and lobbed into the Channel.

I still see the body under the water. Sometimes I don't even need to close my eyes. I reassure myself that this is trauma talking, a keepsake of the day. After all, the sea released me when I freed one of my secrets. You can see through ghosts, but ghosts can see through you, too. The ghost in the sea was Oscar's adoption, haunting me. That's the easiest explanation, and one I am hooked upon if I'm talking with Oscar. He doesn't believe me, not quite.

And he's right. You and I know. You can guess what I

did. The man I murdered; who haunts me. I pushed him over the railings, into the sea, after what he did to me. And maybe the body in the sea is a warning, too. A dead body, yet to be. The body in the sea is me.

So, that's why I don't fish anymore. And I don't eat things from the sea, or venture onto it. I don't even look at the ocean: I give it my back, as it no longer has mine.

Not that I'm telling you this to put you off fishing. I know I can't, and I shouldn't. I'm just telling my tale. You don't have to believe it: I wouldn't. Feel free to dismiss it as a shiver put back in the ghost story quiver, then down your sweet sherry and go to bed. Merry Christmas, mate. May you never dream of the sea and what waits in the deep.

Fifteen

Mara let the last sentence sink into the audience, then re-rolled the story into a scroll. No one moved or made a sound. The silence was more gratifying than a standing ovation. Stunning an audience, removing their mechanism for sound, was the ultimate accolade.

What if, though, she thought, *they were silent because it was bad?*

Just as she was about to pitch into full-blown anxiety, the hush was broken and everyone started clapping. The exception was Robert, who had fallen asleep, mouth wide open, fortune fish balanced on his hand. Mara stayed in her chair, revelling in the praise and the tears Dad had shed during the adoption part. It must have dredged up memories for him, too. Bringing back the first moment he held her. At one point she'd looked at Mum, but she'd been staring at the ceiling rose. Tarn had given her a shiny-eyed smile to get her back on track.

Licking her thumb and forefinger, she snuffed out the candle next to her, and, standing tall, walked out of the library. With every step she felt the character subsiding. She was glad, actually, to cast her off. Rox's nebulous crime left the taste of salt in Mara's mouth.

Tarn was already in the lobby, by the reception desk. She gave Mara another big thumbs-up, but looked upset. Mara was about to go over to her when Mum stepped out of the library.

'I loved the dramatic exit, darling. Very *diva*,' she said, bending to kiss Mara on the temple. 'And you certainly looked like you were enjoying yourself. Did you have a good time?'

'I *loved* it. What about you?' Adrenaline and dopamine were giving her the temporary courage to ask. 'What did you think?'

'Art isn't about *thinking*, Mara, you should know that. It's all about *feeling* and connecting.'

'Okay, what did you feel?' Mara's heart was going too fast.

Dad walked over, wiping his eyes, unintentionally giving Mum an opportunity to think of another way not to answer. 'That was fantastic, darling! So powerful. I couldn't be prouder.' He hugged Mara tight, and she wished it could last all night.

'Adoption was an *interesting* topic to touch on, given our history.' Mum stared towards the staircase as if its steps could sweep her out of the conversation. 'I'm surprised you chose it.'

'It was the story *you* sent *me*!' Mara said. 'I assumed you'd selected it.'

'I didn't send you anything,' Mum said, frowning.

Mara scrolled through her emails to the one from Mum's address and showed it to her.

Mum opened the email and blinked in confusion. 'I

promise, I didn't send it. I've never heard or seen that story before.'

Mara's heart stuttered. 'Then who did?'

A scream came from the library.

She ran towards the sound, pushing past Henry, Izzie and Kimberley to where Celine stood over Robert, holding one of his wrists. On his other hand, the fortune fish was as motionless as he was.

'I think he's had a heart attack,' George said. 'He was rubbing his chest earlier. And knocking back the indigestion tablets.'

'Mara, come here,' Tarn called from the lobby, panic in her voice.

'Not now,' Mara shouted. She locked eyes with her dad, willing him to tell her what to do.

'There's no pulse,' Celine said. 'Who knows CPR?'

'I do,' Anna, George and Mara said at the same time, but Sean leapt forwards.

'Call 999,' he said to Mara, switching into emergency services mode. He seemed two inches taller and two times more sober than he had a few minutes ago. 'Everyone else, help me clear the area.'

As George and Anna moved the furniture to the sides of the room and Sean gently lowered Robert to the floor, Mara took out her phone and dialled for the air ambulance. The signal was too weak.

Running into the lobby, the signal flared as she neared the router in the office, and she was put on hold.

Tarn was standing, stock-still as if frozen, with her back to Mara, facing the reception desk.

'I need your help, Tarn,' Mara said. 'Didn't you hear? Robert Cole-Mortelli has had a—'

Tarn stepped away from the desk, revealing the open dolls' house. She pointed, silently, inside.

The doll of Robert Cole-Mortelli was now lying on the floor of the miniature library, with Sean's doll giving him chest compressions.

Mara was so shocked she didn't catch the first part of the emergency services operator's spiel.

'Is anyone there?' the operator said. 'What services do you require?'

'Air ambulance,' Mara said, jolting back to attention. 'At Aster Castle Hotel on Holly Island, in the Hebrides. One of our guests has had a suspected cardiac arrest.'

'Does the patient have a pulse?'

'I don't think so. Another of our guests is a police officer and is giving CPR.' Mara glanced again at Robert's doll on the floor in a miniature and macabre simulation of reality.

She thought about asking for the police, too, then the operator said, 'We can't get anyone out to you tonight, I'm afraid. The storm has grounded all air ambulances, and the coast guard can't get out that far. Could you please let me talk with the officer giving compressions?'

'Of course.' Mara was about to go when Tarn grabbed her arm and pointed to a scroll of paper next to Robert's doll. She gingerly picked it up and unfurled it, showing Mara the words.

Told you there'd be consequences.

Sixteen

Edie watched from the doorway to the library as her son battled to save a man's life. All the while, the emergency services operator encouraged him on loudspeaker through Mara's phone. Ten minutes passed. Then twenty. After half an hour, Sean looked over to Edie and shook his head. Confirming the time with the operator, he declared Robert Cole-Mortelli dead.

The fire died down as if bowing its head in respect. Lucy and Henry stood to one side of Edie, George to the other. He'd fetched her a chair when Sean started chest compressions and given her a blanket. He, though, was the one shivering.

'You don't expect to see something like that,' George said. 'It's shocking.'

Edie grasped his hand briefly. 'And so it should be.'

Sean stood, unsteadily. He was grey faced, out of breath. 'Right,' he said. 'Must follow procedure.' Fumbling out his phone, he took pictures of the body.

'Why are you doing that?' Lucy asked. 'He clearly died of a heart attack. It's not like you need to investigate anything.'

'Robert *did* mention cardiac problems to me earlier,' George said.

'When was that?' Edie asked.

'During dinner, on his way back from the toilet. He said he'd seen me taking Rennies at afternoon tea and asked for some, said he had indigestion all the time, ever since having heart problems.'

'And then he died holding his left arm,' Henry said, with some authority given that he could hardly stand up straight. 'Clear signs of myocardial infarction. I've had several myself.' He paused. 'Although I was lucky enough to survive mine.'

'Wouldn't we have seen or heard him if he was suffering?' Anna called over. She and Celine were on a nearby sofa in the lobby, huddled under a blanket. 'Surely someone can't die in the same room, and no one notice?' She shuddered.

'Mara was the only one facing him,' Felicity said. 'Did you see something, darling?' she called to Mara, who was standing by reception, in front of the replica dolls' house.

'She was busy telling the story,' Ivan said quickly. 'She's hardly going to be checking everyone's state of health.'

Mara came over slowly. When she reached them, her eyes were unfocused. She looked the most shocked of everyone present. 'What is it, Mum?'

'You had the best view of Mr Cole-Mortelli,' Felicity replied. 'Did you notice anything while you performed?'

Mara shook her head really slowly. 'I don't think so. I thought he'd just fallen asleep.'

'And you were used to that as an actor, right?' Felicity said, attempting a smile.

'People can just die, though,' George said. 'Especially if they have health conditions. My uncle died after Christmas dinner one year and no one knew till later. We thought he was asleep until I tried to wake him up for *Call the Midwife*.'

'No matter how Mr Cole-Mortelli died,' Sean said tersely, 'I'm the only police officer in attendance and am therefore taking responsibility for the scene. Now, would you all please get out of this room? But don't go far.'

Leaving Sean in the library with the body, Tarn took Mara to one side, hopefully to give her some hot sweet tea. The others congregated in the lobby – Edie, George, Anna and Celine on the sofas; Ivan, Felicity, Lucy and Henry in the armchairs. When Henry went over to sit with the other group, a little too close to Celine, Lucy marched across and pulled him off the sofa. His usually amiable face took on a storm front, brows crashing down, teeth bared.

Izzie was the only one alone, standing at reception, pressing a hole puncher again and again, with no paper for it to eat.

Edie leaned forward. 'I think Izzie might be in shock,' she said to Ivan and Felicity. 'As well as Mara.'

'I'm sure Izzie's fine.' Felicity didn't even glance the young woman's way. 'And Tarn will look after Mara. She always does. Well, not always.'

Ivan grabbed Felicity's arm. 'This isn't the time, darling.'

'And when *is* the time, *darling*?' Felicity asked, spittle landing on her lip.

Ivan gave Edie a tight smile, then led his wife away by

her pointed elbow. Her Ghost dress billowed as they climbed the staircase, heads together, fists clenched.

Edie had been thinking of going to bed – her limbs ached, and her head was streaming images of gasping fish, haunted seas and dead financiers – but someone should do the right thing by Izzie. *Besides, Riga will hate that she missed this drama. At least if I stay, I'll catch all the details.*

Edie walked stiffly over to Izzie, wishing she'd brought her stick. The young woman's face was as grey as a bank holiday. 'After something like this,' Edie said to her, 'it's good to be in company, even if you're like me and don't like people much.'

Izzie smiled weakly. 'I like *some* people. I've just never seen a dead person before. I didn't think it would be so *real*.'

'It's a shock, isn't it? George was saying the same.'

Izzie's reply was a big, slow tear.

'Come and sit with me, Anna and Celine,' Edie said. 'Unless you really would rather be alone?'

Izzie shook her head. 'I'll come.'

As they walked back, Tarn came from the direction of The Star restaurant, smoothing her pinafore. Her eyes were red. 'I'm so sorry that the evening has taken a sad turn. Please bear with us while we deal with it as best we can.' Clocking Izzie's shock, she sat on a footstool by the young woman and put her arm round her.

Lucy came over, Henry stumbling behind. 'Isn't there a protocol in place for deceased guests?' Lucy said to Tarn. 'After all, it's a common occurrence in the hospitality industry. Isn't there a statistic that sixty odd per cent of hotel rooms have had someone die inside?' She shook her head as if despairing of the hotel's failings before she'd even received a response.

'For fuck's sake, Lucy,' Henry said. 'This isn't the time. Give them a break.'

'You're on thin ice, Henry,' she snapped. 'I'd be quiet if I were you.'

Henry slumped into a nearby armchair. 'I *always* have to be quiet, don't I? That's how you like it, controlling everything. Not letting me do anything, talk to anyone.'

Lucy's rage bloomed under her face powder. 'Are we seriously going to do this in front of everyone?' When Henry didn't reply, she said, 'Fine. Tarn? I'd like you to find Henry another room to sleep in tonight.'

'Of course you would,' Henry sighed, crossing his arms and resting his head against the wingback. Edie suspected this was not the first time they'd had this conversation. Or the second.

'No problem, Mrs Palmer,' Tarn said calmly. 'We want you to have as comfortable a night as possible.' She shifted her body slightly, making it clear she was now addressing all assembled guests. 'Ryan is making hot chocolate for anyone who wants it, served here or in your rooms, and Kimberley, our resident pastry genius, is rustling up something carby and comforting.'

Mara hurried out of a door behind reception and into the lobby, her phone in her hand. Her eyes were red, her make-up smudged, her forehead scrunched. She looked as tired as Edie felt. 'They can't send anyone to get Mr

Cole-Mortelli's body until Boxing Day morning. It's the storm plus a lack of staff. They've requested that we keep him here till then.'

Felicity stood up, hands on hips. 'Perhaps we should discuss this in private before worrying the guests, darling.' The 'darling' was glazed with the sticky honey of passive aggression.

'It's a bit late for that,' Lucy said.

'And the guests deserve to know what's happening,' Mara replied to her mother.

Sean walked out of the library, rubbing his temples. On seeing Mara, he asked, 'Any news of the air ambulance?'

'No chance of one till first thing on the twenty-sixth,' Mara repeated. 'They're as understaffed as we are.' She covered her mouth as if to take back the last part.

'Can't Swindon take it away tomorrow morning?' Felicity asked Ivan. 'He has to pick up the three other guests anyway, he might as well drop off the body.'

'"It"?' Edie repeated. 'I didn't take to the man when he was alive, but how can he be an "it" already? And "drop off" suggests the school run, not delivery of the deceased.'

Felicity's returning glare contained none of her previous grace or charm.

'*Of course* you can't take him on the hotel boat and drop him off, Mrs Morecombe-Clark,' Sean said, voice tight. 'Certain procedures must be followed now the death has been reported. And there's no need to pick up Liam and the kids tomorrow. I've already phoned him to say that he and the kids should stay at home.'

'No!' Edie cried. 'They've got to still come.'

'It's not an appropriate atmosphere, Mum. Juniper has had enough traumatic Christmases. You should understand that, at least.' The strain in Sean's voice reminded her sharply that he, *their* father and *her* son, was the important one here. 'Swindon can take you and anyone else who wants to leave in the morning.'

'You as well, right?' Edie said.

Sean pressed the sides of his head, a sign that one of his stress headaches had kicked in. 'I'll talk to whoever I can reach at this hour to see what the procedure might be. I suspect, though, that I'll need to stay until the body is taken away.'

'I'm sure that won't be necessary,' Mara said gently, coming over to Sean's side. 'You should get back to your kids.'

Edie managed to stop herself saying they should've gone back when she'd suggested. She'd say it to Riga in the morning, though.

'We'll see,' Sean said. 'For now, I'll need help to move Mr Cole-Mortelli to a more appropriate place.'

'I'll do it,' George said. Mara looked at him with gratitude.

'Thank you, George. And,' Sean said, now addressing Mara, 'this is a very delicate matter, but do you have anywhere cold that we could store the body?'

Mara blanched. 'We have a walk-in cold room in the kitchen. More than big enough for—' she gestured towards the library. 'There's also the old ice house in the grounds, but that's full of garden furniture.'

'Then we'll use the walk-in cold room. No one is to go inside there, or the library, without my permission. Both will be padlocked, and I'll have the keys.'

'We'll have to sort out something else for all the food,' Tarn said. 'The staff are usually in and out of the cold room all the time.'

'I'll leave that to you,' Sean said to her. 'And before we all retire for the night, do any of you have reason to think his death was due to anything other than natural causes?'

'You make it sound like that bit in the marriage ceremony where they ask if you know of any impediment,' George said with a nervous chuckle.

'This isn't a joke, Mr Delt,' Sean said, still looking at the whole group. 'Does anyone have anything suspicious or worrying to report?'

Tarn turned to Mara, raising her eyebrows; Mara shook her head very slightly. Ivan bit his lip; Felicity opened her handbag and peered inside. Lucy glared at Anna; Anna plaited Izzie's hair. Celine stared serenely out of the window. Owain folded his arms in apparent boredom.

'Tell him now or forever hold your peace!' George said, laughing.

No one said a word.

Seventeen

December 25th – Christmas Day

Three in the morning. The killer hadn't needed to set an alarm. Adrenaline had kept them up, as excited for Christmas morning as they'd been as a child. They'd had to act 'normal', though: stumbling to their room around the same time as the others, washing their face, turning out the lights, changing into night clothes and slipping into bed, all to support the story they'd tell the next day. Narrative was everything.

Now, though, it was time to put the next part of the plan into action. Robert had exceeded the killer's expectations, dying without a sound, right on time. As a last act, it was one of uncharacteristic generosity. They hoped their next victim would be as giving.

In the corridor, the killer didn't need to watch out for CCTV – all the cameras in the hotel had already been detached from the system. They could dance dance dance through the hallways after the kill and no one would know.

The key turned silently in the lock and the killer walked into the second-best suite in the hotel. A sitting room in the east turret; a chaise longue looking out to sea. Not that the killer would get to enjoy that view. Opening the curtains might wake her, and the style of kill would be compromised.

Besides, she looked so peaceful in the king-size bed. Her hair was under a knotted silk bonnet, one foot sticking out of the duvet. She was on her back, drooling very slightly. Her left hand, curled like a paw under her chin, twitched. The killer wasn't good enough to hope she was having a pleasant final dream. This woman had caused as yet untold harm. *May it be a nightmare.*

Leaning over to fetch a pillow, the killer placed it over her face and pressed. A minute passed before she rose out of the deep. The fight back was weak, and brief. There was breath, and then no breath. She would harm no more.

Closing the door on the dead woman, the killer crept down the hallway and took the stairs to the lobby. The dolls' house castle was lit by a lone lamp. Opening its doors, the killer rearranged the figures inside. Little arms straightened. Pillow placed just so.

When they'd played enough, the killer stood alone, listening to the castle's ghosts. They could almost see the Magliani children who had inspired them to avenge kids who had experienced loss, or who had been lost. Maybe someday the killer would feel they had been found.

But not today.

Then the killer danced. A one-person waltz across the lobby, in the hotel of the dead. Their soft shuffles showed that, even after death, no nights were truly silent.

Eighteen

Mara woke, heart thumping quicker than the knocking on her door. 'Who is it?' she shouted, stumbling out of bed.

'It's me,' Tarn whispered.

Mara checked her watch – four thirty – and let Tarn in. 'What's going on?'

Tarn was in her tartan pyjamas. Her eyes, wild, unable to focus, flitted round the room. 'Oh God, Mara, what's the detective going to say?' Her voice was ragged and dry. 'We should've told him about the dolls' house last night. No, before that. We should've told the police like you said, before they arrived. Cancelled the whole thing. And he's in there now, with the body.'

Mara tried to tesselate Tarn's words, make them make sense. 'Sean's with Robert's body? In the walk-in fridge?'

'No!' Tarn grabbed at her head. 'Henry Palmer is in their room, with *her*.'

Mara sat Tarn on the bed and handed her a bottle of water. 'Take a swig then tell me what's happened.'

Tarn automatically unscrewed the bottle and raised it to her lips, but didn't drink. She just blinked, over and over, as if trying to process a slow film running through her head. 'Henry, Mr Palmer, called me on the number I left them. He could hardly talk, saying she wasn't breathing. That he couldn't wake her up.'

'Who?'

'His wife! Lucy. I ran up to their suite and found him lying over her body, crying.'

Following Tarn's thoughts was like trying to find stepping stones in the dark. 'I thought Henry was in another room?'

'He was, I put him down the corridor from their suite, but he said he woke up in the middle of the night and kept thinking about their argument so he couldn't get back to sleep. He went to their room to tell Lucy he was sorry. That's what he told me, anyway. He also said that when he arrived, she was dead. And she was. *Is*. I ran up immediately and there she was, on the bed. Her eyes, Mara, they were open, staring into me.' Tarn's own eyes were owl wide and just as unblinking. 'I put a fresh sheet from the laundry over her and came straight to you.'

'You left him alone with her?' Being in a room with your dead spouse would be the most alone you'd ever been.

'I didn't know what else to do. And it's happened again.'

'What?'

'The dolls' house. Lucy's doll is lying on her replica bed, a pillow over her tiny face.'

Mara swallowed rising bile then threw on her dressing-gown. 'Go back up to their room and sit with Henry,' she whispered to Tarn as she opened the door. 'Don't

142

leave him.' Down the hall another door opened, but she couldn't deal with other staff members now. She had to find DI Sean Brand-O'Sullivan.

Running up the fire-exit steps, she tried to practise what she'd say to him, but no words felt adequate. She'd not only failed at running the hotel before it had even greeted its first paying guests, but she'd also failed at being a good human. *What's the worst thing I've ever done? Kept vital information back from a police officer because I felt tired and confused.* The image of her mum's scorn when she found out scorched through her mind.

Banging on the door of Suite One, she thought of how minutes before it had been Tarn at *her* door. She wished she was still asleep, and not dealing with more death.

Sean was in his boxers and a T-shirt, his hair at all angles. He screwed his eyes up at the sudden light of the corridor. 'What time is it?'

'Please get dressed and come with me,' Mara whispered, afraid of waking the other guests. 'I need your help.'

Sean nodded and disappeared back into his room. Hushed voices came from inside. Three minutes later, he was fully clothed and striding down the halls next to her. Neither spoke till they got to the Palmers' suite.

Henry was on a chair in the turret area. Staring at the bed where Lucy lay under a sheet. Lines from last night's story resurfaced: '*Under the sheet of water, the body was still there. Legs, arms, torso, head. The sea was a shroud.*'

Tarn had pulled herself together enough to start making him a cup of tea. Mum often threw that phrase, 'pull yourself together', at Mara, and it had never made sense, and hadn't worked, but watching Tarn move around the suite, getting Henry a blanket, pouring hot water on the tea bag, was like watching the idiom in action. Her breathing deepened; her eyes focused. The scattered woman who'd turned up at Mara's door was slowly adhering to herself again.

Sean was scanning the room, taking everything in. 'Do you have any plastic gloves?' he asked Tarn and Mara. 'Cleaning gloves that come already sealed?'

Tarn's face crumpled. 'I should've anticipated that.' She left the room, coming back a minute later with a bag of hygienic gloves.

'I'm so sorry, Mr Palmer,' Sean said, crouching by Henry's chair and putting on some gloves. 'But I have to ask you to go elsewhere so that we can begin to discover what happened to Lucy.'

Henry's gaze never left the bed. 'I can't leave her like that. She can't see with that sheet on her.'

Tarn took his arm, encouraging him to stand. 'Let's go back to the room you had last night. Lucy will be okay here. Sean is looking after her.'

'I will take the best care of her,' Sean said solemnly.

Henry nodded and let himself be led away. Sean closed the door after them, and then gently lifted Lucy's shroud. Mara looked away, but not before the still of Lucy's grey face and blue lips burned into her memory.

'I have to leave too, right?' Mara said to Sean. 'To preserve the scene as much as possible?'

'We *both* do,' Sean said, not looking up from making notes on his phone. 'I should be in a full forensics suit.

I wish you'd told me what had happened before we got in here.'

'I'm sorry, I wasn't thinking straight. I should've told you everything.'

'Hard to know what to do in these situations.' Sean stood, knees crunching. 'While I *am* in here, I want to make some preliminary investigations. Would you mind getting me a coffee? I need to wake my brain up. And could you send the murder investigation team straight here when they arrive.'

'Have you called them, then?' Mara asked.

'Meaning that you *haven't*?' Incredulity threaded through his voice.

Mara couldn't believe it either. She supposed that when Tarn told her what had happened, she'd thought that fetching Sean was literally telling the police. But, *of course*, she had to ring the emergency services. Another death had taken place in her hotel.

'Never mind, I'll do it now,' Sean said. He switched to his phone keypad, dialled for the emergency services. 'I can't join the Wi-Fi,' he said after a minute. 'Try yours.'

Mara took out her phone, but had no connection either. 'I'll call from the office and then get a coffee sent up. They'll knock on the door and leave it outside.'

'Thank you.' Sean looked up from his phone. 'Before you go, you said yesterday that the spare key to the library and walk-in cold room were in the office. Are the other spares in there too?'

'You want to know who could've got in here,' she guessed. 'Then, yes, anyone could have, as I keep all the spares there.'

'Locked up, though, right?'

Mara didn't reply, just shook her head. She felt wretched enough as it was without wrapping her failure up in words. 'There's something else I need to tell you,' she said.

'Call the police first,' Sean said, rubbing sleep from his eyes. 'Soon I'll sit down with you, and you can tell me anything you know.'

Downstairs, in the office, Mara found the router turned off. No wonder it wasn't working. Switching it back on, she checked the cupboard where she kept the spare keys. None was missing. But that didn't mean the key to Suite Two hadn't been taken then returned.

Heavy, running steps came from the lobby. Peering round the door, Mara saw Swindon lurch to a stop at the reception desk. He was breathless, his chest rasping. 'The boat,' he said. 'It's been vandalised.'

'How? What happened?'

'I woke up early and went to see if she had any storm damage, and saw someone had smashed up the controls. They also did something to the engine. I can't get it to start. Doesn't even stutter.' Swindon started crying, allowing tears to fall without wiping them away. 'I won't be able to get Sean's husband and kiddies.'

Mara had gone to bed exhausted, forgetting that Swindon, off work for the evening, would know nothing of what had happened. 'I'm so sorry, Swindon, I should've let you know. Mr Cole-Mortelli died last night of a heart attack, or at least that's what we assumed, and so all our plans are up in the air. The Brand-O'Sullivan family aren't coming anymore.'

There was a pause. 'You said "at least that's what we assumed" – does that mean Robert Mortelli *isn't* dead?' Swindon was clearly confused. Mara was getting everything wrong. How had she ever thought she could run a hotel or achieve anything?

'No, I'm afraid he died, but now another guest has, too, which puts things in a different light. Or rather puts us in the dark. Two guests are dead and we don't know why.'

'And now we can't leave the island.' Swindon's words were weighted down by what he didn't need to say – he'd had heated discussions with Mara's mum in the lead-up to the launch, arguing that the hotel needed a back-up boat, but Mum had refused to consider even a small speed boat on budgetary grounds. If she'd listened to him, they'd be able to sail away. As it was, they were trapped.

Fear tightened Mara's throat as she checked to see if the Wi-Fi was working. If they couldn't get off the island, it was even more important that the police arrived. Soon.

The usual flashing green lights on the side of the router, however, remained still and red. Turning it over, she saw that the base had been tampered with, the wires cut.

'What about the satellite connection?' Swindon was one step ahead of her, getting out his iPhone. 'It's not showing up for me.'

Mara woke up her desktop and tried to link with the satellite. Again, she failed. The whole programme had been messed with. She had no technical knowledge – it had been installed by an expert, and now it was corrupted.

Someone didn't want them to leave the island this Christmas.

Nineteen

Edie was at the big bay window, binoculars trained on the harbour, waiting to see if Swindon had returned. A few minutes ago, he'd run from the boat to the hotel. The floodlights had caught him slipping twice in the knee-high snow. Edie had also caught his look of anguish. Perhaps the storm, which had somehow left the sea looking-glass-flat, had damaged the boat.

'What's going on?' Riga asked, sleepily, from her pillow-surrounded cocoon in their bed. She pulled off her silk eye mask embroidered with the words 'FUCK OFF' and blinked.

'Mara woke Sean up for something urgent, and now Swindon is acting strangely,' Edie replied. 'Oh, and Robert Cole-Mortelli died last night. But Happy Christmas morning!'

Riga sat up with a yawn. 'I don't understand.' There was a different, coffee-bitter note to her voice.

'Neither do I.' Edie put down the binoculars and took a sip of tea. Now *this* was tea, not the stuff they'd served in the library last night. *This*, her own blend, was as strong as an Oxo cube and as dark in the pot. She'd made it when Sean had left, along with coffee for him. 'But I'm going to.'

'Come back to bed,' Riga said as Edie went through her clothes in their walk-in wardrobe. 'I need to talk to you about something.'

'I'm taking Sean his coffee,' Edie replied, coming out in the red-and-navy Drunken Tailored Westwood jacket that she'd got for a song, if the twelve-inch version, on Vinted.

'You're interfering, you mean.' Riga snuggled back down, putting her arms around a goose down pillow. Edie half wanted to climb back into bed, as Riga had said, and talk about whatever Riga wanted.

'It's all a matter of interpretation and synonyms,' she replied instead, the other half of her winning out. 'Some "nag", I "remind"; some "interfere", I "intervene": when I involve myself, it's for the greater good.'

'Don't give me that. It's because you are as curious as your cats.'

'And by "curious" do you mean that I'm strange, or that I'm nosey?' Edie asked, knowing the answer. Who'd have thought she'd find love and someone to 'banter' with in her eighties?

'Both, obviously. And I love you for it. But you're so busy solving things out in the world that you don't always see what's going on right in front of you.' Something was buried beneath Riga's words. Edie never had been good at such subtleties; she just knew they were there.

'I can stay and talk, if that's what you want,' she said, looking to the door and wondering what Sean was up to.

'Don't worry,' Riga replied, looking down at her new rosary. 'As long as I get your undivided attention later.'

'You will, don't worry. I just have to find out what's going on first.'

'Here's a warning to that curious mind of yours,' Riga said. 'You might not always like the answers.' She pulled her eye mask back on. 'Now let me get more sleep,' she said, though her mask said, 'FUCK OFF'.

Edie waited a few minutes until Riga's breathing had slowed to rest state, then carried the coffee into the corridor. She tried phoning Sean to see where he was, but there was no signal, so she'd have to wander around till she found him. When she got to the lift, however, Sean was walking up the corridor that mirrored theirs. He looked tired already, as if he'd been up all night.

'I brought you Christmas-morning coffee,' she said. 'Thought you might need it.'

They hugged, and she was glad to see him smile when he replied, 'You mean you needed to know what was going on.'

'That too.' She paused, waiting for him to tell her. When he didn't volunteer the information, just kept smiling at her frustration, she said, 'Well, go on, then!'

Sean sighed. 'Fine. Henry Palmer apparently found his wife dead at around quarter past four this morning. She hadn't been dead long, an hour or so, judging from her temperature, but obviously I'm not a pathologist.'

'Obviously.'

'Although I am going to hazard a guess that the pillow he found over her head was her cause of death.'

'Ah.'

'Now I'm guarding the room,' he said, pointing to the

far end of the hall, 'until someone assigned to the case arrives. Luckily, Mara said that no other guests are on this corridor, apart from Mr Palmer.' He pointed to a room at the other end, which must have been the one assigned to Henry when Lucy threw him out of theirs.

Mara appeared at the top of the first flight of stairs. 'No one's coming.' Her words came out in a rush. 'The Wi-Fi's been damaged and the satellite link's blocked, so we can't call anyone, and the boat's been—'

'Sabotaged, too?' Edie guessed.

Mara nodded. 'And that thing I should've told you yesterday.'

Sean's jaw clenched slightly. 'Go on.'

'I had a dolls' house made of the hotel, to give to Mum and Dad for Christmas.' Mara's words tumbled like falling dominoes. 'At some point, someone broke into my room and did this to the doll of my father.' Mara scrolled on her phone to an image of a tiny doll lying on a dolls' house bedroom floor, a sheet over it, suggesting that it was dead.

'Is he okay?' Edie asked.

'I went to the cottage to check on him and Mum, and they're fine. Although I haven't told them about Mrs Palmer yet. I wanted to ask you what to do. Especially as,' she scrolled to another image and pointed to a small clipboard held by another doll, dressed in scrubs, 'this says that my daddy will die, by poisoning, at quarter to six today.' Her voice fractured on the words 'my daddy'.

Sean breathed out slowly and audibly, a sign he was trying to calm himself down. 'If you'd told me when I arrived, or even when Mr Cole-Mortelli died, I—'

'You would've been able to do something,' Mara inter-rupted. 'Yes. I know. I keep going over it in my head. But there's more. When you were trying to resuscitate him and I was trying to call emergency services, Tarn found *his* doll in the dolls' house, in exactly the same position as he was. With your doll standing over him.'

'*My* doll?' Sean said.

'But there was nothing wrong with my son's doll, right?' Edie said.

'No, Sean's doll was giving Robert's chest compressions. And next to him was a scroll that said something about "I told you there'd be consequences".'

'Consequences? As in the game last night?' Edie said.

'As in the ice-breaker: "What's the worst thing you've ever done?"' said Sean. 'So, the consequence for him not declaring his worst act was death?'

Edie started replaying the conversation from last night when no one apart from George, she suspected, had told the truth about their most heinous deeds.

Mara was pressing her fists against her chest, her face stricken.

'There's something else you haven't said, isn't there?' Edie guessed.

Mara nodded.

'Lucy's doll is in her bed, with a pillow over her head?' Edie guessed.

Mara's eyes filled with tears. 'I don't understand any of it. Who's doing this? And why was Dad's doll in there, but he's not harmed?'

Edie's brain was flying, skimming over facts to try and

connect them. 'It's *your* dolls' house, *your* hotel. I suspect that you've been given a warning, on top of the ones the killer has already given.'

'What warnings?' Sean asked.

'It's something to do with the crackers,' Edie said. 'The weird fortune fish instructions are all about guilt, and the ice-breaker was clearly supposed to gain confessions. Although I don't know how we're supposed to spill our darkest secrets to strangers.'

'Did you tell *anyone* about the dolls?' Sean asked Mara.

'When I saw Dad's doll in the weird tableau, I told Tarn, asking her if we should call the police,' Mara replied. 'And she thought it must be a prank.' She folded her lips into each other, her dimples twitching just as Riga's did whenever she tried to suppress her feelings. 'But it's not her fault, it's mine. If she'd thought I was in danger, she would have acted, as she's looked after me more than anyone else.'

I'm glad someone has, Edie thought. She'd watched Mara wince and quail at her mother's barbs yesterday. After only a day, she'd wanted to tell Mara to slice the apron strings and fly far from her parents.

'I thought too much had gone into the Christmas event to stop it,' Mara continued.

'The sunk-cost fallacy,' Edie said. 'Always costs more in the end.'

'I also couldn't bear the thought of letting my parents down.' Mara resembled a yearning little girl, not a woman in her late thirties with a hotel to run; but then most people looked like children to Edie, leaving her at once very annoyed and wanting to mother them all. She remembered the looks that Felicity had given her daughter during her performance – glances that lay somewhere in the greens between envy and jealousy.

'If no one is coming until Boxing Day morning,' Sean said, 'and we're stuck here with, I have to now assume, a murderer, we must find them before they hurt anyone else, including your dad.' Edie bet he was thinking of the kids and how he wouldn't see them now until after Christmas, because that's what she was thinking, too.

'Do we know for sure that the emergency services will arrive then?' Edie asked. 'Did *you* talk to them, Sean?' She could feel Mara's agitation without looking at her.

'That's what I was told,' Mara said defensively. 'And I've got no reason to doubt them.'

But do we have reason to doubt you? reverberated in Edie's head but remained unsaid.

'Could I have a word with you, just inside the Palmers' suite?' Sean asked Edie, turning away from Mara.

Mara's glance at him was either surprised or hurt, Edie couldn't tell. 'You said no one should go in, that it could compromise the crime scene.'

'That was before we got cut off,' Sean said. 'And I became aware of a clear death threat.' Nothing changed on his face, but Edie had never heard such a sharp point to his voice.

Mara must have heard it too – she flinched as if cut and backed away. 'I'll be in the kitchen if you need me.'

When she was out of earshot, Sean opened the door to the Palmers' room. 'Without going inside,' he said quietly, 'can you look and tell me if you see anything notable?'

Edie stepped forward, feet on the purple-and-gold corridor carpet while leaning into the suite. Lucy Palmer lay dead on the bed. Her eyes were still open.

'You probably can't see from there, but her skin is grey, with tiny red marks,' Sean said.

'They were like the ones on the skin of the man who was suffocated in the jigsaw case?'

'Exactly,' Sean said.

'Then I'd guess it must be the pillow, as I can't see a mark around her neck. Strange, though, that her arms are by her sides. I'd expect her, or anyone, to fight automatically to remove the obstruction. Unless she was drugged.'

'Or maybe she did fight back,' Sean said, 'then, after her death, the killer arranged her arms and hands.'

Lucy's left hand was curled like a monkey's paw, palm upwards. Something red peeped out between her thumb and forefinger, like a tongue.

'Is that a fortune fish?' Edie asked.

Sean zoomed in on one of the photos he'd taken. 'It is! Just like Cole-Mortelli.'

'Two people dead, each holding a fortune fish. Unlikely to be a coincidence, given those instructions.' Edie spotted something white between Lucy's salmon-pink nails in the photo. 'What's in her other hand?'

Sean started. 'I didn't think there was anything.' He magnified the image further, this time showing a thin strip of white between the fingers of her right hand. 'Stay here. Don't let anyone in,' he said, setting off down the corridor.

'As if they'd dare try.'

Two minutes later he was back with a pair of tweezers held in plastic-gloved hands. 'I'm going to retrieve whatever she's holding – could you video me entering the crime scene? In case there are procedural worries later.'

Edie filmed Sean moving to the bed in a few long strides then, bending and extracting what looked like a strip of paper from between Lucy's fingers without touching her. It looked like an outsized, macabre version of 'Operation'.

Sean stood in the doorway, straightening the paper with gloved fingers. 'It's one of the riddles from dinner yesterday.'

Edie, still filming, zoomed in on the words:

With one big foot, in a torn cloak,
I oversee the spinning folk.
On twelfth night The Bright One acted,
Shook her head; a Star redacted.
Disobey and touch the treadle:
I'll stitch you up with sweat and pebbles.
WHO AM I?

'It's Frau Perchta,' Edie said, her brain at last throwing her the fact. 'Also known as Frau Holle. One of the gift-bringing Frauen, anyway.'

'You're going to have to give me more than that,' Sean said.

'You know how Santa is supposed to reward nice kids with gifts, but naughty ones get nothing, or maybe coal? Well, Frau Perchta, or Berchta, or Percht, is an Alpine legend associated with the Feast of Epiphany, sewing – hence the big foot or treadle – and the revelation of hidden things. She brought coins to good children and stuffed the stomachs of the bad with straw and stones, then sewed them up.'

'I think I prefer Santa,' Sean said.

'The star part confuses me, though,' Edie mused. 'It could refer to the wise men following the star and Epiphany, but it doesn't quite fit.' When creating crossword puzzles, she always looked for ways to indicate clues that stood out. This was one of them.

'The hotel's restaurant is The Star,' Sean said.

'True, after Aster, the girl who died. The one from the tragic family who built this castle.'

'That's got to be connected. But why would Lucy be holding this?'

'Didn't she say it was Henry's riddle?' Edie said, playing back last night's conversation. 'Maybe she was trying to tell us he's her killer?'

'But the riddles could easily have got mixed up on our table,' Sean countered. 'Henry could've won the cracker they pulled together or just picked the riddle up randomly from a pile near him.'

'Well, there's one way to find out if it's a message from the killer,' Edie said. 'But it means revisiting Mr Cole-Mortelli.'

'To see if he's holding a riddle,' Sean said.

'And, if so, which one.'

Twenty

Mara stood in her office, paralysed by questions that fell as fast as the snow in the dark beyond her window.

What was the hotel manager etiquette when two guests were amongst the dead? Room temperature, for example. Should she turn up the air conditioning in Suite Two? Crank up the heating elsewhere to treat the living for shock?

And was it right to lay the breakfast tables in the style that had been planned? The crackers seemed frivolous; the brass name plates now resembled coffin plaques.

Should she be helping an investigation to prevent harm to her guests or remain neutral? Was it right to worry about her dad more than the people she'd invited here?

None of the hospitality courses had trained her for this. The lift pinged, releasing Edie and Sean into the lobby and Mara from inertia into action. As they moved towards the kitchen, the key to the cold room in Sean's hand, Mara met them at the door. 'I was in shock earlier, Detective Brand-O'Sullivan, and too defensive. You should question me more. It's the right thing to do. I should set an example to the staff.'

'It's my intention to interview everyone in the hotel this morning,' Sean told her. 'Staff and guests alike. And, yes, we'll start with you.'

Mara's heart beat faster. Doing the right thing was scary.

'I need to check on Mr Cole-Mortelli,' he continued. 'And arrange for Owain to help me move Mrs Palmer's body. Ms Morecombe-Clark, with my mum's help, could you please set up a suitable, private room for the interviews?'

'Of course,' Mara said, watching him open the cold-room door and switch on the buzzing, neon light. In his pinstripes, limbs stiff, Cole-Mortelli's body looked like a large ventriloquist's dummy who'd lost his voice forever.

'Hard to deal with, isn't it?' Edie was watching Mara closely. 'Seeing something like that.'

'Can't say I *am* dealing with it. I need to focus on the next thing, which is finding an interview room.'

'How about we use your office?' Edie said, suddenly striding out of the kitchen.

Mara went after her, instinctively wanting to refuse the suggestion, but before she could work out why she minded or object out loud, Edie had, surprisingly quickly, crossed the lobby to the dolls' house and opened the office door. Nodding, she then slipped behind the desk.

Following Edie into her own office, Mara found the elderly woman in her swivel chair.

Easing her lilac hair up to a punkish point, Edie looked around the office. 'This will do nicely. Central but private. And I bet you have tea and coffee facilities.'

Anger twisted and climbed inside Mara. 'This *won't*

do. Not at all. I still need to run the hotel, and this is *my* workplace. He can use another room. We have lots. It's a hotel, after all.'

Whenever Mara stood up to her mother, Mum always reacted with her daughter's rage squared. Edie's response, however, was a broad and unexpected grin. 'Well done!' she said. 'I was wondering when you were going to show some backbone. I bet that felt great.'

Mara blinked, realising that, yes, she *did* feel good. Really good. 'You're not angry?'

'About you defending your space? God, no. I respect it. I *am* pissed off with you, however, for not cancelling this whole event as soon as you found your miniature father under a sheet. If you'd been as brave then as you were a minute ago, you'd have saved the lives of two people, and I'd be spending Christmas Day with my grandchildren.'

'You're right,' Mara said, sitting down hard on a chair. 'I'm not good at standing up for what I want.'

'You only get good at something by doing it badly first. Keep doing the thing and you'll improve.'

'It'd help if I knew what I really wanted.'

'Start there, then.' Edie shrugged as if that was easy.

'I never even knew what I wanted on my Christmas list as a child. I'd choose from the list of things Mum had written down for me.'

'Maybe begin by imagining every possible option and then discussing it with someone you trust – and I'd suggest not your mum. Your dad, maybe? He seems more accepting?'

Mara felt herself smile. 'He's the best dad I could ask for. Kind, generous, supportive . . .'

'He's the interior designer for the hotel, right?' Edie asked. 'Has that always been his job?'

Mara laughed. 'No, he used to work in the city, but it's difficult to imagine now. He hated it. Gave it all up to follow his dreams.'

Edie's eyes were fixed on Mara as if she were a puzzle to be solved. 'I bet he's got some stories to tell. You meet all kinds of people working in the city, not all of them savoury.'

'Oh, I see,' Mara said, turning away, surprised at the hurt she felt that Edie's interest wasn't really in her welfare. 'You're trying to find out why someone would threaten him.'

'And who they could be,' Edie replied. 'For instance, did he know Lucy? They both worked in the city.'

Mara remembered reading an interview with Edie in *The Times*, in which she compared solving a crime to completing a jigsaw – 'place the known facts as cornerstones and build inwards, making connections, until the picture is clear.' She was trying to find connections.

'If he did, he never mentioned it, and I'm sure he would have when I told him they were coming. He didn't even know who Henry was.'

Edie pointed to Mara's desktop. 'Can you access all the hotel's CCTV cameras on here?'

Baffled by Edie's hairpin turns in this conversation, Mara just nodded.

The older woman shifted her chair and beckoned for

Mara to bring hers closer. 'Then show me the corridor outside Suite Two, the last few hours. Then we'll track Cole-Mortelli's activities in the run-up to his death, though presumably that will take longer.'

Mara shook her head, annoyed that she'd only just realised what Edie was doing. 'That's the reason you burst in here, right? It had nothing to do with choosing an interview room.'

'Yes, it did! But I'm also nosey and like to see behind the scenes. I wanted to see where you keep the spare keys, too – presumably in that.' Edie nodded to the dark brown cupboard on the wall.

'Bullseye,' Mara said, walking over and opening the cupboard to show Dad's beloved first dartboard, with keys hung on the inside of the doors.

'Novel storage method,' Edie said, 'if not the most secure.'

'Dad said that keys used to be in plain sight behind the reception desk, so this felt relatively protected. And as you've seen, we do have cameras *everywhere*.'

Coming back over, Mara sat at the computer and opened the CCTV application, searching for the files from camera seven on the first floor. Nothing came up. She tried looking at recent files, as they were automatically recorded every minute. Nothing.

'Try a different camera,' Edie said. 'The one by the lift must show the entrance to the corridor.'

Mara clicked on camera nine. No files saved.

'Is it because the Wi-Fi is down?' Edie asked. 'The footage isn't uploading?'

'It's on a separate system,' Mara replied, panic rising,

'saved to the hotel's main hard drive. Or at least, it should be.' Selecting the previous day on the programme calendar, she again found no categories.

'What about the footage from the staff quarters,' Edie suggested. 'Your dolls' house was first tampered with a few days ago, is that right?'

Now Mara was angry at herself. 'I was going to check it, then completely forgot.'

Edie raised her pencilled eyebrows.

Instead of defending herself (she wasn't sure she'd believe herself in Edie's position), Mara looked through the day before, and the few before that. The last recorded film was five days ago. 'Someone's either disconnected the camera or otherwise disabled the system.'

Sean entered, holding a sealed plastic bag containing a slip of paper. He held it up and nodded at Edie. 'You were right. It was in his other hand.'

'Which riddle?'

He read aloud from his phone:

"My first another word for 'pack',
My next another name for 'cat'.
To punish I will use a birch,
But how? You must do your research.
I'm horny and have Schnappsy breath;
I run from my harm, my name means death.
WHO AM I?"

Which you, Mum, worked out was Krampus. Of course, now his name really does mean death.'

Edie rubbed her face. 'It always did. Mortelli. I should've seen it. That's on me.'

'You can't have anticipated anyone dying based on a riddle,' her son replied. 'You're not a murder butler.'

Mara looked from the detective to his aunt. 'What do you mean about the riddle?'

'Where did all the rubbish go from last night's dinner?' Sean said urgently, not answering her question. 'We need everything from the crackers.'

'In the recycling bins, I suppose,' Mara said. 'Izzie cleared up after the gala dinner.'

'Take us to them,' the detective ordered.

'Not until you explain.' Mara slammed her hand down on the desk. 'I'm the manager. I want to know what is happening in my hotel.' She retreated from her own anger, scared of herself.

'See, you *do* know what you want for Christmas, after all,' Edie said.

As Mara led mother and son the back way into the kitchen, no further on in her search for an explanation, Edie looked at her watch.

'I might skip the bin dip,' she said. 'Riga will be wondering where I am. We normally have our first cups of tea of the morning about now. And I've got her a stocking this year.'

'You haven't?!' Sean said, real joy ringing in his voice. 'Edie O'Sullivan as Mother Christmas. Who'd have thought it? Go. I'll have to do the search anyway.' He pulled another packet of gloves from his pocket.

While Edie's footsteps hurried away, Mara opened the outside door and started down the steps to where the bins were kept.

As the security light came on, Sean grabbed her arm. 'Wait. There's something down there.'

In the alley between the basement and garden walls, a shape lay in the snow. A body, arms and legs at impossible angles that made her think of the Isle of Man flag.

The detective pushed past her, running towards the corpse. He crouched down, then looked back at her. 'It's Owain. He's dead. He must have fallen, recently, given the lack of snow over him.'

Mara looked up. Part of the railing surrounding the roof terrace had been twisted apart, leaving a gap.

'He fell from the roof, or was pushed,' Sean continued, holding a slip of paper in his tweezers. 'While holding the riddle for Santa.'

Twenty-One

The lift doors had only just opened when the fire alarm went off. The skinny scream followed Edie down the first-floor corridor as she hurried, hands over her ears, to their suite. She imagined Riga's candy-cane-thin arms reaching for Edie as flames engulfed her.

Riga, though, was sitting up in bed, headphones on, calmly reading through the programme of events. 'Says here,' she shouted, 'that the first event of the day is breakfast. No mention of a fire alarm. I'd prefer bagpipes myself.'

Nicholas the pug was glaring at the alarm on the ceiling, growling.

'You *must* get up when you hear an alarm,' Edie said, helping Riga out of bed. 'You can't just lie there!'

'I could sense you were on your way,' Riga yelled, eyes twinkling. 'It's probably a false alarm anyway.'

Edie eased her into the wheelchair that Tarn had left in the suite's vestibule the night before, then plonked Nicholas on her lap. 'Unlikely. This hotel has been full of justified alarm so far. We're getting out.'

When they got to the lift, Henry and Tarn were waiting for it to descend. Tarn put her hand to her chest as if relieved to see them, although Edie noted that she hadn't gone to get Riga. Henry seemed not to see them, or anything, at all.

The lift doors opened. George was inside, his scarf wrapped around his head, covering his ears. Seeing the four of them standing there, though, he sprang out to make room. 'Race you down!' he shouted, heading for the staircase.

The alarm was even louder in the lobby, if that was possible. George waved at Edie from halfway down the stairs. 'You win!' he mouthed.

Sean was standing at the foot of the staircase. His shoulders were back, chest bone lifted. He looked strong, in command. It was only when Edie got close to him that she noticed the panic in his eyes.

Swindon was with Mara, shaking his head as if that could stop the tolling of the alarm. Mara was holding a clipboard to the side of her head, looking as if she'd aged in the last ten minutes. They both followed Sean over to join Edie and Riga by the Christmas tree.

Hearing quick footsteps, Edie looked up to see Anna and Celine hurrying round and round down the staircase so smoothly, hair flying, that it was as if they were on a helter skelter. Izzie then emerged from a door to the side of the bar, followed by Ryan. Ryan's arms were folded, his hair not as carefully askew as last night.

'Where have they come from?' Edie asked Mara.

'Staff quarters,' Mara explained, leaning in. 'In the basement. Those are the back stairs.'

'Took their time,' Swindon shouted. 'I knocked on their doors five minutes ago.'

Kimberley appeared from the kitchen, and Mara ticked her name off the list on her clipboard. Catching Edie watching, she blushed. 'I know. It's like a bigger version of the clipboard in my dolls' house. I feel weird using it.'

But that wasn't why Edie was staring. Three names had been struck through instead of ticked: Robert Cole-Mortelli, Lucy Palmer and Owain Spencer. What was Owain doing on that list?

Edie placed her finger next to Owain's name and said, 'Is he . . . ?'

Mara nodded, then wrote under the list of names.

We found him. Fell off the roof.

Edie felt the air go out of her as if there *were* a fire, sucking oxygen from the room. They had been in the hotel barely more than twelve hours and three people had died. She'd checked the dolls' house not long ago for any more strange tableaux, but had seen nothing odd, other than the dolls' house itself. Close up, the miniaturised details, replicated down to exactly the same shades of Farrow & Ball, were uncanny.

Mara scribbled out her own words and placed her index finger over her mouth. Then she tapped her pen on her parents' names, biting her lip. 'I should go and get them,' she shouted.

'Where are they?' Sean yelled.

'Far end of the back lawn – there's an outbuilding, then their cottage,' Mara replied.

'I'll go,' Sean mouthed, but just then Ivan and Felicity Morecombe-Clark walked in from the restaurant.

From where she was standing, Edie couldn't hear what Felicity shouted, but she could lip read clear enough: 'What the fuck is happening?'

Mara rushed over to the control centre by the front doors, re-setting the alarm. For a moment, Edie thought it hadn't worked, but the bells were just echoing in her head.

'Is there no fire?' Celine was asking. At the same time, Anna was wrapping herself in one of the hotel blankets and saying, 'Can we go back to bed now?', while Mara murmured to Ivan and Felicity in the corner. Judging by how Felicity covered her eyes as if to see no evil and Ivan suddenly steadied himself against the bar, their daughter was telling them about the deaths.

Sean climbed a few steps of the staircase. 'Everyone gather round. I'm sorry about waking you on Christmas Day with a fire alarm but it was the only way to get you all here as quickly as possible. I'm afraid that two more of our company have died.'

Celine gasped. Anna looked around the crowd as if to work out who was missing.

'How?' Ryan asked. 'Because it wasn't my food. I know that for a fact.'

Sean's lip twitched. 'We don't know exactly how, nor can I talk about it other than to say Lucy Palmer was killed—'

Lucy's suffocated face flashed into Edie's head. Lucy had been annoying, as had Owain, and Cole-Mortelli, but death lessened all that.

'Owain Spencer fell to his death from the roof terrace

not long ago. I've made a preliminary examination of the roof and discovered that the railing through which he fell was damaged.'

'Deliberately?' George asked, in apparent shock.

'We won't know until there's a full investigation. Meanwhile, the roof terrace is out of bounds, as is the alleyway beside the basement.'

'Is that where Owain is?' Izzie asked, starting to cry.

'It's where Ms Morecombe-Clark and I found him, yes. His body has been covered for now but will be moved once the scene has been secured as much as possible.'

'But he'll be cold,' Izzie said. When Ryan awkwardly patted her shoulder, Kimberley placed her arm around the younger woman, removing his hand.

'Do we know what he was doing up there?' George asked.

'It's unclear if he was meeting someone,' Sean said. 'Or how he fell, if he did indeed fall and wasn't pushed. The fact, however, that three people have died in short succession suggests that it may not have been an accident, just as Mr Cole-Mortelli's suspected heart attack may have been due to something other than natural causes. All three of the deceased had similar items in their hands when they died. As such, I am deeming this a murder investigation.'

So, Owain must have had a fortune fish and a riddle in his hands, too. If Sean wasn't spelling it out, however, he must be keeping specific information from the guests.

'We're facing a very difficult twenty-four hours,' Sean continued. 'The boat has been tampered with, so we have no means by which to leave the island; the emergency services won't arrive until tomorrow morning and all means of communication with the outside world has been vandalised or dismantled. It seems we are in the company of a killer who wants to keep us here.' He surveyed the small crowd, and the crowd surveyed itself, everyone eyeing each other with suspicion.

'Then *I'm* going back to my room till tomorrow morning,' Ryan said, walking towards the back stairs. 'Reckon you'd all be wise to do the same.'

'Stay here, Mr Dreith,' Sean commanded. 'You are now a suspect in a murder investigation, as is everyone in this room.'

Edie moved closer to Riga, who grasped her hand.

'I need to interview each of you,' Sean said. 'This will take a while, so I want you all to stay in the lounge area of the lobby until breakfast, at which point we'll all eat together in the restaurant, then I'll resume questioning.' Edie thought of the Sean who'd arrived here in the boat, as excited as a little boy, compared to the Sean whom everyone was looking at with respect, and some fear. She loved both versions.

'How are we supposed to prepare and serve breakfast if we're in here?' Kimberley asked.

'I'll leave the logistics to Ms Morecombe-Clark – we're only just working it out between ourselves, but I imagine meals will be pared down to necessities,' Sean said.

'I would say "over my dead body",' Ryan said. 'But that seems unwise in the circumstances. If I'm forced to be around these people, then I'm cooking exactly what we planned. When this hits the press, the story will be how I kept on cooking.' He stared into the distance as if imagining himself, top off, in heroic manspreading stance on the covers of men's magazines.

'What if me and Kimberley don't want to work with *you*?' Izzie said, glaring at him.

'Then I'll do it all myself. It's not like there's many to cook for, and they're getting fewer all the time.' He was the only one laughing. 'Fuck off for all I care. I don't need anyone. Never have.'

Izzie turned her back on him, hiding her tears.

'Well, that works out for everyone,' Kimberley said, walking Izzie away from the chef. '*You* could be the murderer.'

'If *I* were a killer,' Ryan said, 'which I'm not, Detective, don't pop the cuffs on – but if I *were*, I'd be a good one. The best. For a start, I wouldn't trap myself on an island with my victims so they could interview everyone and track me down.'

'At least that saves you interviewing him now, Sean.' Edie's voice showed more sarcasm than the Christmas-tree-displayed baubles.

'That's a good point,' Anna said, hope in her voice. 'Do we know for sure that the killer is still on the island? What if they arrived on a small boat, stowed it somewhere and have already left?'

'The only place you can land on the island is the harbour or the beach,' Ivan said. 'Sheer cliffs surround the rest of it.'

'I'd know if another boat had arrived,' Swindon added. 'Or left.'

'We're not ruling anything in or out at this stage,' Sean said. 'Does anyone else have any questions?'

'I don't understand why we can't return to our rooms and lock the doors. How will all of us being in the lounge or restaurant keep us alive?' Celine asked. 'Mr Cole-Mortelli died right in front of us.'

'I understand, and it's a good point. But last night most of us,' Sean glanced quickly at Mara and Tarn, 'were unaware of any danger. We know now that there's a threat, so if we're all looking out for each other, and for questionable behaviour, we're more likely to stay safe. As for sleeping arrangements tonight, well, I'll talk that through with Ms Morecombe-Clark.'

'One of us *isn't* trying to keep everyone safe, though,' Anna said. 'They're trying to kill us.'

'Could be more than one murderer,' Ryan added.

'Thank you, Mr Dreith,' Sean snapped. 'True, but not helpful.'

'What can we do to help?' George asked, bringing over a chair for Henry, who slumped into it, his head in his hands.

'A very welcome question, thank you, Provost Delt. If you, and everyone here, could think about anything that you've seen or heard since you got on the boat, that could help. Similarly, I'd be grateful if anyone who knew Mr Cole-Mortelli, Mrs Palmer or Mr Spencer *before* this trip could be ready to give their impressions of them, and any connections between the victims.' He turned to Mara. 'Anything to add, Ms Morecombe-Clark?'

Mara joined him on the stairs, staying a step below. 'I

just wanted to say to guests and staff alike, how very sorry I am that these terrible, tragic events have taken place here in the hotel. I don't know how we'll recover from it. And although we cannot possibly make up for all this, my parents and I will endeavour to make the remainder of your stay as comfortable and comforting as possible.'

Felicity strutted forwards. 'I think that's a rather pessimistic view, Mara. After all, there are many intelligent people here. Perhaps together we can solve the case and stop a murderer!'

'This isn't a murder mystery weekend, Mrs Morecombe-Clark,' Edie said. 'Catching a killer is not on your programme of events.' As she said it, she thought of last night's entertainment – the ghost story read by Mara. One of the lines rose up – *made my stomach turn and twist like a fortune fish*. Edie felt that fizzy jigsaw feeling she got when she put the first tricky piece of a puzzle in place.

When Sean had sent everyone to either prep breakfast or wait in the lounge for him to call them, Edie said to him and Mara, 'Can I have a look at one of the fortune fish that the victims were holding? Not the actual item obviously – your photos.'

Sean got out his phone and Edie swiped through the images he'd taken, finding one in which he was holding up an evidence bag as if he'd won a dead fish at a funfair.

Zooming in, she could just make out small black letters on the polymer. 'Can you read this?' she asked Sean. 'Something's printed on the fish.'

Sean enlarged the image further. '"Make a ghost of those that haunt you,"' he read out.

A chill swam across Edie's neck. *Make a ghost of those that haunt you.* Was that a threat or an invitation? 'The ghost story you read yesterday said something like that, didn't it?' she asked Mara.

'More like *"say* what haunts you", I think,' Mara said. 'I remember it as I found the idea of having to confess to something otherwise it'd follow you forever terrifying.'

'Similar to saying, "what's the worst thing you've ever done?"' Edie suggested.

Mara nodded.

'Where did you find the story?' Edie asked.

'I'd been thinking of reading an M. R. James tale, or one by E. Nesbit, as Dad used to read them to me on Christmas Eve, but Mum said a modern one might be better, and that she'd send one to me. When "Swim, Little Fish, Swim" arrived from her email address, I assumed she'd sent it.'

'Are you saying she didn't?' Sean asked.

'*Mum's* saying she didn't,' Mara replied. 'Even though it came from her account. So, either someone cloned her email or used one of her devices, or she's—'

'Or she's lying,' Sean interrupted.

Mara looked across the lobby to where her mother sat on a sofa. Her eyes flashed. 'It wouldn't be the first time. You should ask her about it, question her before me, especially about where she got the crackers. She had them made especially.'

Twenty-Two

'The crackers?' Felicity Morecombe-Clark was reclining on the chaise longue in one of the hotel's suites. Sean sat in one armchair, conducting the interview, with Edie in another, making notes. 'I commissioned them from a very charming man at a Christmas-in-July crafters market on Mull. I loved his on-the-shelf ones and, when he said he could make them bespoke, I asked him for a hundred in the hotel's colours and with our crest. He did a lovely job, too. *And* made sure they were delivered on time.'

'A hundred?' Sean repeated. 'Isn't that a lot for a two-night break?'

'It was the minimum for a personalised order. And it's not like they'll go to waste – we wanted them at every meal. And we'll have our own little Christmas when this is over.'

'Even after what's happened?' Sean asked.

'It's not Christmas' fault that some psycho is killing people, is it, now?' Felicity gave him a reproving look. 'Besides, what better way to cheer you up than a cracker? They're one of the best parts of Christmas, don't you? Everyone in their silly hats, reading silly jokes, the little snap . . . it brings out the child in everyone.'

Felicity smiled fondly as if she loved the thought, which was strange for a woman who didn't seem to like her own child that much. Edie would have said so, but Sean had said in the lift on the way up that he needed her to be there, to take notes and make connections, but she shouldn't ask questions in case it compromised the procedural integrity of the case.

Sean didn't return Felicity's smile. '*These* crackers have been part of every crime scene. We need to know more about this man, the supplier.'

'He's got a website, "Nice" something. I can find it— Oh,' Felicity said. 'No Wi-Fi, and I haven't looked at it recently, so it won't be saved. But you can check the box the crackers came in. It's downstairs, in the kitchen store-room. Not the one where the bodies are being kept, thankfully.'

'Are the remaining crackers inside?' Sean asked.

'Aside from the ones laid out for breakfast, yes.'

Sean glanced at Edie, eyebrows raised. He was probably thinking the same as her – did the killer have more riddles for them to crack? And more victims in mind?

'Tell me about the ghost story your daughter read out,' Sean said. 'I believe it was sent from your email address.'

'And yet I'd never heard or read it before Mara performed it. It's a conundrum,' Felicity said calmly. 'I've no idea how that happened. I'm not up on "tech".'

'What about this Christmas event?' Sean asked. 'Whose idea was it, and who invited the guests?'

'Mara came up with it all. We're very proud of her,' Felicity said. 'When Ivan told her about his dream of

178

running a family hotel, she ran with it. She found the island, researched luxury hotels and guest experiences, talked with experts . . . Celine was especially helpful. She suggested a special launch event to get some good PR and marketing, and then Mara thought: *What better than a Christmas break on Holly Island?*' She laughed. 'Now, of course, *anything* would be better.'

'You seem strangely sanguine given that three deaths have occurred in your hotel. Aren't you worried?' Sean asked.

Edie leaned forwards, keen to hear the answer.

'Worried about what?' Felicity said, frowning.

'Your livelihood, your reputation and your retirement fund for a start. As your daughter said, it's hardly good publicity. I'm also surprised you're not concerned about the likelihood of a killer currently being on the premises.'

'Detective Inspector,' Felicity said, crossing her legs and looking out of the window to where the sky had lightened slightly. 'If you knew my history, you'd understand that little can throw me these days.'

'Can you say more?' Sean asked. 'What is it about your background that means things don't get to you?'

'Let's just say I've had epiphanies that have left me somewhat anaesthetised to further shock.'

'And can you say what these revelations are?'

'Oh, I could. But I don't want to. And it has nothing to do with this situation.'

Edie wished she was allowed to speak. She'd say that you never knew which detail mattered in a case. Which clue provided the connection point.

'It wouldn't throw you to know, then, that a replica

doll of your husband was found in your daughter's dolls' house, covered by a sheet? Or that standing next to it was a doll in a doctor's uniform, declaring your husband dead at five forty-five this Christmas Day?'

Felicity reached into her pocket and took out a lip balm. She swiped it slowly across her lips. After a while, she said, 'It doesn't please me, but it doesn't alarm me either.'

'Maybe it should, Mrs Morecombe-Clark.'

'Maybe, but I tend not to feel as I should. The Morecombe-Clarks are known for their lost hearts.' She continued to apply lip balm, as if the layers of grease could stop the chafing of unwanted feelings.

Questions were building up inside Edie. She hadn't been quiet for this long in a very long time. She tried to convey to Sean via eye contact and whatever psychic projection she could muster to *Ask her what she means by that!*

'Do you know why someone might target your husband?' Sean asked.

Clearly Edie had no psychic powers.

'As everyone will tell you,' Felicity replied, 'Ivan is a kind and gentle man, with exquisite taste in soft furnishings and wives. What possible cause could there be for someone to kill him?'

'That's the question I'm asking you, Mrs Morecombe-Clark. Is there anything in his past, for example, which might cause him to have an enemy?'

'If you remove the mystery, what do you get?' Felicity asked. 'When the Victorians raided Egyptian tombs, they came back to the UK with mummies to unwrap at dinner parties and grind up for paint.'

'I'm not following your point, I'm afraid,' Sean said, understandably.

Felicity sighed and rolled her eyes. 'I don't prize the past and I have never prised Ivan from his. I much prefer to behold the present before it loses its paper.'

Edie suspected Felicity would be a great riddle-maker. Lines from last night's ghost story resurfaced again: '*We have to say what's beneath the sea. The shapes we've all seen under the water. The ones in our past. We must speak the whispers.*'

'Thank you for clearing that up,' Sean replied with faint sarcasm. 'Can you tell me where you were in the early hours of this morning, Mrs Morecombe-Clark?'

She beamed. 'I've always wanted to be asked that! I was in our cottage from around eleven o'clock last night until the fire alarm rudely woke us. Ivan was with me, of course – all night, if I need an alibi.'

'And you didn't see or hear anything suspicious during that time?'

Felicity tipped her head to one side. 'I don't know about suspicious, but I saw Ryan Dreith and Izzie having an intense tête-à-tête in the snow when we walked across the lawn to get home, so about half ten, maybe? After that I was out like a snuffed candle. It's been a very tiring run-up to this event.'

'And Owain Spencer. When did you last see him?'

'Last night, I suppose, on our way to bed? He was in the lobby, trying to chat up the lovely young women and failing miserably. Not as miserably as Henry Palmer, but quite amusing to watch, nonetheless.'

'By young women you mean . . .'

'Celine and Anna, and Kimberley was there too. It's not like you could count our Mara as a young woman anymore! Nearly forty and you wouldn't catch her flirting. She wouldn't know how. No grandchildren for me from her, I suppose. Not that it really matters.'

'When did you last check the railings on the roof terrace, Mrs Morecombe-Clark?'

She laughed. 'Obviously *I* haven't. You'll have to talk to Swindon about that, but those railings were *very* expensive. Ivan commissioned them and the chap who brought them over was *very* attractive so I can't imagine they, or we, are at fault. Swindon finished them off, though, so, as I say, talk to him.'

'Do you trust Swindon?'

'As much as I trust anyone, which is very little. You learn not to. But he has been an excellent worker, and very reliable. Older than us, yet far more energy. He's even listened to me moan more than once.'

'You seem very detached from the fact that a young man in your employ fell to his death from the top of your hotel. Or indeed that two of your guests are dead, and your husband has been threatened.' Sean shook his head in amazement. 'Perhaps this connects to your previous statement about the Morecombe-Clarks' lack of heart. Can you say more about that?'

Perhaps Edie's psychic powers worked after all, albeit on a delay.

'Oh, I doubt it,' Felicity said. 'I tried once or twice, but I'm not sure there's any point. But don't worry about me. I'm fine. We'll all be fine. We always have been before, so why not again? The hotel will be fine, too. You'll see. Ryan was right about the press paying attention after this. The hotel will be notorious. I guarantee that, after this becomes public, we will be booked up for years to come by rubberneckers and dark tourists.'

'To some,' Sean said, 'that might sound like motive.' Edie had been thinking the same thing.

Felicity shrugged. 'I truly do not, and cannot, care.'

Twenty-Three

Mara's mother sailed out of the interview room as blithely as if she'd been to one of her Oban brunches with 'the girls' rather than an interrogation with a detective. Her upper lip, though, was weirdly shiny. 'Your turn is it, darling?' she asked Mara. 'Well, he has lots to ask you, but I'm sure you'll be fine. You take after me. In some ways.'

Mara didn't know how her mum managed to make her feel like an unwrapped and unwanted present. If it wasn't so hurtful, it'd be impressive.

Edie was in the corner of the room, in one of the wide armchairs that Mara's dad had reupholstered in purple; Sean was sitting alongside her in its pair. Mara sat on the desk chair, turning it to face them, away from the mirror. She didn't want to see what she looked like right now. She'd only just managed to change out of her pyjamas into her suit and only had time to apply one layer of foundation. She hated the thought of people being able to see through her mask.

'You might be comfier on there,' Sean said, pointing to the chaise longue.

Mara shook her head. She'd feel like she was showing off – the worst of sins, according to Mum. *I don't know about acting for you, darling. It's another one of your theatrics, whims and suchlike. Showing off is for other people, not the Morecombe-Clarks.*

'What we need from you first,' Sean said, 'is anything you remember from last—'

'I've been thinking about it,' Mara said. 'I thought I hadn't seen anything, but then remembered that I saw Henry having a tense conversation with Ryan in the kitchen during dinner. I was preparing for the ghost story at the time, so I didn't think much of it. Then later I saw George going up the internal stairs to the roof, at about midnight, or maybe half past. This was after catching Owain trying to follow Celine up to her room. But I can't imagine George being involved in anything sinister. He's too gentle and nice, and I don't think he has the audacity to take chances.'

Mara caught the detective exchanging a glance with his mum and could tell that they understood each other without the need for words. She envied them their closeness. 'I woke up sometime after two and heard someone moving in one of the rooms above mine,' she went on.

'Which guests are in those rooms?' Sean asked.

'Sound carries strangely in the castle, so it could have been George, Anna or Celine.'

'Could you give us a run-down of how this event was set up? Go right from when you thought of having a Christmas break for marketing purposes.'

'Hard to say when I first had the idea. It emerged out of chats in the hot tub in Switzerland, talking with Dad over tea cakes at Stirling Castle, watching travel TikTok . . . I imagined Celine in the castle doing reels and videos, presenting this beautifully decorated building. And I thought a good review from Henry could be used to appeal to US visitors – "come and stay in a Scottish castle next Christmas." Now it's "come and stay in the murder hotel."'

'Your mum thinks that'll bring in loads of business,' Sean said lightly.

'Even if it does, I'd end up being little more than a ghost tour guide: "In this room, Lucy Palmer was suffocated in her own bed, and here's the library, where a banker met his end during a spooky tale and ended up in his own ghost story."'

Edie laughed. 'You'd be very good at it,' she said, then mouthed 'Sorry!' to her son.

'I don't want to do that, though,' Mara said.

'Knowing what you don't want is a step towards knowing what you do,' Edie replied, then put her hand over her mouth and did the 'zip up' motion. Sean had clearly told her not to interject during the interview. Mara supposed Bring Your Mum to Work Day might not go down well when he presented a report on the investigation.

'Let's get on to how you chose the guests that you invited,' he said.

'As I said, I met Celine and Anna while on my research trip; Celine then introduced me to Henry. Dad has known George for a long time – they're both in the same golf club. And George is on the board of the charity that auctioned off the place won by Cole-Mortelli. Cole-Mortelli was going to bring a plus one, then, for some reason, decided not to. Two days before.'

'What about the staff?' he asked.

'Tarn has been with my family pretty much forever.

She was nanny for me when I was adopted, and for my brother and sister, then worked as a P.A. and sometime housekeeper for Mum and Dad. Mum calls her our "right-hand woman".'

Edie and the detective shared another glance that looked meaningful.

Mara felt as if she was on the other side of the glass. Unable to bear it, she asked, 'What is it? You're both thinking something.'

'You say it,' Sean said to Edie. 'I officially give you permission to talk.'

'Oh, thank fuck,' Edie said, as if she'd been holding her breath, not her peace. 'I thought I was going to explode! It's not good for you, keeping all those words inside like a snapper in a cracker. It's why I compile crosswords.'

'And what are the words you need to say?' Mara asked, irritated and a bit delighted by Edie's outburst. She wished she could do that more.

'Since you read that ghost story yesterday,' Edie said, 'fishing lines from it keep apparating into my head. I didn't know why – I mean, I liked it, and you read it well, but there was no reason for it to haunt me into today. But when you mentioned adoption just now, I remembered that the story has that at its centre. Maybe that's why it's stayed with me. My life changed when I adopted Sean, and Sean's changed when he and Liam adopted the kids.'

'So, you were just sharing a moment about adoption?' Mara asked, hoping she wasn't revealing her disappointment that the story had stayed with Edie because of its emotive content, not her performance.

'No, don't you see?' Edie said, her frustration showing. 'Statistically speaking, it's unlikely that such a small group of people would include three adoptees and four adopters.'

'That we know of,' Sean said. 'There could be more.'

'I was wondering,' Edie said, getting a notebook from her pocket, 'if it was related at all to the Santa riddle. Owain had that in his hand, right?'

When Sean nodded, Edie read from her notebook:
'Named a dad with no known child,
A housebreaker beatified,
I punish those who're on my list,
Yet no one knows my naughtiness.
I've many names, yet posts still find me;
I leave cookie crumbs behind me.
WHO AM I?'

'He could have a kid that was given up?' Mara said, with doubt in her voice. 'Though he was only twenty-something. He never mentioned it, not that I've known him long.'

'He was more than old enough to father a child,' Sean replied. 'It's a theory, at least. And it makes the selection of that story interesting, especially as we don't know where it came from.'

'Are you saying that the killer has been pulling the strings, *my* strings, all along? To bring these people to this place, now, and that my adoption is something to do with it?' *What's if it's my biological mother?* Mara thought, but didn't say.

'How do you and your parents feel about your adoption?

I only ask because Edie adopted me when my parents died, and it's been difficult at times.' Sean turned to Edie with an apologetic look.

He went on, 'All adopted kids carry trauma, and they and their adoptive parents need support. I also know from going to adoption classes that there can be stigma about adopted kids, even if it's internalised.'

'Honest answer?' Mara asked.

'It'd save time,' Sean replied.

'Mum really wanted another child after my brother, but it wasn't happening biologically for her and Dad, not till later. So they bought me. Just like you'd buy a handbag or a pair of heels.'

'Or a hotel?' Sean said.

'That's right,' Mara replied ruefully. 'Only I was harder to give back when I wasn't what she wanted.'

'Which was?' he asked softly.

'I don't know. Whatever it is, I've never been able to be it.'

Sean asked Mara more questions about how she found the other members of staff, and while she answered them, her mouth speaking about Swindon's support, of her conflict over hiring Ryan, about poaching Kimberley from a London restaurant and finding Izzie and Owain through the agency, her mind was ghosting her, thinking instead of the stranger who had given her up, and whether she might be a killer.

Twenty-Four

Edie didn't think she was hungry, and then she walked into the lobby. Smells of pastry baking and bacon frying cut through her thoughts of death and drew her straight into The Star restaurant, where Riga, thanks to Tarn's earlier help, was already at their table, feeding Nicholas bites of sausage. Sean was by the entrance to the kitchen, watching Tarn tong croissants onto a plate and place them on a table.

Edie went over to the buffet and grabbed two croissants. 'You were right when you told me that interrogation requires carb-loading. I'll never doubt you again.'

'Can you tell Liam that?' Sean replied.

Ryan marched out, slammed a platter of fruit on the table and then, going back into the kitchen, slammed the door behind him.

'He's been extra touchy the last couple of days, which is saying something,' Tarn said. 'No idea why.'

Edie returned to Riga, placing one of the croissants on her side plate and kissing her on the head. The tables were set as they had been yesterday, with two places removed. Crackers had again been placed at every setting. Yesterday, they'd promised festive fun. Today, they threatened menace. There were two differences to yesterday's crackers – none of today's were named, and they were much lighter.

Anna and Celine walked in together, with none of the joy they'd had yesterday. They sat down, both glancing at the empty space where Robert had sat last night. Anna placed an Aster Aurelio cocktail in front of Riga.

In contrast, Felicity and Ivan walked in, arm in arm, waving as if they were royals at a gala. Ivan had a glass of Champagne in one hand, the bottle in another.

Ivan gestured towards Riga's drink. 'Enjoy!'

Celine picked up the cracker in front of her. 'It can't be tradition to pull these now, in these circumstances?'

Edie and Sean had talked about this on the way down. Sean had considered taking all the crackers and opening them by themselves, but there was a reason the killer wanted them to be cracked at breakfast, and they might reveal themselves more this way. But it was a risk.

'We're gonna open them,' Edie replied, holding one out to Riga. 'It's Christmas after all.' Seeing this, Sean came over and sat on her other side. The whole table was now crossing arms, making her think of 'Auld Lang Syne'. Robert, Lucy and Owain were new rather than old acquaintances, but she'd never be able to forget them.

On the other table, Felicity shrugged and smiled and wobbled her cracker at her husband. Taking it, he shared his with George. Henry shook his head and stared down at his name plate. He was holding another, Lucy's presumably, on his palm.

'One, two, three, pull!" Celine said quietly. The crackers jolted; their innards spilled. Fortune fish rained down like a red plague but there were no gifts inside this time. Just fish, hats and riddles.

No celebration this time either as those holding the winning ends looked inside. Anna fished out a hat but didn't put it on; Sean unrolled a slip of paper. He scanned through it once, looked at Edie, then read out:

'*A mother who has scoffed at kids,*
A crone who jettisoned bad kin
Into a cooking pot of herbs,
Trolling with denying words.
Instead of loving your huge cat,
Embrace instead your reject brat.
WHO AM I?'

'This riddler sure has Mummy issues,' Edie said.

'Who doesn't?' Celine said, making Anna laugh then cover her mouth.

Edie read through the brainteaser while running through her list of festive gift-bringers. One mother stood out. 'Grýla, a mythical Icelandic troll-woman who takes – or eats, depending on the source – wicked children. She is mother to thirteen of her own very naughty children, the Jólasveinar, otherwise known as the Yule Lads, who each visit children over Christmas until Twelfth Night.'

'Are any of those "reject brat"s?' Sean asked.

'Not that I know of,' Edie replied. 'Although I bet Window Peeper, Door Sniffer and Meat Hook try her patience.' When Anna's eyes widened, Edie said, 'Yes, those are their real names. Nominative determinism playing a strong role there.' She turned back to Sean. 'Grýla does have a massive cat, though. Lucky woman.'

The other table snapped into action.

'I've got a riddle!' Ivan shouted. He didn't seem fazed in any way – maybe he too, like his wife, was never thrown. Or perhaps neither Mara nor Felicity had told him about the death of his miniature figure. Or maybe the wine was hiding his fear.

'Man of stars, to those I'm fixed.
A bag of gifts and harsh rods mixed.
Make amends, turn the bad to good.
A beard of straw, masking the truth.
Whistle and blow a stop to
Winter. Poor foal adopted.
WHO AM I?'

He left a pause, then said, 'Fucked if I know!'

Felicity clapped, hooting. Mara, sitting next to her, closed her eyes.

'Man of stars,' Izzie said. She'd joined the other table, on strike from her work. 'That could be Ryan! He wants stars more than anything else.'

'He wants to *be* a star more than anything else,' Celine said.

'Can I see the riddle, please?' Edie asked, and Ivan got up unsteadily and handed it over. As she read it through, the image of a man in a wooden mask, with a wicker basket for a hat, came back to her from researching the gift-bringers. 'I think this is Gwiazdor, a Polish figure who wants to know about children's good and bad deeds. His name is derived from the Polish word for star.' The word 'star' again. And 'adopt'.

'How do you remember all that?' Anna asked. 'My memory's shit. I have to write everything down otherwise it's gone.'

'Don't do yourself down. You remembered which drink I liked yesterday,' Riga said, making Anna smile.

'It's not always a blessing,' Edie said. 'Recalling everything is tiring and traumatic as well as tremendously useful in pub quizzes.'

'We've been banned from my local because she kept on winning,' Sean said. 'Anyone else got a riddle for Mum to solve?'

'I have!' George said:

'Alleged patron saint of bairns,
Your intercession grants her prayers;
Exchanges made to the offspring –
Gold coins or a little plaything.
The relics of your deeds are kept
Inside your digs, like your secrets.
WHO AM I?'

'That's St Nicholas!' Edie shouted, realising that the dopamine hit from finding solutions was overriding her sense of urgency in working out what the murderer meant by them.

'Isn't that the same as Santa?' Anna asked.

'Santa *is* based on St Nicholas,' Edie explained, 'but he's a different visiting figure. In Ukraine, for example, St Nicholas, also known as Cold Nicholas, brings gifts on December sixth, or "Magic Night". He also delivers the first snow by shaking his big beard.'

'I've got a riddle too,' Anna said:
'*Spooky witch of Christmas time –*
If you're vile I'll give you grime;
If nice there'll be festivities.
Agent of Epiphanies,
I bring sweetness to the chosen,
Sweep away the sinful frozen.
WHO AM I?'

'You could be the spooky witch, Riga,' said Edie.

'I'll take that as a compliment,' Riga replied, but she wasn't smiling.

'I'd say that was one of my favourites,' Edie said. 'La Befana. In Italian folklore she's a witch-like woman who delivers gifts or sweets to good children on Epiphany Eve, and coal or dirt to the naughty ones.'

'I found a repeat from yesterday – Krampus – but there's also one more.' Henry read aloud:
'*My mum dispensed with naughty kids;*
Our pet those wearing threadbare kit.
I'm one of thirteen brothers who
In December blesses shoes
With gifts each night, yet have flaws all:
Mine is cruelly beating portals.
WHO AM I?'

His voice, stripped of all previous bonhomie and bombast, unintentionally gave the riddle the solemnity it merited. Everyone was listening to him with the reverence reserved for the bereaved. A few moments of silence and then Riga said, 'Makes me think of one of the Yule Lads. I once went to Iceland – the country, not the shop – at

196

Christmas and all the shops had wooden decorations of them. I came back with a suitcase stuffed with Lads. Can't remember which one this is, though.'

Edie searched her mind for the right memory box and smiled when she found it: 'That's Door-Slammer, or Hurðaskellir. He arrives on December eighteenth and, well, slams doors.'

'Door-Slammer? Now that *does* sound like Ryan!' Izzie said.

'Not the most malevolent of our characters, then?' Sean said to Edie. He was trying to work out what that meant, too.

Edie unfurled the inner tube of her cracker and found, as she'd suspected, another ice-breaker. 'You should all look inside the crackers,' she called out, holding hers up.

Everyone peeled back the crepe paper and velvet, and uncurled the cardboard.

'Another question,' Anna said, then read out, '"What is your darkest secret?" So basically, the same question as yesterday.'

'Only most of us didn't answer it,' Edie said. She raised her eyebrows at Sean, indicating that maybe the group should be encouraged to spill their secrets, just like the characters were in the ghost story.

'While I can't tell you everything,' Sean said to them all, 'you should know, I think, for your own safety, that there's a theory that the killer is trying to get us to confess to events in our past that are haunting us, or someone else.'

'But why?' Anna asked. She was trembling, her wide eyes darting round the room.

'We don't know what secrets they're looking for us to spill,' Sean said, 'or why. But I think at least two people have been killed for not "coming clean". So, if there's something you think you're being targeted for, I suggest you confess.'

'They're trying to work out if we're naughty or nice,' Celine said.

'Who wants to start?' Edie asked.

Everyone looked at each other. No one spoke.

'There must be something to help us pin down which wrong the killer wants us to discuss,' Henry said shakily. 'What should my Lucy have said?'

'That's a good place to start,' Edie said, taking out her phone and scrolling to Lucy's Frau Perchta riddle, then handing it to Henry. 'Can you see anything that links your wife to this riddle?'

He put on his glasses and read it through, then shook his head. 'I don't understand what it means, let alone how it relates to Lucy.'

'Did Lucy have anything to do with sewing?' Edie asked. 'She was given a gold-plated sewing machine decoration as a cracker gift, and Frau Perchta oversaw spinning.'

'As she said herself,' Henry replied, 'she never picked up a needle. I'm the one who mends things at home.' His face crumpled, remembering, perhaps, that home would never be the same again. He tilted his head. 'Although she does have investments in clothing companies and is on the board of at least one in China.'

'Dodgy clothing companies in China?' Anna asked.

'She never said so,' Henry replied. 'But then, she didn't

like to bother me with her business stuff. Said it was boring compared to my job.'

'The link between Lucy, her riddle, her gift and her investments might come to nothing,' Sean said, 'but I'd like everyone to think of the presents they got in their crackers, and how they could relate to your misdeeds. And tell us as soon as you can. It looks like making a public confession is important.'

Edie felt for her new keyring, now attached to her skirt with the large safety pin it had come with. If she had committed a terrible crime, she would have done it in Vivienne Westwood. Riga took her new rosary out of her pocket and scrunched it in her hand.

'The buffet breakfast is ready,' Tarn called out from the back of the restaurant. 'I'll be bringing round fresh pots of tea and coffee and rounds of mixed toast but otherwise help yourself to anything on the tables.'

While most left their chairs to fill their plates, Sean, Edie, Riga and Mara checked all the slips of paper to make sure no riddles had been missed, but all they found were plastic fish. So many fish.

Edie placed one on her palm and watched the head and tail move. 'Looks like I split the jury.'

Sean suddenly took the fish from her. 'What if the killer attacked those who touched the fish yesterday?' he said. 'Based on what the fish did?'

'I don't think so,' Mara replied. 'I'm sure Anna or Celine held one yesterday, and they're both fine. Dad did too.'

Just then a crash came from behind them. It was

Ivan – he was on the floor, holding on to the tablecloth. Plates had fallen around him, covering him with fruit and pastries.

Mara ran to her father. 'What happened?' she asked her mum, voice taut with fear. Edie joined them, with Sean by her side.

Felicity's lip was trembling, her eyes unblinking. 'He's not breathing.'

Sean crouched by Ivan, checking his wrist and listening to his chest. 'He has a pulse, but it's weak, as is his respiration. I don't like his colour.' He prised open Ivan's fist and found a fortune fish. 'Or this.'

'Maybe he was just holding it because he picked it out of his cracker?' Mara said with heart-breaking hope.

Sean reached for Ivan's other hand, encouraging it to uncurl and release the tablecloth, and a slip of paper with the riddle for Gwiazdor.

The man of stars had fallen in The Star.

Twenty-Five

'What does all this *mean*?' Mara's mum was saying as Tarn and Sean carried her dad to one of the booths in the Gold Bar. They laid him on the banquette, and Mara pulled up a stool as close to him as she could, her heart crumpling. 'This can't happen. Not to him,' Mum kept repeating.

'What do you mean?' Sean asked Felicity sharply. 'Why *not* to him?'

'It's not allowed,' was all she would say.

Mara moved her dad's hair out of his eyes, then jerked her hand away. 'He's burning up and sweating. How can this have come on so quickly?'

Dad convulsed, mucus spittling on his paling lips.

'Could be poison,' Sean said. He, too, was perspiring, wiping his temples with his wrists. 'But without the internet I can't look anything up.' He turned to Riga, who was standing between Edie and Anna, rubbing a rosary between her thumbs and middle fingers. 'Any ideas?'

'What would she know?' Mara asked, more harshly than she'd intended.

'Riga has knowledge of herbal remedies,' Edie said. 'Although I doubt there's an herb garden here.'

'We can treat the symptoms and try to bring down his

201

temperature, but we really need to know which poison he's ingested,' Riga said gently.

When she heard the word 'ingested', Mara remembered seeing her dad at the breakfast buffet table, loading his plate and raising something to his lips. Seconds later, he'd started fitting.

'Did you see what Dad was eating just before he got ill?' she asked Tarn.

Tarn's eyes shifted to the left in recall. 'I think he had bacon, egg, tomatoes and sausages, same as everyone else. Although Ryan made him a special black pudding on tattie scones.'

'And no one else had that?'

'I don't think so.'

'Then we need to talk to Ryan,' she said, the stool toppling as she stumbled off it. 'Has anyone seen him?'

'He's still in the kitchen, I think,' Sean said.

As Mara ran back into the restaurant, she tried to think why Ryan would want to hurt her dad and came up with nothing. But if *he* wasn't the killer, he'd at least know who'd been in contact with Dad's food.

George was still sitting with Henry in The Star. 'How's your dad?' he asked as she sprinted past.

'Not good,' Mara spat out, anger spiralling again. How could they just sit there while Dad was on the brink of death?

Bursting into the kitchen, she looked around for Ryan, trying not to think of the bodies in the cold room. Kimberley was putting a loaf of bread into the oven. 'Where's Ryan?' Mara asked.

Kimberley shrugged. 'Vaping in the courtyard last I saw him, kicking at the wall. If he's wise, he'll be trying to keep this latest of his career opportunities. But he's not wise. He's an idiot. And horrible. Whatever he said or did to Izzie yesterday has left her in an absolute mess. She's absolutely stricken but won't tell me why.'

Mara scanned the room. 'Where are the pans he used to cook Dad's black pudding and tattie scones?'

Kimberley looked around. 'No idea. I keep to my own station.'

Mara stormed through the kitchen and out of the back door, past the tarpaulin that she and Sean had used to cover Owain's body, and into the courtyard.

Footsteps showed in the thick snow, leading to what used to be the ice house, now used for storage, and, it seemed, for vaping.

As she entered, all she could see were garden tools and stacked garden furniture waiting for summer. But Ryan was there somewhere – his raspberry ripple ice cream vapour stank out the cold air. 'Ryan? I need to know how you made the food that was just for Dad, and who was in the kitchen with you.'

No reply.

'Honestly, Ryan. I need your help. Dad could die and we need to know what happened. It looks like his food has been spiked, and I don't know if it was just his plate, or the black pudding, as no one else seems sick. I know I'm grasping at straws, and you're not one for sentiment, but I'm begging you. He's my dad.'

The room's silence itself felt cold.

As Mara moved further inside, she knocked a pair of sharp shears off their hook. Fear iced her back as she realised she'd followed a potential murderer on her own, into a room filled with weapons.

Picking up the shears, she crept past the wall of parasols that hung like grey ghosts and slowly looked behind the seated lawnmower. More tarpaulin lay on the floor. And a human shape lay beneath.

Maybe Ryan was trying to scare her. He'd heard her coming and slunk underneath. Aware she was afraid of everything, he was lying under the plastic sheeting, knowing she'd be too freaked out to look.

Well, that wasn't going to happen. One good thing that was emerging from the last twenty-four hours was that she'd found a sliver of bravery. Crouching, shivering, Mara picked up the edge of the tarpaulin and, in one movement, flicked it away.

Ryan Dreith *was* beneath. But he wasn't hiding. He was dead on the floor, in a jus of his blood. His own knife in his heart. A fortune fish in one hand, a riddle in the other.

Twenty-Six

Ivan was shivering, despite being covered in three tartan blankets. He was on his side, but Tarn had to keep clearing his mouth to make sure he didn't choke. Felicity, meanwhile, was pacing back and forth behind the bar, muttering.

'Please,' Tarn said to everyone crowding round, holding out her arm as a barrier around her employer. 'He needs some space.'

'Of course,' Edie said. 'We'll be nearby if you need us for anything.' She, Riga and Sean went into the adjacent booth. With no idea what Ivan had been poisoned with, there was nothing any of them could do for him medically. And Tarn was making sure he was as comfortable and safe as possible.

'I still need to interview everyone, but things keep happening, and everyone's in shock.' Sean opened his rucksack and showed them the box of crackers, with ten left inside. 'We need to focus on the crackers, what's inside them,' he said. 'Find out what the riddles and games mean. They're true clues, and I think the killer actually wants us to solve them, to find out and publicly lay bare the victims' crimes. I've also got a list of the cracker presents, including the ones that the staff received, that Mara wrote up for me earlier.'

Edie checked that no one could overhear them, but the other guests were elsewhere, Ivan was too delirious to hear, and Tarn was unable to care as she dabbed at the tears she'd shed on his forehead. 'We also have to find the murderer and stop them before they kill again.'

Ivan's rasps grew louder; Felicity's pacing quicker.

'From the riddles we had yesterday, the ones I found in the recycling and the ones at breakfast, six have been repeated over and over. Four of them have been found in the hands of the victims, which suggests—'

'That the killer intends there to be two more victims,' Riga finished for Sean.

'We should open the remaining crackers,' Edie said, her heart beating hard at the thought of Sean or Riga being one of the two. 'To make sure there are no more riddles. I presume the killer intended us to pull them at Christmas lunch and reveal the last part of their game. This way, we stay ahead. Or at least, one step less behind.' She took a cracker out of the box and, instead of offering it to Sean or Riga, pulled both ends herself. The others did the same. These crackers, though, were louder – the snap more of a bang, smelling of the cap guns Edie used to love.

'What the fuck was that?' Tarn said, peering round the edge of the booth. Seeing the cracker halves, she said, 'I never want to see another one of those again.'

'I've only got a riddle and a fortune fish,' Riga said, staring into the tube. Her slender fingers pulled out the paper, and then she showed it to Edie.

'*WHO AM I?*' was all it said.

'I suppose it's still a riddle, of sorts,' Sean said, showing that his was the same. All the crackers, in fact, were the same, with '*WHO AM I?*' on the paper, a plastic fish that pledged to make a ghost of the one who haunts you and an ice-breaker printed onto the cardboard tube: 'Who have you hurt the most?'

'These crackers are getting less and less festive,' Edie said at last. 'Not one paper crown to be found.' She picked up the box. The makers traded under the name 'The Naughty and Nice List', which tolled a bell in her head, presumably from the many times Santa's creepy inventory, surely a breach of GDPR, had been mentioned this Christmas. She had been right to distrust him.

'So, the presents were only in the first batch and were specific to each person. What did each of the victims receive?' Sean asked.

'Robert had a wooden-handled screwdriver, Lucy had the gold sewing machine decoration and,' Edie paused to check the list, 'Owain got a gold-plated laptop decoration.'

Riga gave a sardonic laugh. 'That's a clear clue to his transgression. I wonder what naughty things he got up to online?'

'The answer will be in the Santa riddle somewhere,' Edie said, shuffling the papers till she found it. '"I've many names but posts still find me." If it was referring to Santa, then it would be "post still finds me", but this is "posts", as in "posting" on social media or in forums. Which also goes with "cookie crumbs" and his laptop decoration.'

'So, he was probably a menace behind an online silhouette. A troll, basically,' Sean said.

'That probably describes a quarter of the people in the UK,' Edie said. 'Everyone is brave behind a screen. But Owain must have been a troll who did something sufficiently bad to be judged not only "naughty" but not worthy to live.'

'That's one extreme festive visitor,' Sean said. 'What was it you said about Santa yesterday? "What gives him the right to adjudicate over us?", or something like that?'

'Something like that.'

'Well, the killer thinks it's their right,' Sean went on. 'But what brings someone to that point? And how do they know so much about everyone? How have they gathered us all together?'

'The good thing, if I can call it that,' Riga said, 'is that Ryan was right when he said that the killer has trapped themselves along with us. It must be one of our group.'

'Unless,' Edie said, 'they're hiding out elsewhere on the island. We only have the Morecombe-Clarks' word that no one else is here, and even they could have missed someone arriving by boat, however much Swindon insists that's impossible.'

'Without the ability to conduct a proper search of the island, I suppose that's a possibility,' Sean said, looking more glum by the moment.

In the next booth, Tarn was holding Ivan as he was sick into an ice bucket. Still Felicity didn't help.

'We should concentrate on Ivan's riddle,' Edie said. 'Try

to work out his "darkest secret". See if there's a way that we can save him.'

'Where do we start?' Riga asked, looking over the print-out of the Gwiazdor puzzle.

Man of stars, to those I'm fixed.
A bag of gifts and harsh rods mixed.
Make amends, turn the bad to good.
A beard of straw, masking the truth.
Whistle and blow a stop to
Winter. Poor foal adopted.
WHO AM I?

'References to stars again, and to adoption,' Sean said. 'And obviously Ivan and Felicity adopted Mara. It must be something to do with that.'

'Mara said she was "bought" as a child, but where from?' Edie asked. 'Are we looking for a disreputable adoption agency, maybe? The one that Mara was adopted from? Perhaps the babies were unethically sourced? It says in the riddle that a whistle can be blown – is that what he's supposed to blow the whistle on?'

'I'll ask Felicity,' Sean said, jumping up and crossing the room. Riga and Edie watched for a moment as he joined her behind the bar, casually poured himself a Coke and started talking. Felicity shook her head, then Sean pointed across to where Ivan was lying.

Felicity bowed her head, her mouth moving.

'I hope he's getting something useful out of her,' Riga said.

'If she does have anything to say, she'll have actually come through for her family,' Edie replied. She re-read the riddle. 'There's something about the last line, the reference to the foal. It keeps jumping out at me, as I'm not aware of Gwiazdor being associated with horses. There's another connection, I can feel it.'

'It'll come,' Riga said, a look of pride in her eyes. 'It always does.'

Something from the ghost story was tickling Edie's brain, but she couldn't remember what.

'What about the "make amends" bit?' Riga asked. 'Is that giving him a chance to confess?'

'He's the only one who has so far survived an attack,' Edie said. 'But what if he was meant to? What if he's being given another chance to make up for his past?' Again, just like in the ghost story. She needed to read it, or hear it, again.

Sean returned. 'Felicity said Ivan arranged the adoption. He told her that the agency whose books they were on – and she claims she never knew their name, which I find unlikely – rang them to say that a baby had been left outside a police station on the winter solstice, and that she, Mara, could be theirs. For a hefty fee.'

'That doesn't sound right,' Edie said.

'Morally or logistically?' Riga asked.

'Adoption doesn't work like that, surely,' Edie said to Sean. 'You had to jump, twirl, paraglide through the tiniest hoops and still wait for ages to get Juniper and Rose. Even if they paid a fortune, there must still have been legal requirements.'

'There are ways to circumvent pesky things such as the law,' Sean said, 'but that would involve child trafficking, or going abroad, not getting a child from a British police station and taking it home for Christmas. So, either Felicity is lying, or Ivan lied to all of them.'

'Then the question is, where did Mara come from?' Riga said.

'And is a dodgy adoption the worst thing Ivan's ever done, or is there something else? Something darker?' Edie asked.

The door into the bar from the restaurant slammed open, and Kimberley and Izzie burst in, half carrying, half dragging Mara.

'Oh, God,' Tarn said, her hand going to her chest. 'What's happened?'

'I f-found Ryan. Outside.' Mara handed Edie the St Nicholas riddle and stared at her with the wide, imploring eyes of a doll. 'He's d-dead.'

'Where was he?' Sean asked, already putting on his coat.

'In the ice h-house.' Mara's teeth were chattering as if she'd been kept out there all night.

Felicity started to laugh, a strange gurgle of a chuckle that wouldn't stop. She bent over with laughter that seemed to physically hurt her. 'Another body! Another corpse! It's a good job we built a big cold room.'

Twenty-Seven

Mara knew she was wrapped in blankets but she couldn't feel their warmth. She couldn't feel *anything*. *Maybe that's a good thing*, she thought. *Who wants to feel at a time like this?* Not that she even knew what the time was; all she knew was that her mother had lost it, and her father was losing his life. She didn't want to feel a thing.

'Try and drink something,' Anna was saying, placing a mug of hot chocolate in her hand. 'You're in shock. The sugar should help a little.'

Hot chocolate was the drink Dad always made her on Christmas morning, while Mum drank Bucks Fizz. You didn't get marshmallows in Bucks Fizz.

Anna helped bring the mug to Mara's mouth, making Mara think of when she used to have tea parties with her dolls, and she'd get them to 'drink'. She was like a doll now.

'Everyone, listen.' Sean was standing in front of the shining gold counter, clapping his hands. He looked handsome, the light bouncing off his face. People paid attention. Even Mum had stopped laughing and was gazing at him.

And everyone *was* suddenly here. When Mara had left

the bar to find Ryan there had only been a few people, but now Henry and George were sitting on stools, Izzie and Kimberley standing close together in the corner while Anna and Celine hovered over her, tucking her in as if for a bedtime story. Swindon was nearby, holding his head in his hands as if it were too heavy for his neck.

'Since we met here nearly twenty-four hours ago,' Sean said, 'four people have died. Mara has just found Ryan Dreith in the storage area outside, stabbed in the heart. He was here, serving breakfast, not more than an hour ago, and now he's gone.'

Anna and Celine bent their heads in unison. Izzie folded over, sobbing.

'How is it possible for that to happen in daylight, with so many people around, without the killer drawing attention to themselves?' George asked. 'Are we looking at a professional hit?'

Celine laughed. 'I can't see any of us being an assassin!'

'It feels too personal to be professional,' Edie said. 'Someone's heart is in this. It might be a warped heart, but there's emotion and a twisted sense of justice. They're on a mission. Once we know *why*, we'll be able to stop them.'

'I see your point,' George said quietly. 'But maybe it's a professional with a personal mission? Think about how well it's been executed – sorry, forgive my poor choice of language.' He blushed. 'But everything has gone right for them so far, to the point of Robert dying in front of us without any of us knowing. And then there's all the methods: different poisons, suffocation, stabbing and quite possibly pushing from the roof. That's a varied set of modus operandi.'

'As if they're trying to do it differently each time,' Henry said thoughtfully.

'And it would be easy for a professional to hide out somewhere on the island,' George continued. 'Keep the castle under surveillance and strike at the right moment.'

'You two seem to know a bit too much about these things,' Mum said.

'I have a lot of time to read and watch films and telly,' George said sheepishly.

'But this isn't telly,' Izzie said. 'Ryan's a real person, rude and obnoxious and talented and—' She covered her mouth and coughed as if choking on her unsaid words.

'I know this is a very difficult time to ask, Izzie,' Sean said, 'and in public, too, but I think it's important that we all stay together from now on. It's too dangerous to be separated. So, forgive me, but I need to know why you are so upset.'

'He was my father,' Izzie said through her tears.

Mara let out a gasp. The resemblance was there, once you knew. Or maybe resemblance, or the lack of it, was found after the fact, the confirmation bias effect shown in the way that people would say that she looked like her dad, or sometimes her mum, and then be mortified when she explained that she was adopted.

'But he didn't want to be my *dad*,' Izzie continued. 'He and my mum were a thing, briefly, in their teens, but then she moved away when she got pregnant.' Kimberley held her until her cries subsided.

215

'That's what you were arguing about yesterday?' Sean asked.

Izzie crossed her arms around herself. 'I told him that I was his daughter, and he said he didn't care. It's the only reason I'm here. I thought he'd be pleased.'

Kimberley was staring at Izzie. 'I thought he'd taken advantage of you,' she said. 'I thought . . .' She stopped speaking and just shook her head.

'Is there something you want to say about Ryan, Kimberley?' Sean asked.

Kimberley didn't look up or reply.

Sean paced the length of the bar, giving Mara something to focus on. She was coming back to herself again.

'As there's a limited time frame in which the killer could have struck,' Sean said, 'I need to know where everyone was in the last hour, what they were doing and who they were with.'

'I was on the boat,' Swindon said, 'trying to find a way to fix her. No alibi. No hope of it working but doing it anyway.'

'Thanks for trying,' Sean said.

'You're welcome, but it's for my own benefit,' Swindon replied. 'I can't stand being abandoned somewhere. The thought of being stuck here . . .' He trailed off, staring through the window to the trees.

'Who else doesn't have an alibi?' Sean asked.

'I was with Henry most of the time, but went outside by myself about thirty minutes in,' George said, 'to get some fresh air. But I didn't see Ryan or anyone else.'

'And when George went out, I suppose I don't have an alibi either,' Henry added.

'I went to my room,' Anna said.

'And I went upstairs with Anna, then when she went to her suite, I checked out the gym,' Celine replied. 'But I decided not to use it and went for a walk by the harbour instead. I saw Swindon at the boat, swearing.' She smiled at him, and his gruff grin back made Mara feel that maybe things would be okay.

'I went outside briefly,' Tarn said, 'to have a word with Ryan about lunch. He was vaping by the storage area, but didn't really want to talk, so I left him to it.'

The brief, pregnant pause suggested that, like Mara, the room was thinking that the 'it' Tarn had left him to was his death.

'You haven't put yourself forward as not having an alibi, Mara,' Sean said. 'But you're the most obvious one.'

Mara felt like she'd been stung. But, of course, he was right. She'd found the body, alone. And she'd been seen going after Ryan, angry, passing through the kitchen, where he kept his knives. 'I hadn't thought of it like that, because I know I didn't kill him. But anyone could say the same. I see that. And what can I say? I went to ask him about Dad's breakfast and saw a shape under the tarpaulin. When I moved it, there he was.'

With everyone else accounted for and witnessed at all times by someone else, Mara looked from Tarn to Swindon, Anna, Celine, George and Henry. One of them could be the killer.

Twenty-Eight

Edie looked between Henry, George, Anna, Mara, Celine, Tarn and Swindon. It *seemed* like one of them was the killer, or was something else going on? Whoever was behind the riddles had a fascinating brain. Dangerous, but fascinating. And George, one of the suspects himself, had a good point about the skills, training and experience required to pull off their plan. Of all the people in this room, who had the Christmas riddle killer's heart, brain and ability to harm? The fact that she couldn't imagine it of any of them suggested that whoever it turned out to be was a very good actor, too.

In the next booth, Ivan screamed. He'd raised his head and was staring into the air above him, face curdled with fear. 'You can't take Mara. She isn't a suspect,' he rasped, coming to slightly. 'She's my baby. My Pudding.'

'Shush, darling,' Felicity said, going over to him from across the room for the first time in an hour. She looked at the others. 'He's delirious, the fever isn't coming down.'

'Why don't you have a face?' Ivan said to the ceiling. 'Take off your mask, or is there nothing behind?'

'I think he's seeing Gwiazdor. He thinks he's come for him, or for Mara,' Edie said. Standing up, she went round to Ivan's booth. 'Tell Gwiazdor what he needs to hear, Ivan. Blow the whistle. Maybe then he will leave you both alone.'

'But I tried to tell them,' Ivan cried to the sky. 'I went to HR about the environmental pollution in our sister company. They were pumping toxic waste into the rivers and the sea. I said I'd tell the press, tell everyone if they didn't stop.'

'That was a brave thing to do. And then what happened?' Edie said, softly pressing for a confession.

'They offered me a settlement,' Ivan said, tears falling. 'More money than I had ever imagined, and I knew we could retire, and I could be what I wanted, maybe even be a better man this time. Not let anyone down.'

'You never let anyone down,' Mara said.

Edie closed her eyes in pained empathy. If she was right, Mara would soon know that Ivan had let many people down, especially Mara herself, and her mother.

'I took the money, Pudding. That's what this place is built on. Look,' Ivan implored the Gwiazdor only he could see. 'I turned bad to good! Isn't that what you want? And I did it all to protect my baby, as I always have.'

'Mara told you she didn't want you calling her that,' Felicity said, her face red.

'But she *is* my baby,' Ivan said. 'You can't say otherwise. You can't reel me in with your riddles.'

As he spoke those words, theories and memories skittled and collided in Edie's head. It all came back to the ghost story. That's how she'd prove it.

Mara kissed her dad's cheek and, despite the circumstances, looked the happiest that Edie had yet seen her, until he sank back onto the banquette, his eyes closing. Gwiazdor had left the building.

'Mara,' Edie said, gesturing for the two of them to talk away from the others. 'I know this is an odd request, but could we please hear "Swim, Little Fish, Swim" again? And, if possible, I'd love a copy to read along at the same time.'

'Of course,' Mara said with a half-smile, as if afraid to commit to full beam. 'I'll print another copy.'

'Did you talk to anyone else apart from your parents about the story?'

'Tarn and I planned the programme of events together. In fact, she suggested that I perform something, although I don't think the idea for a ghost story came from her. She thought I should sing carols, which I probably should have done instead.' Her laugh was sad, rueful. 'Maybe then no one would be dead.'

'You don't need a ghost story for someone to die,' Edie replied. 'Though something needs to die for it to be a ghost story.'

Mara forced a laugh. 'I suppose so. Where would you like me to read? Sean has asked that we keep the library out of bounds until forensics has cleared it, whenever they get here.'

'Either here or in the lounge.' Edie glanced back at Ivan, who was slumped on the banquette, sleeping. 'We should stay here. Your dad shouldn't be moved if we can help it.'

While Mara went off to print another copy of the ghost story, Edie read through the riddles over and over, committing them to memory. The better she knew them, the easier she could make connections. Finally, Mara was back, and Edie was ready.

'If you could make yourselves comfortable,' Edie said in her strident public-speaking voice. 'We are lucky to have a repeat performance of last night's ghost story narrated by Mara Morecombe-Clark.'

Henry shook his head. 'I don't think that's a good idea. I'm not superstitious, but it feels like inviting spirits in, when we are already surrounded by the dead.'

'What better way to venerate those we've lost,' Felicity said, placing her hand on top of her husband's.

Candles gave any location a hazy, sleazy, in-between-worlds-y feel, but they couldn't make the Gold Bar feel like the right place for a ghost story, no matter how many votives Anna and Celine lit. The only chains spectres would be rattling here would be Annoushka and Tomfoolery. Still, this time the candles were for the dead. Maybe lighting candles during ghost stories was always for the dead.

Mara could feel the difference, too. It was clear from how she sat on her hands to stop them shaking; from the metronome swing of her legs on the bar stool; from how she kept scrolling and unrolling the story on the gold-leafed counter; but mainly from how she kept looking at her dad. He was lying in the booth at the back, his head on her mum's lap, the table moved so, if he opened his eyes, he would have an unobstructed view of his daughter. His skin was now the colour of old snow.

Edie looked away from Mara and down to her doodle

pad. In the last few minutes, she'd been drawing crossword squares without realising, her mind boxing and unboxing thoughts and theories.

Henry was in the next booth along with George. Every now and again he'd mumble, out of nowhere, 'But she was with me yesterday. How can she not be here? She has to open her present.'

George patted Henry's back. He was always so *nice*, so generous with his time and kindness. Was anyone really that good? Even his darkest secret was one that was completely human, vulnerable and even a little likeable. It would be an excellent move from an arch-manipulator, and whoever had planned all this had manipulated Mara and others to perfection. What *really* lay beneath the Provost chain that hung over George's heart?

Tarn came in and, after handing out breakfasts that no one could face eating, joined Anna, Celine, Izzie and Kimberley in their corner booth.

'Are you sitting comfortably?' Mara asked.

Dad, slow as a sloth, hovered a thumbs-up sign an inch above the banquette then let it fall.

Tears in her eyes, Mara picked up the ghost story. 'Well, isn't this a strange way to spend Christmas Day?'

George laughed encouragingly from his booth.

'Yesterday,' she continued, 'I augmented the tale, saying someone had told me about it in the pub. The scarier thing is that I don't know where "Swim, Little Fish, Swim" has come from, who sent it to me or what it means. Something, though, is lying under its surface, shouting at us from the deep. We need to catch its meaning and understand what the killer wants, before someone else dies.'

'How?' Henry's voice was small.

'By listening out for clues to the worst thing you've done. To the one you've hurt the most,' Mara replied. Her cheekbones seemed to widen as she spoke, her eyes becoming wiser. Yet this was her improvising. In character, yes, but the words were hers. 'Tie yourself to the thing that haunts you, even if you don't yet know it, and throw yourself on the sea's mercy.'

In the hush that swelled around them, Mara read the ghost story again. Edie closed her eyes, following the words like rosary beads, waiting for the ones that would toll. Echoes and coils of resonances and whispers surfaced then submerged, but there was nothing that Edie could catch.

And then they landed in her lap, in the air and on the page.

'*Symbols of a birch tree, a cotton reel, a catfish with long whiskers, a door, a horse and a cradle.*'

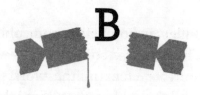

Twenty-Nine

Edie applauded, and with good reason. Mara's narration had had a darkness that was missing the first time round, giving the tale the spectral gleam of a moonless sea. Her eyes now carried more knowledge, as if she'd seen things she hadn't known about herself before. The definition of epiphany.

The rest of the audience felt it, too. George was clapping, Ivan slowly nodding. Anna and Celine were finger-cymballing in time.

Riga was staring down at her rosary. Some of the beads looked too shiny, as if tear coated.

'What is it?' Edie whispered. 'What have you realised?'

'Nothing concrete,' Riga said. Her voice carried the cracks of time that separated her from whatever she was keeping from Edie.

'It's the rosary, right?' Edie continued. She knew she should back off, let Riga come to her, just as Edie would do with all regal cats, but her heart was beating hard, the insides of her chest scratchy with fear. What if Riga was the next victim?

'I told her she'd be fabulous,' Felicity said to the whole room and no one in particular. 'She takes after me.'

Edie realised she was hoping that, should the final two riddles *have* to find their victims, Felicity would be one of them. Of all of those remaining, surely, she'd done the worst thing? No killer would target Riga when they could take Felicity from the world.

No. Now she was thinking too much like the murderer. Human life either had value or it didn't, and everyone was of equal value. In theory. Until you met them.

'If you have even the slightest idea of what you're supposed to confess to, and to whom, then just say it to everyone. If it's not what the killer's looking for, it doesn't matter, at least you tried,' Edie announced into the ensuing silence, Mara still hunched on her stool before them.

'I can't,' Riga said. 'There may be consequences for the person I "wronged".'

Anger swirled and coiled in Edie's chest. 'But there will be consequences for you, and therefore for me, if you don't. Have you seen the latest dead dolls in the dolls' house?' Her words were coming out as snaps. Each word a fired cap.

'You know I haven't. I've barely moved today.' Riga wasn't even giving minimal eye contact now. Her hands were folded in her lap. Nicholas was at her feet, blinking up in pug confusion at the change in atmosphere.

Edie just wanted to say, 'Whatever you want, I don't mind. I just want to help. Be there for you. Share it all,' but the words corroded and instead she said, 'I checked the dolls' house earlier. Four dead doll bodies are stacked in its cold room, mirroring the real one. And mini-Ivan is lying in state in the miniaturised Gold Bar, and the rest of us are there too, bowing round his banquette. Even Nicholas. It's like the strangest Nativity scene you've ever seen.'

Sean strode up to stand next to Mara. 'Now that we've all had another chance to listen to the story,' he announced, 'has anyone recognised clues in the riddles, cracker presents and ghost story that have led you to realise your "worst" actions, or at least the misdemeanours that the killer accuses you of?'

Anna looked as if she was about to say something, then shook her head.

'Are you sure, Anna?' Sean said. 'Because I reckon it's better to confess to something and find it's not what you've been accused of, than keep something in and potentially leave here in a coffin.'

'It's more likely that they'll be taken out in body bags,' Henry said. 'I've been thinking of Lucy. She hated anything that rustled.'

Edie felt an irreverent giggle surge at the thought and tried to catch Riga's eye. Usually, they'd share a glance at something like that and talk about it later. Riga, though, was fixed on her beads, mouthing a silent prayer.

Even Anna, in the booth on the other side of Riga, wasn't showing a hint of a grin.

George put up his hand.

'Yes, George,' Sean said, trying for a smile. 'I like that you put up your hand, but you don't have to.'

George hesitated before speaking. 'Something in the story chimed for me. When I was first looking after Mum, I was in the beginning stages of a relationship, and I ghosted them. I kept my heart in a jar, like the story said.

She was amazing, but I didn't feel worthy of her. The feelings I had were like a tidal wave, crashing around me. So, when she went away for a month, I ghosted her. I haven't loved anyone new since.'

'I think it's unlikely that this is one of the dark secrets the killer has asked for,' Sean said, a kind, honeyed-whisky warmth to his voice. 'But thank you anyway. Though it would be useful to know your activities last night and this morning, just so I can plot who was where when.'

'Before I went to bed, I went up onto the roof terrace, to look at the sky. I'm an amateur astronomer and there is so little light here – the sky was so dark it looked like it recessed into caves. Like starlit chasms.'

Mara was staring at him as if *he* was starlit.

'Did you see anyone, or did anyone see you?' Sean asked.

'At one point the floodlights came on in the courtyard, showing up Izzie and Ryan arguing – that was presumably about him being her dad, sorry Izzie, and then I saw Ivan stumbling down the lawn.'

'By himself?' Sean asked. Felicity had said that she and Ivan went back to their cottage together.

'Yes, he was swaying and almost fell down a snowbank into the trees.' George lifted his hand in apologetic acknowledgement. 'Sorry, Ivan. For a moment I thought you were going to dive headlong into a silver bir—' He stopped mid-sentence, a look of surprise crossing his face. 'I just remembered something else that bubbled up during the story.'

'About you?' Sean asked.

'No, about Robert. It'll be no surprise to anyone who

was on the boat or saw me around him that I wasn't his greatest fan. If I like you, you'll know it. And he knew I didn't like him when he tried to bribe me and several other council members to give the go ahead to his development. Now, the parent company behind his corporation was called Birch, a word that came up in the Krampus riddle he was holding when he died: "I will punish you with birch." It's also mentioned several times in the story – it's one of the symbols on the box of secrets.'

'I bet the wood used on his screwdriver was made from birch,' Edie said.

'That's all I've got, really,' George said, chuckling his awkward chuckle that had nothing to do with mirth. 'I don't know his *specific* crimes, other than trying to bribe me. He's probably been more successfully corrupt elsewhere, but I also heard there were accusations against him that were hushed up. Although, that's hearsay, of course.'

'Of course,' Sean repeated. 'So, you don't know of anything specific that would cause someone to kill Mr Cole-Mortelli?'

'No, and if I did, I'd tell the police. Not some Christmas cracker vigilante with a riddle fetish. Only a truly bad Santa would do those things.'

'No arguments from me,' Sean replied. 'Has anyone else made any connections to themselves or to someone they know here who has died?'

Henry raised his arm. 'I think . . . the ghost story might be based on Lucy.' He took a deep breath. 'She told me once that she knocked over a homeless man when she was at university. She'd been drinking before driving back to her halls, in the middle of the night in the Kent countryside, and she ran into him and over his leg. She thought about calling an ambulance, but she was studying Law. She knew she'd be breathalysed and, instead of helping, she left him barely breathing at the side of the road. She never knew if he survived or died right there.'

'So, you think Bella's crime involving an animal in the story was actually Lucy's hitting a man in real life?' Sean asked.

'It didn't haunt her, though. At least, I don't think so. She was kind of laughing when she told me. She was explaining why I shouldn't trust anyone, even her. Which was true: she constantly accused me of cheating, but she was the one having affairs while she was away in China on business trips. I knew it all, and I loved her in spite of it. Or because of it.'

'Of course, Lucy's not here to give her reply,' Edie said. 'You could be finding a reason for someone else to kill her when you were the one most likely to, with clear means, opportunity and motive, by the sounds of it.'

'Let's be honest,' Celine interjected. 'It wasn't Lucy who kept leering at me and Anna, or putting her hand on my knee.'

'You don't understand,' Henry said, starting to sweat. 'That was part of our game. Making her jealous was the only way I could get her attention. If she thought I wanted someone else, it made her want to—'

'Reclaim her property?' Anna suggested. When Henry

nodded, tears falling, she said, 'I've known men and women like that. It's exhausting. And never worth it.'

Henry shrugged. 'It was for me. I loved Lucy. I didn't kill her. I was a plant that only grew in her shade. She has been writing most of my columns for years.'

'If we could move on to your alleged argument with Ryan Dreith,' Sean said, trying to steer him back on course. 'You were observed exchanging heated words by George.'

'Ryan wanted me to give him a glowing quote there and then,' Henry said. 'He didn't intend to stay here long – he said he had family issues he wanted to attend to, so he was going to leave. He wanted a reference to take to his next employer.'

'I assume you refused?' Sean said.

'I said I didn't feel comfortable based on one meal at what was supposed to be a two-day event, but that my Boxing Day report would have some pull quotes,' Henry said. 'Ryan became aggressive, blaming me for his career blips because I wrote a scathing review of his first restaurant.' He paused. 'That was one I actually did write. I've forgotten how to since then, I think. Forgotten how to think at all, maybe.'

Sean wrote the details down in his notebook, then asked, 'Anyone else?' He looked again to Anna, whose bob was hiding her face. She didn't look up.

'I'm Door-Slammer!' Felicity said, standing up abruptly and waving as if she'd won at bingo. 'It's all there. I'm one of seven siblings, which isn't thirteen, but it's too many. I can only think what my mother must have thought when she found out she was having a seventh: calamitous, I'm sure. I also "arrived", as in I was born, on eighteenth December.'

'And she's been known to slam doors,' Mara said. The adrenaline of her performance must have been keeping her fight alive. Long might it last. She might need it to survive.

'You sharing a birthday with Door-Slammer is interesting,' Sean said, 'but he has already been claimed, as it were. Ryan was holding the riddle.'

'Oh,' Felicity said, smiling wider, a little manically. 'That's good, then!' She was nodding, over and over again, and reaching for Mara's hand. Mara pulled away.

'Let's take a break so we can sort out what's happening for lunch,' Sean said, defusing the awkward moment. 'As my mum will tell you, investigating is hungry work, and we're all doing it. Well, one of us is only pretending to.'

Everyone looked at each other, sizing their neighbours up as the killer. Edie hoped at least one of them thought *she* was the murderer. Elder ladies tended to get overlooked in these areas, and she was all for equity.

Sean beamed at the group, making them even more unnerved. 'Don't go far – no one is to go to their rooms until bedtime, and keep to the ground-floor public areas, specifically the lobby, lounge, toilets and bar. Only staff in the restaurant and kitchen, and *no one* in the library, cold room, alley or on the roof terrace.'

With the group's attention now diffused, Edie turned back to Riga. 'How are you feeling?' She stroked Riga's hair and kissed her forehead, the ache to have tender contact again appeased for now.

'Like I need to talk,' Riga replied, holding the rosary beads between both palms and raising them to her nose.

'I'm right here,' Edie said. 'Where would you like to start?'

'With all their tales, I suppose. I thought they were aweful, with an "e", and inspiring in the way they revealed what was hidden, like a poppy opening in time lapse,' Riga said, her usual bite tempered by something else. 'They were so full of loneliness, fear and desperation. These sad vignettes. Like dolls' house tableaux.'

'I can see that,' Edie said carefully. 'Although most of them think that the story is about them in particular. Instead of trying to search for symbols and clues, they're using the ghost story like a fortune fish – reading too much into something that has nothing to do with them. I want to know *your* ghost story. Your ghosts.'

Riga smiled slightly. 'I don't mean to keep them from you. I keep them from myself.'

'We all do,' Edie said, and didn't understand when Riga turned her head away.

'What do you think about all the adoption talk?' Riga asked, her voice unusually monotone.

'Psychologically, I'd say the killer is someone who has been adopted and is taking out whatever mother wounds and abandonment issues they have on—' Edie stopped.

Riga was crying, holding the beads to her chest. 'You don't understand. I can't talk to you.'

'Please,' Edie said, confusion scattering her thoughts as she tried to string the two of them back together. 'I can try. I don't know what we're talking around.'

'No. You don't. And for someone so perceptive, how do we always manage to spiral back to here, where you see nothing.'

'Riga, please, I—'

Riga didn't look at her. 'If you don't mind, I'd like to be by myself for a while.'

The formality hurt almost as much as the abrupt cutting of all contact – eye, skin, heart – their connection severed.

Thirty

Mum was still shaking when Mara sat down next to her. Dad was slumped in the corner but no longer dribbling. To see both of them so reduced made Mara feel like a dolls'-house doll forced to live a bigger life. Mum and Dad had always been there, telling her what to do. And now they were both looking to her.

Where was Tarn?

'This isn't how it should be,' Mum was saying, swinging her head back and forth.

'Mum, what's wrong? The way you're talking, and about that riddle, and your laughter before that . . . It feels like you're . . .' Mara's words dropped away as she realised she had no idea how to say what was happening to her mother. What was it? Metamorphosis? Breakdown? Both?

'The thing you need to understand, Mara,' Mum said, 'is that we always meant what's best for you. Or at least I did, anyway.' She laughed again, high pitched this time.

George looked around from his booth and mouthed, 'Are you okay?'

Mara nodded, but wanted to say, 'No, George. Come and save me.' Although that wouldn't change anything.

'Leave it, Felicity,' Dad said, his voice barely more than a whisper but his tone as cool as the cold room.

'I can't,' Mum said. 'It says we must tell her.'

'What does?' Ivan asked.

'The cracker, otherwise there'll be consequences,' Mum said, grabbing hold of Mara's hands and squeezing them, holding her gaze in such tight eye contact that it felt like her eyeballs were being squeezed, too.

'And who are you going to tell? Me?' Mara asked.

Mum nodded. 'It's time.'

'It. Will. Never. Be. Time.' Ivan's features had hardened, his warm eyes swapped out for ice.

'You can cope with it, Ivan. You can compartmentalise. I can't. If I could, I'd've been a better mother, but it's always there, whispering, like in the story. "Wishwish-wish", as I wish for something different, for you not to have—'

'NO!' Ivan shouted, lurching forward and slamming a palm on the table. His body rocked with the effort. 'I won't allow it.'

'I should have said "no" back then,' Mum said. 'I shouldn't have allowed *any* of it.'

Mara looked from Mum to Dad but couldn't see her mother and father. They were changed. Gone. Replaced by replicas gone wrong.

'I have to say something,' Mum was pleading with Dad, grasping at his hands. 'It's scratching away, on the underside of my skin. I have to get it out of me.'

Then Mara understood. Felicity hadn't changed in her

being; she'd only changed state. She was the same selfish Felicity, shaken to the point that she'd switched from solid to gas. But everything was still all about *her*.

And it was time Mara was solid, not bouncing around a space someone else had contained. 'When you're ready to tell me, Mum, I'll listen. Or I'll work it out myself. But right now, I need to look after the people in my hotel. You two can look after each other.'

Sliding out from the booth, Mara walked towards the kitchen, thinking *Be solid, not gas. Place roots in the earth.*

Tarn was with Kimberley, looking down at Ryan's scribbled messes of menus, laid out on the counter. Looking round to see Mara enter, Tarn must have clocked the distress on her face, as she held out her arms. 'Come here, love. You can help us decipher Ryan's plans for Christmas lunch.'

Mara sidled up to the older woman and leaned into her. In front of them was a torn page of A4 with a recipe for sprout crostini and turkey soufflé. On the side were dozens of ramekins containing tiny, diced vegetables and micro herbs.

'We've got a load more veg, haven't we?' Mara asked, trying to push her shakiness down inside.

Kimberley nodded.

'And a whole salmon, plus two turkeys that we were going to have when the guests left?'

'Yup,' Tarn said.

'Then,' Mara stated, 'assuming anyone here trusts us not to poison them, we're going to serve up a delicious traditional Scottish Christmas dinner, with all the trimmings. It won't be till tonight, now, so we'd better get something hearty and filling for lunch, such as—'

'I bunged some jackets in earlier,' Kimberley said, 'and I've made two pizzas and bits and bobs. When Izzie's not stuck behind the bar, I'll get her to help me cobble together the kind of Christmas buffet I had at my Nan's in Kilmarnock.'

Mara's words of gratitude were interrupted by Edie's arrival, her usually sharp eyes that scrutinised people as if 3D-scanning their souls fixed on the ground. 'Can I help with anything?' Edie asked quietly.

'You can peel the thousands of tatties we're prepping for tonight,' Tarn said, taking charge and heaving a bag of potatoes onto the counter.

'So, we're not having the Dreith Dreary Festive Dinner, then?' Edie asked. 'Because I was worried about the mackerel macarons.'

Kimberley was busy writing out a new menu on the board:

Roasted side of salmon
Roast turkey
Nut roast
All the tatties
All the fucking trimmings

Mara had come in here in the middle of a family fight that would rival an *Eastenders* Christmas, and was sharing her hotel with a serial killer, but somehow, they were

238

pulling together and making the best of it. Being solid, together.

'What are we doing for pudding?' Edie asked.

'We?' Mara laughed.

'I make a mean Dorset Apple Cake,' Edie said, 'but we could call it Holly Island Cake and stuff a piece of holly on the top?'

'Don't worry, I've got pudding covered,' Kimberley said.

'By which you mean you've got custard or cream?' Edie replied.

'Even better.' Kimberley rushed out into the storeroom and came back rolling a huge, old-fashioned dessert trolley. The wheels squeaked. 'I got this on Ebay for hardly anything, then it cost me a hundred to get it delivered. Ryan wouldn't let me do anything with it, but today I'm going to fill it up. He'd said I couldn't bake for his dinner, but I secretly made a trifle, a Black Forest gateau and three Christmas puddings in case his tiny soufflés didn't rise.'

All four women laughed, then looked at the cold room door where Ryan and the other bodies were kept.

'What was the deal with you and Ryan?' Tarn asked Kimberley quietly as if the dead could hear. 'It was like the whole kitchen was a cold room with you two in it.'

'I worked for him in his first London restaurant,' Kimberley said, 'and reported him to HR for exposing himself during service. *He* was moved to a different restaurant in the fancy hotel chain, and *I* was fired. When he discovered I was working here, he tried to get me sacked again, but Mara refused.'

239

'My fear of him wasn't as great as my fear of losing you on our team,' Mara replied.

'You're doing better on that,' Tarn said with a proud smile. 'I've seen you standing up to your mum more.'

'What *is* going on with your mum?' Edie asked. 'I know your dad is in a terrible state, and I understand her falling apart, but it just feels like there's something else going on. And I won't say I don't want to pry, because I fucking love prying, and Sean and I do need to know what's going on.'

'I wish I knew,' Mara said. 'It looks like the environmental damage cover-up wasn't their darkest secret, maybe just a light-grey one.'

'Ah,' Edie said. 'I wondered as much. They should tell Sean, as soon as possible.'

'I think it's something to do with my adoption,' Mara said hesitantly. 'I've always thought it weird that they—'

An anguished cry seared through from the bar. *Dad.* Mara ran, her hand over her mouth to catch the sobs she was sure would drop when she got there.

Dad, though, was sitting up, pointing towards the corner booth. It took Mara a moment to understand what was happening. Riga and Anna were head-to-head, leaning against each other like dolls waiting for animation. Their eyes were closed, their lips blue. Fortune fish danced on their palms.

Celine was backing away. 'I only went to the loo for a few minutes. When I came back, they were like this.'

Mum stood and moved towards the booth, as if she would have any idea what to do. 'Tarn!' she shrieked. 'Get in here *now*.'

Mara knew she'd feel the sting of that later, but for now she was solid and anaesthetised by adrenaline. With Celine's help, she moved Anna onto the floor in the recovery position, and laid Riga in the same on the banquette. Riga's eyelids flickered, her lower lip straining as if she was trying to speak. Her thin fingers shook around the slip of paper in her grip.

Celine was checking for Anna's carotid pulse, awkwardly slipping her fingers beneath the turtleneck. She shook her head, eyes panic-wide. 'There's nothing.'

Mara bent down and gently pressed the pads of her fingers against Anna's wrist. Not even the faintest of flutters. She placed her hand above Anna's mouth, hoping that her first aid training was letting her down and she'd feel a faint exhale. Again, nil.

Sean was standing over them. 'Out of the way,' he said, and Mara was glad to step back and watch him carry out the same checks. But he, too, shook his head. 'I'm afraid Anna is dead.'

'Oh, God, no.' Edie was rushing over, her jaw unhinged. She slid into the booth next to Riga and took her hand. A slip of paper fell out, landing on Edie's other palm:

A mother who has scoffed at kids,
A crone who jettisoned bad kin
Into a cooking pot of herbs,
Trolling with denying words.
Instead of loving your huge cat,
Embrace instead your reject brat.
WHO AM I?

'If you're Grýla,' Edie said, clearly fighting to control her voice, 'then I think you've been hiding a secret from me for a very long time.'

A tear slipped from Riga's eye.

Sean looked down at poor Anna. He gently removed the riddle from her hand. 'La Befana,' he said. 'The spooky witch of Christmas time.' His voice was shaking. He kept glancing back at Riga, wincing as she fought for breath. He closed his eyes and breathed out slowly, as if gathering himself back into a police detective. 'We can't leave Anna here in the public area for any length of time. She's already been moved anyway, so we'll have to put her in the cold room.'

'But she'd hate that,' Celine said, huge tears streaking down her cheeks.

Sean, Tarn, Swindon and George carefully lifted Anna, supporting her head, hips and legs as if carrying her in a coffin. Mara went ahead, leading them through the restaurant and into the kitchen, using the keys Sean had handed her to open the cold room door. She tried not to look at the bodies, but it was impossible not to. There was just enough space for Anna to lie next to Ryan.

'Put this down for her,' Celine said, wiping her running nose with her sleeve and handing Mara one of the hotel blankets.

Anna was laid gently on the tartan, a cushion placed under her head. Her cheekbones seemed even sharper, as though death was already carving into her. Looking down at her friend, Mara remembered lying next to Anna in the Swiss spa, drinking Bellinis and dreaming of their new ventures. Sean had tried to get Anna to open up several times, and she'd seemed nearly ready, but she hadn't been able to disclose her darkest secret. Now the darkness, and her dreams, were permanent.

Thirty-One

The killer had to keep their head down. *Stay calm. Lie low.* They'd got away with their act so far, but they mustn't draw attention to themselves, not now the job was very nearly done. The naughty targets had been dispatched; Ivan had admitted one of his bad deeds and thus had been given a little reprieve, but unless he fully confessed, he, too, would die. He deserved it. Soon everyone would know why.

It hurt that Riga hadn't spoken up, although she had clearly been torn. The killer understood the conflict, but there were several big reveals to happen yet, they hoped. If Edie could keep her detective head when her heart was breaking.

Right now, she was murmuring 'Stay with me, stay with me', over and over. 'You've got to live,' she said. 'You're my Riga. I can't wait till I'm eighty and then find love, just for it to die. You are not allowed to die, Riga Novack.'

If anyone were to stand in front of the Grim Reaper and shake his own scythe at him to scare him off, it would be Edie. He wouldn't come for her for a long time yet.

Riga, though, was another issue.

The killer really didn't want Riga to die. It felt wrong

to take the life of a woman with so little time and so much to do. But Riga needed to do the work. Everyone did. Look beneath the surface.

'She's got a steady pulse,' Sean was saying to Edie. 'And her blood pressure is low but not worrying. I just don't know if we can keep her stable without knowing what she's been given.'

'How did it happen?' Edie asked. How could she know that the poisoner, the smotherer, the pusher, the stabber was right there with them? But she must suspect who the killer was. They'd seen a question in her eyes several times as she'd gazed at them, and then away. Surveying. Taking it all in. The killer had designed everything to suit Edie – catered the riddles to her tastes and skills, written the story with her magpie mind in mind.

'Stay with me, Riga,' Edie said.

Stay with me, Riga, the killer whispered in their head.

Thirty-Two

Edie held Riga, the love of her life, in her arms. Glass-bauble frail, she felt Riga could smash at any moment. She kept trying to speak, but no sound came out. Edie said it for them both. *Stay with me. Don't go.*

Celine sat at a nearby table alone, staring towards the kitchen as if Anna would walk back out at any minute. George had tried to show support, but had retreated to the next table when Celine, like Riga, had said she wanted to be alone.

In his booth, Ivan was sitting up straight, his colour had returned slightly, and he had the strength to pick up and sip a cup of tea. Felicity was at her own table, re-doing her make-up. The Felicity that Edie had met yesterday was slowly coming back into filtered focus.

'Do you think you were given an antidote at some point after you confessed?' Edie asked Ivan. 'Did you feel a needle in your skin, or were you given something different to drink?' She eyed Izzie, who had been bringing everyone drinks and snacks from the bar.

'I don't know,' he replied. 'Only that I felt a real improvement not long after talking about the pay-off. Both physically and wherever the conscience lives.'

'I'm surprised you can feel it,' Edie said acidly, 'it shows such little sign of life.'

'What do you mean?'

'Nothing,' Edie replied. 'I'm glad you're showing signs of recovery. You worried us all there.'

If Riga confessed in front of everyone, would the same thing happen? And how could she catch the poisoner administering the antidote?

Of course, if Edie had been a better listener, and had understood what Riga was implying, Riga might well have confessed her darkest secret and would be lightly teasing Edie right now.

Edie usually tried not to think of a time when Riga would no longer be here, but it came crashing in now. No more hearing her breathe. No more laughter. Silent nights.

She pushed the thought away again. At least for now there was some movement – Riga was reaching for her rosary. Edie handed it to her and watched as Riga slowly moved between each station.

If she was strong enough to do that, then—

Edie grabbed her bag and plucked out her crossword notebook, placing her pen in Riga's hand.

'Write it down,' Edie said. 'As much as you can. Everything I didn't understand and that you want to express. It's the darkest secret and has such weight, but I want to carry it with you.'

Riga wrote agonisingly slowly, the words falling with as much focus as prayers on the beads:

I was pregnant at fifteen. Too young. Long time ago. You gave up kids for adoption then. No other options for me. My child. I gave them this rosary. It haunts me. Shames me. To blame. I think my descendant is here, and they may be a killer. Still, I want to hold them.

Edie read Riga's note out loud, watching for reactions from the others. Celine was nodding, Swindon sat open-mouthed, George had his hand over his heart, Henry seemed shocked, Tarn was looking at Mara, Izzie didn't even look up from her phone.

'So,' Edie said, loudly, when she had finished, 'if the killer is in earshot, and I bet you are, you've just heard Riga embracing the "brat" that she was made to give up, so give her the fucking antidote.' She gazed around. 'It's weird looking at you and wondering who's related to my love. If you're a great-grandchild, then Celine? Izzie? Kimberley? If a grandchild, then Tarn, George or Mara, maybe even Henry? And if a child, then Swindon, Ivan or Felicity?'

Nobody moved, nobody said a word, nobody delivered an antidote.

Riga's breath was now ragged, delivered in jagged bursts.

'What more do I have to do?' Edie asked the room, stroking Riga's cheek, desperation cracking through her. 'Write a letter to one of the festive gift-bringers? "Dear Santa, there are only two things on my Christmas list: save my Riga and let me see my grandkids this Christmas?" That's it. Now I've just got to hope I'm on your nice list.'

Because the killer of course had their own naughty and nice list. They were the ultimate arbiter, and the assassin.

Through the fog of grief and fear, something snagged in Edie's brain – something said on the boat that made sense of everything and yet was, must be, impossible. But if she got this right, she could flush out the killer. And then force them to give Riga the antidote.

Thirty-Three

Mara needed space. She'd slipped away from the others, and was in the restaurant, polishing cutlery, when Edie rushed in. 'Is Riga okay?' Mara asked at once.

'She's fading,' Edie replied, her voice cracking with emotion. 'I need your help to save her.'

'Anything,' Mara replied. 'What can I do?'

'Gather everyone in the lounge, around the fire.'

'Everyone?' Mara asked. 'Because Kimberley and Izzie are preparing lunch and Swindon is out clearing snow from the pathways.'

'No one can be left out, as any of them could be the murderer.'

'Oh, God,' Mara said, covering her mouth in excitement. 'You're going full Agatha Christie.'

'I'm going full Agatha, baby,' Edie replied. 'Underestimate Christie or me and regret it. I'm going to reveal the killer in front of everyone, then force him or her to give Riga the antidote.'

'Sounds simple,' Mara replied with uncharacteristic sarcasm.

Edie continued as though she hadn't heard her. 'I need you to arrange the armchairs around a central point, where I will stand, and leave enough room for me to make a grand entrance down the staircase and into the middle of the group. Let's say a full wingspan.' She held out her arms in her Westwood cape.

'When do you want them in position?'

Edie checked her watch. 'Half an hour, during which time I must find concrete evidence before I confront the murderer. Riga's life depends on getting this right. While I'm busy, would you look after her for me?' Edie's tear-magnified eyes pleaded with Mara. When Mara nodded, Edie grasped her hand briefly, then strode to the reception desk.

Opening the front of the dolls' house, Edie nodded, took a picture, then closed it again. On her way back to the bar, Edie peered through the library door windows and nodded again. 'Just as I thought,' she said.

Mara wondered what it would be like to spend a day with the brain of Edie O'Sullivan. Probably absolutely exhausting.

Heading to the lounge, Mara set to work, creating a wide circle of chairs around the fireplace, leaving enough room for Edie to sweep in and confound them with her conclusions. Then she checked in with Riga, who was asleep in the corner of her booth. Her skin was always pale, but now it had taken on the plastic sheen of on-coming death.

Nicholas lay next to her, front paws crossed, staring at his owner as if he too was worried she'd fade away. Maybe dogs weren't so scary. He sneezed once, shaking his head.

'Bless you,' Mara said.

When twenty-five tense minutes had passed, Mara corralled the staff and guests through into the lounge. The fire rose up to greet them, giving their skin a burnished glow.

Swindon helped Riga into her wheelchair and gently rolled her over. 'Nicholas likes to get close to the fire,' she told him weakly. 'He'd climb in there if I let him.'

'Good job he's got you, then,' Swindon twinkled.

'Is this compulsory?' Henry asked. The plum-coloured sags under his eyes seemed darker than this morning, as if his grief was grading his complexion.

'I can't force you to attend,' Mara said, 'but Edie said it's essential that everyone turns up. Kimberley and Izzie have put lunch on hold until after.'

'I'm not hungry anyway,' Celine said. She was wearing a blanket around her like a shawl, as if it would bring her closer to the dead friend who lay on a matching one in the cold room.

As the clock struck half past, the crystals of the chandelier shimmered and quaked together. The wind whispered in the chimney.

'Well, isn't this a lovely view!' Edie said from the first-floor landing, peering at them over the curved wall, then slowly walking down the coiling staircase.

'What's she up to?' Henry said.

'I don't care,' Celine said, 'but if we're all together, I feel safer.'

'I don't,' Kimberley replied. 'Because it means we could be in here with the killer.'

When she was halfway down the stairs, Edie stopped.

'I bet you're wondering why I brought you here,' she called out. Then she barked a laugh that Nicholas echoed. 'I've always wanted to say that.'

'Are you going to tell us, then?' Izzie asked. 'Only I've got coleslaw to make.'

'There are few things more important than coleslaw, Izzie,' Edie replied. 'But murder is one of them. You are all here to bear witness to the reveal of the Christmas Cracker Killer, as I'm sure the tabloids will delight in calling them.'

'You know who it is?' Ivan said.

'Of course she does,' Celine said. 'Edie is the queen of the crime scene!' In her French accent it sounded extra chic.

'Thank you very much, Celine, but I'm a republican, with a small "r",' Edie replied as she reached the bottom of the stairs and walked into the centre of the circle. She glanced at Riga, frail in her chair. 'No need for fancy titles, although I *will* take the money.'

'Can we get on?' Swindon leant against the wall by the front doors. 'I want to clear the paths before it gets dark. I don't want anyone tripping on late-night walks. It's going to be a beautiful evening.'

'I take your point, Swindon,' Edie said. 'Time and tide wait for fuck all, of course. And I took far longer than I'd like to work out who was behind this intricate plan and, even now, I still need some of the jigsaw pieces to be handed to me. So, who better to ask than the murderer?' She swivelled round and pointed at Celine.

Mara gasped, her heart racing. It couldn't be Celine. Celine was her friend, and one of the sweetest people she'd ever met.

254

'Me?' Celine said. 'But I didn't—'

'Kill anyone?' Edie interrupted. 'But then you *would* say that. As the person who not only persuaded Mara to take on a chef that you wished to kill, but were also involved in so many of the decisions made in planning this event.'

'Because she's my friend and has more connections than anyone else,' Mara replied, indignantly. She hadn't arranged all this for Celine to be wrongly accused.

'A very convenient position to be in,' Edie said. 'As is being a travel influencer. Frequent flights, speaking several languages and a ready-made excuse to film would give you the perfect cover to be an assassin. And that's what we are dealing with, as George rightly suggested earlier. This assassin targeted six people and brought them together.'

Celine raised her hands in disbelief. 'You think I could be an assassin?'

'I have no doubt,' Edie said, 'that you *could* be. You are a very clever, resourceful woman, with a likeable nature. But no, I don't think you are our killer. If anything, I believe you are in the killer's good books – on the nice list, if you will. Your cracker gift related to your darts hobby, simply reflecting your interests. The same went for me, as I'm obviously nice—'

Riga's little laugh morphed into a cough.

'—and I got the reward of a Vivienne Westwood keyring. George got his train, Henry his coin, Mara a gold Oscar decoration because she loves acting, and so on. The people who were targeted received presents that alluded to their suggested misdeeds.'

'Take us through them,' Sean said.

'Thank you, darling, I shall. Robert Cole-Mortelli was given a wooden screwdriver, most likely made of birch, to tie in with his associations with a dodgy company – Birch. But that didn't seem enough. I kept reading his riddle – the one based on Krampus – and, aside from the capitalised "Birch", the line that stood out was its rhyme: "do your research". And where do most people do their research?'

'The internet!' Celine said.

'True,' Edie replied. 'But I was thinking more of the original depositories of knowledge, and pornography.'

'Libraries,' Mara shouted, then watched, fascinated, as Edie strode across the lounge and over to the library where, flipping her keyring up, she used a key to open the library door.

'Where did you get that?' Mara asked.

'Exactly where you showed me,' Edie called back. 'From your office, in the dartboard cabinet.'

Moving into the library, Edie grabbed a bunch of the box files from the shelf and, in doing so, knocked over a pile of books.

'Don't worry,' she said, 'nothing's broken. Just a Dickens novel hitting the floor.' She brought the files over to the group. 'I noticed these during last night's ghost story since they felt incongruous in a Victorian-style study. Then when I was told to do my research, I did.'

Edie handed one file to Mara, another to George, the third to Izzie, the fourth to Kimberley. 'Our killer is an extremely good researcher themselves. They have done more than a deep dive on their targets; they have done a

Mariana Trench descent to uncover the depredations of the first four victims.' She turned to Mara. 'If you'd open your file, please, Mara, and read the top sheet.'

Mara opened it and, after flicking through a hefty stack of financial records, arrest warrants, witness statements and other documents, read the summation sheet lying on the top. She had to take a breath and compose herself to make sure she didn't cry when she read it out loud: 'Mr Robert Barnes Cole-Mortelli raped a sixteen-year-old child, Dana Birch, who was a part-time holiday cleaner at one of his investor hotels.'

Celine covered her face. 'That's awful.'

'In her report to the police,' Mara continued, 'Miss Birch detailed the attack, including the cherry Schnapps on his breath. A witness in the hotel, who heard screams coming from his hotel room and knocked on the door only to be told to "mind your own business", redacted his statement after a large sum of money was transferred into his account by a company traced back to Cole-Mortelli. Miss Birch,' Mara stumbled, the catch in her throat becoming a lock, 'died by apparent suicide before the case could come to trial, yet the circumstances of her death remain suspicious. Thirty-two further reports of sexual assault, harassment and rape have been made against Cole-Mortelli by girls of between fourteen and seventeen. As yet, none has gone to trial.'

Edie placed her hands on her hips, surveying each of the assembled group. 'I haven't been through all the documents in these files, as I only managed to pop into the library and have a look while Mara was looking after Riga—'

'Oi!' Mara said.

Edie shrugged. 'But the evidence is damning. Witnesses have been paid off, victims made to sign NDAs. Now, of course, he is dead, and will never face trial. But would he ever have anyway?' She left a pause, then said, 'George, would you read the top statement in your file, please?'

'Lucy Emma Palmer,' George read out, 'is an investor-owner of several clothing factories in Changshu, Jiangsu Province in China, where forced labour of children is endemic. A typical fourteen-year-old employee works twenty-eight days a month, from 7.30am to 10pm, sometimes more, and is also forced to work overtime yet is paid a fraction of the salary of other workers. At least a third of the factories' employees are under sixteen, are beaten if judged to be misbehaving and only get paid at New Year. Children frequently become ill from cheap adhesives and fillers; one child died using old machinery, another by suicide. One child, called Xing, meaning "Star", simply didn't wake up, dying of exhaustion.'

'Lucy didn't know about any of that,' Henry said, his chin quivering. 'She'd never have allowed it.'

'Lucy Palmer was informed of these and other deaths,' George read, voice wavering, 'and, when asked whether new machinery or working conditions should be introduced, replied, "That's not necessary." Orders with her signature stated that she refused to comply with United Nations Sustainable Development Fund requirements and sought to keep global turnover below the threshold that, if exceeded, could bring inspection under the UK Modern Slavery Act. And they did *not* want that, as they'd fail.'

'I don't believe it,' Henry said, shaking his head. 'I *won't* believe it.'

'Perhaps you'll believe the victims of someone who *wasn't* your wife,' Edie said, nodding for Izzie to look inside her file.

'It's going to be Owain, isn't it?' Izzie said as she lifted the lid.

'And remember,' Edie said, 'that Owain received a gold laptop decoration, and a Santa riddle that stated he was "named a dad with no known child" and left "cookie crumbs behind".'

'Owain John Spencer,' Izzie read out, 'has been found operating on sixteen internet forums and chatrooms specifically for children under the age of sixteen. With names such as "Daddy15" and "DAD"—' Izzie handed the box back to Edie. 'I can't do it.'

Edie continued with the summary. 'Spencer targets vulnerable young people, pretending to be their age and coercing them into sending pictures and videos. He then blackmails them into giving him money or explicit pictures, stealing credit card details from their family etc., with the threat of exposing screenshots of their chats and images to parents and friends. One of his victims, twelve-year-old Martin, killed himself as he couldn't bear the shame; several others have self-harmed, and many more require therapeutic help.'

'I knew he was a knob,' Swindon said, sounding stricken, 'but I couldn't imagine him doing anything like that.'

'Everyone's a closed file till you open them,' Edie said.

'I think I'd rather keep people shut,' Tarn said.

'I agree,' Ivan added.

'You would,' Felicity replied.

'And I've got the last file,' Kimberley said. 'Ryan. Here goes.' She read in her head first, then out loud. 'When he was nineteen, Ryan Drummond Dreith racially abused and cruelly beat a twelve-year-old boy called Dabeeb, which means "Door" in Urdu, into a coma. He and his friend covered Dabeeb with leaves and left him to die in a wood. If Dabeeb had been taken to a hospital, he maybe could have recovered from his injuries, but he wasn't found for two days. He never woke from his coma. His friend was coerced into not speaking to the police, but has since made a statement to an investigator.'

'Ryan was "Door Slammer" in the riddle,' George said. 'The killer clearly sees themselves as some kind of avenging angel, righting wrongs that will otherwise go unpunished, but they're still a murderer.'

'From their level of skill,' said Edie, 'I think they're either military or secret services trained – a chameleon, so possibly an agent. The word "agent" *was* used in one of the riddles. Plus, spies were mentioned on the trip over, and alluded to in the ghost story. If they're a *retired* agent, maybe they're putting their skills to what they see as better use.'

'It makes them complicated at the very least,' Riga said, sadly.

'They could be one of your relatives,' Felicity said.

'Or one of yours,' Riga replied, making Mara flinch. 'Because the adoption angle won't go away.'

'What do you think that's about, Edie?' Mara asked. 'The adoption stuff?'

Edie sighed. 'This is where it gets entangled and personal. If I'm right, the killer bonded with someone in this room over being adopted, and the idea of exposing deception, lies and generational familial trauma spiralled from that point. They brought everyone here for a reason, be they Nice or Naughty. But we won't know for sure until the murderer is confronted.' Edie walked around the circle, staring everyone in the eyes, deep-diving into their beings.

Suddenly she stopped, putting her hand to her ear. 'And now I've got my final piece of evidence, we can ask the murderer themselves.'

The sound of squeaky wheels rattling across parquet reverberated around the lounge.

'It's my dessert trolley!' Kimberley said.

'What's the evidence?' Izzie asked. 'Kimberley's Black Forest gateau?'

Mara laughed, glad for a release of the tension that had been rising inside her, then stopped when she saw Sean solemnly pushing the large trolley towards them. A pair of handcuffs hung from his wrist. A white sheet covered the trolley's body-shaped cargo.

Unease spread through the room. Flashing back to Ryan's corpse under the tarpaulin, Mara's chest restricted. What, or who, was beneath the sheet?

Edie went over to the trolley. 'Beneath this sheet lies something that may disturb some – well, most of you. As if what we've experienced already today wasn't traumatic enough.'

'Are you sure you want to do this?' Sean asked her.

They huddled together for a moment. Mara had to lean forwards to hear.

'I think we have to. Somebody here has the answer.' Edie turned back to the group. 'I realised something about poor Anna's death. I wonder if anyone else can spot it.'

She ripped away the sheet, revealing Anna's body. Lifeless on the silver trolley, as if it were a gurney and not meant for desserts. She was a life-size doll in the murderer's dollhouse.

A wave of bile burned Mara's throat. 'This isn't right.'

Celine leapt up, backing towards the wall. 'What are you doing? This is disgusting.'

'Come on, now,' Swindon said. 'This isn't a freak show. We're not here for a lecture, to learn from a poor young woman's death. Let me take her back to the cold room.'

Sean shook his head. 'No one move.'

'I don't think she'd like it,' George said. 'It's not respectful. We must give her some dignity.'

Mara couldn't look at Anna, not directly. Anna had been so vibrant when she was alive, that, even now, glancing at her was like looking at the sun: Mara didn't want the image of Anna, dead, scorched into her brain.

'We *should* learn from her, though,' Edie said. 'From her death, we can make sense of the murderer's actions.'

'What do you mean?' Kimberley asked.

'Before she died, Anna gave me the missing part of the picture. When I was reading out Riga's confession earlier, I was pleading to the murderer as if they were one of the Christmas visitors. Sending Santa my Christmas list of saving Riga and seeing my grandkids. I hoped I was on the nice list, so my request would be granted, and then I remembered something.'

Tension winched up in the room.

'Poor Anna,' Edie said, 'on the boat over, said that she'd never put someone on *her* list without good cause.'

Mara remembered Anna saying something similar when they'd first met. She'd been in awe of Anna's gawky elegance, enthusiasm and cheekbones, and now she was too afraid to look at her. Everyone else was the same, staring anywhere other than at Anna.

'*Her* list was an aggregate of hotels for beautiful romantic breaks, nothing to do with human behaviour, but as I was effectively praying to a non-existent man in a red snowsuit, I remembered that the brand who made our bespoke crackers was called "The Naughty and Nice List". And then, of course, everything fell into place.'

From the confused looks on the others' faces, however, they were as behind as Mara.

'How did Anna describe her new venture when we first met?' Edie explained. '"An aggregate of destination romantic breaks. Boutique places that are both saucy and luxury." What phrase would be a great way to sum that up?'

'The Naughty and Nice List,' Tarn said, looking shocked.

'Exactly,' Edie said triumphantly, beaming as if everything now was clear and she was not standing next to a corpse on Christmas Day.

'They're still not following.' Riga's eyes were shut, her skin sallow despite the firelight. Sadness soaked her voice.

'You're standing in front of a murdered young woman,

boasting that you've thought of a name for a company she'll never now be able to open?' Henry said. 'You are sick.'

'No,' Edie said, turning on him. '*Riga* is sick, and I want the antidote, so I will use whatever I can to get it. And this woman was *not* murdered.'

'She . . . killed herself?'

'Yes,' Edie said, simply.

George stuttered, choking up. 'B-but why?'

'Oh, no,' Celine said. 'You're saying *Anna* was the murderer?'

'Yes. Anna murdered Robert, Lucy and Owain, poisoned Ivan and Riga, then killed herself.'

'Then how is she going to help you get the antidote for Riga? Does she have it on her body?'

'I hope so,' Edie said.

'How can you be so blasé?' Kimberley asked, her lips curling. 'I thought you were a good person.'

'Oh, I am,' Edie said. 'And, at the same time, I'm not. Which is why I'm going to frisk a corpse for anti-poison and think nothing of it.'

'Don't you dare,' Swindon shouted.

'I admire you for standing up for your granddaughter, Swindon,' said Edie. 'I'd do the same.'

Mara's world was tipping. 'I don't understand.'

'It's true,' Swindon said. 'Anna *was* my granddaughter. She was adopted, like me, and we only found each other recently. She told me about the caretaker job because she needed me here to prepare for her arrival. To put the dolls in the tableaux as a warning to Mara; to set up listening devices in every room so she knew what everyone was saying.'

'So she'd know when we were sleeping, or awake,' Mara whispered, feeling sick.

'And how to move around the castle unnoticed,' Swindon continued. 'She had an earpiece fitted that couldn't be seen.'

Mara again felt like a doll in an oversized house. All this was too big for her.

'I have lots of questions for you, Swindon, but now, I need the antidote.' Edie's tone was crisp and even.

'If anyone is going to search for it, it'll be me, with respect, and love.' Swindon was tearing up. He suddenly looked much older. 'But not while you're all gawking. I'll take her back to the cold room, and search there.'

'No,' stated Sean. 'Stay where you are.'

'Let her have that dignity,' Mara said. 'How can you be so cruel?'

'Not cruel, pragmatic,' Edie replied. 'Because I know that otherwise he'll escape with her.'

'With her body?!' George asked, horrified.

'Well, yes, I suppose so. Although she'll be there for the ride,' Edie replied.

Mara looked at Anna properly then, realisation dawning. 'You mean she's—'

'She's alive!' Anna said, sitting up on the trolley.

Thirty-Four

The room erupted. 'What is happening?' Mara cried. Nothing made sense to her.

'Thank fuck for that,' Anna said, taking a massive breath. 'I thought my lungs were going to explode. Or implode. It's very hard for me to keep still, you know. But it's easy to play dead.' She reached under her polo neck and plucked out a tennis ball. 'One of these squeezed under the armpit and you'll have no pulse in your wrist.'

'And your neck?' Celine said.

'I took pills that, administered correctly, slow your heartbeat to as low as possible without you blacking out – one of the same drugs I used to attack Cole-Mortelli's dark heart. Plus, wearing turtlenecks makes it difficult to get purchase on a carotid artery.' Anna looked at Edie. 'How did you know I wasn't dead?'

'Once I realised you were the killer,' Edie explained, 'it didn't make sense that you'd unalive yourself. You were still on a mission. So, I looked in the cold room: you were surprisingly pink for a woman in pallor mortis.'

'Weren't you worried I'd run as soon as Sean came to get me?' Anna asked.

'I took the risk that you'd want your moment with

Riga,' Edie replied. 'The antidote, please, Miss Malone. Although that's probably not your real name. What *is* your family name?'

'Nice way to introduce the topic, Gamma Edie. Is it all right to call you that? Since you're practically married to my great-grandmother.' Anna jumped off the trolley and went over to Riga.

'Wait, what?' Mara said, trying to follow the chaos.

Crouching by the chair, Anna took Riga's hand and kissed it. And then Mara understood. Next to each other, the family resemblance between Riga and Anna was clear. High cheekbones, small bumps on their noses. Wide, sparkling eyes.

'When did you know?' Anna asked Riga.

'Since the rosary fell from the cracker,' Riga said, her words strung together in ragged bursts. 'It was the way you were watching me at the table.' She took the beads from her pocket and smelled them. 'I gave them to the orphanage to give to Swindon, not that I knew his name, or even his gender. They took him from me before I could even hold him.'

Swindon's head lowered, his shoulders shaking with the sobs he was clearly trying to sandbag inside himself.

'It also made sense of why Nicholas liked you and Swindon so much on the boat,' Riga continued. 'He must have smelled our genetic similarity. The "DNA strand" hint that Swindon gave me on the trip over.'

Edie made a face. 'I should've thought of that. Why didn't you tell me?'

'I also met Nicholas when I broke into your house one night,' Anna explained, 'to look through your papers.

Sorry.' Taking a pill bottle out of her pocket, she handed two to Riga. Standing up, she leaned over to the mantelpiece and withdrew a glass of black liquid from behind the carriage clock.

'Activated charcoal water?' Riga guessed, taking the glass and swigging down the two tablets.

'With marshmallow root and a few other herbs.'

'That's my girl,' Riga said softly. She held out her arms and they hugged, Anna's eyes closing.

Swindon wiped away a tear.

'What about Dad?' Mara asked, looking over at Ivan, who still had a grey pallor. 'Did you give him enough antidote?'

'No,' Anna said coolly. 'Because he hasn't owned up to the *worst* thing he did.'

'And what's that?' Mara asked.

'How about Ivan tells you privately?' Edie said. 'So that Mara doesn't have to hear it?'

'You guessed, then?' Anna said.

'Hard not to, with the riddles, the brush, and the pony and foal symbolism,' Edie replied, 'evoking grooming. All that, plus their overall weird family dynamic. And, yes, I *am* judging.'

'So am I,' Anna said. 'That's now my job. And it's *very* fulfilling. But it must be declared publicly to count. Darkest secrets, out in the fresh air at last. Open up that stale dolls' house.'

'Pudding,' Ivan said to Mara, wheezing a little. 'This is going to be very difficult to hear. We lied about how we came to adopt you.'

'Who lied?' Felicity asked.

He faltered. 'I did. *I* lied. To everyone.' He glanced over to Tarn, and away again. 'Tarn is actually your biological mother.'

Mara looked from Tarn to her mum, to her dad. Her face became slack. 'No,' was all she said out loud.

'I became pregnant at sixteen,' Tarn said, 'and didn't know what to do. Your father said he and Felicity would adopt you. They'd wanted another baby, but it wasn't happening.' She glanced at Mum, then away again.

Mum folded her arms tight around herself, as she should have done to her daughter.

'Is that the full story?' Mara said. 'Because something's telling me it isn't.'

A brief silence, then, 'When Tarn was fifteen, she was your brother's babysitter,' Mum said, hardly able to control the tremble in her voice. 'And she became close to the family.'

'Euphemisms can be terrible things,' Edie said.

'"Grooming",' Mara said, realising. 'Oh, Dad. You didn't. *Fifteen*? The fucking *babysitter*? You are *disgusting*.' Mara thought she was going to be sick.

'It wasn't like that, Mara,' Tarn said, coming over to Mara. 'It was a relationship. And it stopped, after you were born.'

'It's not your fault,' Mara said, holding Tarn, acting as a mother to her own mother. 'You were *fifteen*.'

'Can I have the rest of the antidote?' Ivan asked.

Anna said nothing as she handed him a pill. Her face said everything.

'What happened to *you* as a child?' Edie asked Anna, gently. 'To end up avenging unseen injustices to children?'

Swindon let out a sob that told a terrible tale.

'Enough to have to decide to do the right thing after I was done wrong,' Anna replied.

'But you killed people, darling,' Riga said. 'That *isn't* right.'

'The people I killed, unlawfully, on this island, committed crimes far worse than those I assassinated on the orders of the government.' Anna's lip curled. 'I was recruited to MI6—'

'While studying languages at Cambridge, like Oscar in the ghost story,' Edie interrupted. 'You've shown us you can speak French.'

'Well done, Gamma.' Anna smiled. 'Yes, I was trained to obtain information, manage and manipulate assets, charm and disarm and, yes, kill. Maybe if I'd had a more stable upbringing, not going from foster parent to foster parent to older, abusive boyfriends, I wouldn't have needed the validation it brought, but who knows? Maybe I just like killing. While I was working in Italy, using my travel agent cover story, I heard about Cole-Mortelli and others like him. If there is a hell, he'll burn as hot and bright as the first part of his name. He deserved an even worse death. Anyone who hurts children does. I'm glad I pushed Owain from the roof; that I suffocated Lucy. And more will follow. At last, I'm putting my skills to good use.'

'What do you mean "putting"?' Edie said, looking concerned for the first time since she'd entered the lounge. 'Your killing days are over.'

'I have a team of experts in IT, logistics and pharmaceuticals, as well as disaffected secret services colleagues, ready to help me punish those who hurt children. They're my elves, my Yule Lads and Lasses. One of them made sure that you, Felicity, would be at the craft fair on Mull by making it seem bougie at your book group; another posed as the cracker maker behind the stall and persuaded you to buy them. Others infiltrated the recruitment agencies hiring the staff, convincing some not to come. We're already working on next year's plans. Please let the world know that the Naughty and Nice List, available on all good dark webs, will get rid of the ghosts that haunt you, and reward those who deserve it.'

'Why should we help you?' Celine, crying, was unable to look at her.

'I know I've hurt you, Celine,' Anna said, softly. 'And I'm so sorry. I used you and Mara for my own ends, but the friendship is real. You're both amazing, and I love you and want you to thrive.'

'You lied,' is all Celine replied.

For the first time, Mara caught a flicker of remorse on Anna's face.

'I did lie, you're right,' Anna said. 'And I will again. I hope you'll all forgive me, and that we'll meet again.' She nodded then to Swindon.

Sean moved towards her, handcuffs outstretched. 'Anna Malone, I'm arresting you for—'

The lights snapped off and all was dark.

'Stay where you are,' Sean yelled.

A head-splitting crack echoed through the lounge and lobby. The smell of silver fulminate choked the air.

Chaos descended as someone screamed and everyone started moving at once.

'Everybody keep still and remain calm,' Mara shouted as she felt her way to the control panel on the wall to turn the lights back on. For the first time in her life, she wasn't afraid.

As the smoke cleared, Mara scanned the lobby. Guests and staff were milling about, confused, but two of them were missing.

'We need to search the island,' Sean said. 'Anna and Swindon have gone.'

Thirty-Five

'She must have been carrying the fulminate with her, in case she needed it,' Edie said. 'I have to applaud her commitment to the cracker theme.' She wasn't sure what she was feeling: admiration? Envy? Both?

'Mum and Dad,' Mara said, not looking at either of them, 'go to your cottage, look there and in the outbuildings; I'll search the house with Tarn, Kimberley, Izzie and Henry.' She seemed a changed woman to the one Edie had met only a day ago. Her eyes were clear and focused on what she had to do, not following her parents round the room. 'Tarn, you and I will take the top two floors; Henry, you search down here; Kimberley and Izzie, search the first floor and the roof terrace.' She strode towards the stairs, then stopped, looking over to the lift.

Tarn raised her eyebrows. 'Really?'

'It's not courage if you're not afraid,' Mara said, and, going over, pressed the up button.

'George,' Edie said, grabbing his shoulders to try and bring his shock into focus, 'search the grounds at the back of the house, and as far as you can into the holly forest; Sean and I will take the front and the coastline.'

With a Clark tartan blanket wrapped around her over

her coat, Edie walked through the revolving door into the snow. The sky was streaked with dusk, whisky-orange against dark clouds.

Sean was at her side, holding her arm. 'We're going to the boathouse first, right?'

'Absolutely,' Edie replied, blinking away snowflakes. 'I'm assuming that either Swindon was lying about there not being another boat, or his was never broken.'

When they got to the path, boot prints heading to the harbour told them they were right. But there was only one set.

'They've split up,' Edie said. 'Very wise.'

'You sound approving,' Sean said. *He* did not.

'Anna is a woman of drive and action trying to do a warped kind of good. But I *don't* approve.'

As they approached the gate at the end of the front lawn, the harbour became visible. Swindon was on the boat, throwing off the ropes. The engine was already running.

'Swindon Marr,' Sean shouted as he burst into a run. 'Stop now, and it may mitigate your sentence of aiding and abetting.'

Edie slowed, unsteady on the ice. If she fell, she might never get up.

'I can't go to prison,' Swindon yelled back, his cape billowing. 'I won't be attached to four walls.' He disappeared into the cockpit, and the sound of the engine shifted.

Sean was now on the harbour wall, running at the speed of Edie's heart. She imagined him slipping, falling into the sea and whatever waited within it.

'Be careful,' she shouted.

276

The boat roared and, still for a moment, it then lurched forwards, sending waves gossiping away.

'This is a final warning,' Sean yelled, only metres away from the boat, the sea churning between them. He looked down, as if thinking of jumping in and swimming after Swindon.

Another motor rumbled, answering the call of the boat. To Edie's right, a speedboat zoomed out from the red-faced bay, plotting a course out to sea. A dark shape was at the helm – Anna, Edie presumed. The silhouette waved, but Edie couldn't tell whether it was to Swindon, Sean, her or the unholy island that they were leaving behind.

Hours later, in Aster Castle, the cursed hotel of the dead, Edie sat in the lobby, having the strangest Christmas dinner of her life.

Candles flickered, holding back the dark. She, Riga, Sean, Mara, Celine, Tarn, Kimberley, Izzie, George and Henry were sitting around the big farmhouse table that had been carried from the kitchen, sharing a feast of roast salmon, roast turkey, nut roast, an allotment of tatties and all the fucking trimmings. Moving anything required a complicated tessellation of platters of spiced red cabbage, roasted sprouts, neeps, parsnips, cheesy leeks, macaroni cheese, green beans, broccoli, cauliflower and peas, as well as ramekins of mustard, pickles and cranberry sauce and, of course, gravy boats.

Edie hadn't eaten so well in years. Detection and death

built up a storming appetite. Mara, though, was hardly eating, pushing mashed neeps around her plate.

'How are you feeling?' Edie asked her.

'I'm not sure. It's complicated,' Mara said. 'I don't want Mum and Dad here.' She glanced at Tarn. 'But I keep thinking of them in the cottage, alone together.'

'That's a good way to put it,' George said thoughtfully. '"Alone together." If I were with someone I loved, I'd want to be in company together.'

'Let's stop faffing, shall we?' Edie said. 'You and Mara are both sweet and strong and fragile people, who could make each other's lives brighter. You like each other, that's clear as pure ice. So, get on with it and get it on, would you?'

Celine tapped her thumb and ring finger together and smiled for the first time in hours. 'Edie O'Sullivan,' she said, 'you bring back the sun in dark times.'

'You know,' George said to Mara, 'I don't feel as nervous around you as I usually do around people.'

'Um, okay?' Mara said.

'No, that's a good thing.' George reached for her hand. 'I tend to laugh when I'm anxious or when I don't know what to do or say. With you I feel calm. Happy. Me.'

Mara held his hand. 'You make me feel the same.'

'That's settled, then,' Edie said. 'Thank goodness. There's plenty of time to ghost when you're dead – put your hearts in each other's jars. But no heavy petting at the Christmas table, get a suite.'

'What are you going to do with the hotel?' Kimberley asked Mara. 'And I'm not asking because I want a permanent job, as there's no way I'm staying here.'

Mara speared a piece of turkey and dipped it in cranberry sauce. 'I'm going to sell up, if anyone wants a notorious dark tourism destination. Give a chunk of money to charities that fight child exploitation and then—' She stopped talking, digging in her pocket for something. She pulled out her little doll and held it up. 'This was on my pillow when I got changed for dinner. Swindon or Anna must have left it there.' The doll held a tiny Oscar statuette in one hand. 'Anna and my mini-me reminded me to find out what I really want, for Christmas and for always. So, I'm going back to theatre school.'

George cheered and Tarn grinned. 'I'm so glad,' Tarn said. 'I thought you never should have left.'

'And you?' Mara asked her biological mother. 'What are you going to do? Tell me you're not going to work for Felicity and Ivan still?'

Tarn took a deep breath. 'I don't know who I am without them. But it's time to find out.'

'That sounds wise,' Izzie said. 'I'm going to stay with my mum for a while. I always blamed her for moving away from Ryan. But I understand now.'

So many family issues around one table. Everyone had shattered baubles in their attics. Trauma was passed between generations like condiments across a festive table, but here, in this moment, the past and present weren't overshadowing the future. Everyone was looking to what was yet to come. And Edie should, too.

Her heart was as full as her stomach as she leaned over and whispered in Riga's ear. 'Will you marry me?'

Riga smiled. 'I will.'

'What's that sound?' Sean asked, jumping up.

As he opened the access door and sprinted into the snow, the whirring of a helicopter blasted through the lobby. Its lights shone through the skylight.

Sean ran back in. 'It's a police helicopter! We're rescued!'

'Anna must have called them,' Riga said with a slight smile.

Edie wrapped her arms around Riga, the best present she could wish for. 'I've got everything I want for Christmas: you safe and well, and now we'll be able to see the kids. Maybe Santa isn't such a carbuncle, after all.'

Epilogue

January 6th

It was Twelfth Night, and La Befana was coming again to Weymouth town. Anna Malone emerged from Riga's shed, stretching her legs. Since her great-grandmother's bedroom light had gone off, ninety minutes ago, she'd been sitting cross-legged on a sack of logs, polishing garden tools. Now, though, it was time.

Riga's conservatory was even more full of plants than the last time Anna had visited, in secret, months ago. Fairy lights, still on despite it being one in the morning, trellised the room. Maybe aspidistras and orchids were scared of the dark; maybe they just loved Christmas.

Taking out her lock-picking kit, Anna inhaled deeply, trying to calm herself. The adrenaline was real enough, though. Her pulse never went over sixty BPM when she killed, yet now, just picking the conservatory lock, her heart was beating as fast as the flashing fairy lights.

Lock dispatched, Anna stepped inside as easily as she had the last time, when she had searched the attic and found the letter. *You really need to up your security, Nana.*

A snuffling came from behind one of the plant pots

and Nicholas trotted out, panting. His little peeking tongue was poinsettia red and just as tasteful.

'And you're not much of a guard dog, matey.' Anna crouched and held out her hand for sniffing. 'Although I suppose bribing you the first time helped.' Nicholas licked Anna's palm, his tiny tail whipping left and right. He sniffed her tote bag with interest.

I need to be quick, Anna thought, walking through the kitchen into the hall. She stopped, though, as she passed the living room. Silhouetted against the dark red curtains was Riga's Christmas tree. It was squat and potted, a little lopsided, and wearing a lot of silver lamé strands. Right in the middle, hung on a branch, were the rosary beads.

At the top of the stairs, Anna placed her hand on the armrest of the chair lift, waiting for Nicholas to catch up. Soft snores called from down the hall. A night light showed Riga on the left of the bed, covered in blankets; Edie on the right, surrounded by cats. Riga's walking sticks leant against the wall like bald brooms.

Worries about Riga flared like coals in a fire. How many more days did she have till her nights were all silent? They'd only just got to know each other, and it wasn't as if Anna could move in with her great-grandmother. Edie, her son and the entire legal system would have something to say about that. For now, though, it was enough to show Riga that she was in Anna's thoughts.

Bending down, Anna carefully took one of the gifts from her bag and placed it in one Riga's slippers, then froze. Something was already tucked inside. A miniature

Befana cake was wrapped in a note, in Riga's scratchy writing:

I knew you'd come, little one. Naughty or Nice, you are loved.

Anna tucked the note in her pocket, trying not to cry.

Slippers placed back under the bed, now containing salted caramel truffles (and a chocolate orange in Edie's shoes, too) and a little card with her own message of love, Anna watched over the two wonderful old women, now fiancées, for a moment, then turned away. She must leave them to their snores and their love, for now. She had the darkest deeds to commit for the lightest reason: there was so much evil under the sun, and she was the shadow. But she knew she'd be back here, before it was too late.

As she crept back out of the house, Anna looked up to the star-scattered sky, praying it would look over Riga and Edie while she couldn't. May they sleep with heavenly peace and wake afresh; may their nights not be truly silent for a long time to come.

Acknowledgements

Thank you as ever to my utterly wonderful agent, Diana Beaumont; the glorious editorial team of Katherine Armstrong and Georgie Leighton (love you both so much); to lovely Laurie McShea in Publicity and the exceptional Rich Vlietstra in Marketing; to Karin Seifried in Production; India Minter in Design; Olivia Allen, Madeline Allan, Rich Hawton, Jonny Kennedy and Nicholas Hayne in Sales; Amy Fletcher and Ben Phillips in Rights; proofreader Charley Chapman; freelance editor Emma Capron; Alice Twomey in Audio; and countless others in these teams, Operations, Finance and Contracts. I am so very lucky to be part of the Simon & Schuster UK family – and am so grateful for your expertise, kindness and commitment. Thank you, too, to the publishers of my books in other territories – you're fantastic.

Hugest of thanks to my husband, Guy – you are everything, and I couldn't do this without your love and support; Verity, the very best Pickle in the universe; Di and Antonio for Pickle wrangling, garden whispering and general brilliance; Mum and Dad for all your support; Lin and John; David, Sofia and Carolina; my whole family; Roz; Karen and family; Michelle, Lou, Steve,

Kirsty, Caroline, Nigel, Sam and all at Supper Club – I toot and salute you on my mini harmonica; Steph and Susi; Colin Scott; Judith; Lou L; Angie; Barny; Charlotte and Kit; Laura, Paul and Aby; Emma O'Leary and Andy Duckmanton for sorting my writer's back/shoulders; The Unthanks and Douglas Pipes whose *In Winter* album and Krampus soundtrack accompanied my tapping; Colin Scott; my mentees; Flow Club; Write Magic; Forest at Nui Cobalt; Black Phoenix Alchemy Lab; Guy at Marjacq; Emily Hayward-Whitlock; PATCH; Roland in Waterstones Eastbourne and Nicola in Waterstones Bluewater; all booksellers, bloggers, vloggers, librarians and readers.

May you all have a cracking Christmas!

Alexandra
xxx

Ice-breakers!

Questions to ask over Christmas dinner, if you dare . . .

1. If you were to murder someone, who would it be?
2. Would you make a good MI6 agent?
3. If you could choose a location where you thought you might be able to murder people and get away with it, where would it be?
4. Give three reasons why you should be on the Naughty List.
5. Give three reasons why you should be on the Nice List.
6. What's the worst present you were ever given for Christmas?
7. What's the best present you were ever given for Christmas?
8. Excluding your own, if applicable, biological or not, who would you have liked to have as your parents?
9. What celebrity would you like to adopt? And why do you think you would be good as their parent?
10. What's the worst thing you've ever done?

Answers to Games 2 to 5

Game 2

Edie's favourite punk songs:

1. 'Kimberly', Patti Smith – p. 35
2. 'Liar', The Damned – p. 3
3. 'Ether', Gang of Four – p. 33
4. 'Pretty Vacant', Sex Pistols – p. 19
5. 'Vindictive', The Slits – p. 33
6. 'Nostalgia', Buzzcocks – p. 62
7. 'Career Opportunities', The Clash – p. 203
8. 'Jigsaw Feeling', Siouxsie and the Banshees – p. 175
9. 'Warrior in Woolworths', X-Ray Spex – p. 98
10. 'See No Evil', Television – p. 170

Game 3

Anagrams of Christmas films:

1. *It's a Wonderful Life* – 'a fortune. Wildlife's', p. 54

2. *Arthur Christmas* – '**armchair thrusts**', p. 79
3. *Santa Claus: The Movie* – '**a seventh: calamitous**', p. 232
4. *White Christmas* – '**theatrics, whims**', p. 186
5. *Scrooged* – '**codger so**', p. 24
6. *Violent Night* – '**novel hitting**', p. 256
7. *Last Christmas* – '**starlit chasms**', p. 228
8. *The Holdovers* – '**sloth, hovered**', p. 223
9. *Bad Santa* – '**and a stab**', p. 15
10. *The Polar Express* – '**relax, prophetess**', p. 93

Game 4

Books and films set in hotels:

1. **White Christmas** (1954, dir. Michael Curtiz) – p. 5
2. **The Lobster** (2015, dir. Yorgos Lanthimos) – p. 21
3. **The Shining** (1977, Stephen King; 1980, dir. Stanley Kubrick) – p. 213
4. **A Room with a View** (1908, E. M. Forster; 1985, dir. James Ivory) – p. 71
5. **Grand Hotel** (1932, dir. Edmund Goulding) – p. 104
6. **The Silence** (1963, dir. Ingmar Bergman) – p. 127
7. **Death in Venice** (1912, Thomas Mann; 1971, dir. Luchino Visconti) – p. 26
8. **Jamaica Inn** (1936, Daphne du Maurier; 1939, dir. Alfred Hitchcock) – p. 26
9. **Evil Under the Sun** (1941, Agatha Christie; 1982, dir. Guy Hamilton) – p. 283

10. *Dance Dance Dance* (1988, Haruki Murakami) –
    p. 139

Game 5

Ghost Stories for Christmas:

1. *The Ash Tree* (1975, dir. Lawrence Gordon Clark; based on 'The Ash-tree' by M. R. James) – p. 84
2. *Whistle and I'll Come to You* (2010, dir. Andy de Emmony; based on 'Oh, Whistle, and I'll Come to You, My Lad' by M. R. James) – p. 72
3. *The Signalman* (1976, dir. Lawrence Gordon Clark; based on 'The Signal-Man' by Charles Dickens) – p. 23
4. *A Warning to the Curious* (1972, dir. Lawrence Gordon Clark; based on 'A Warning to the Curious' by M. R. James) – p. 114
5. *Lost Hearts* (1973, dir. Lawrence Gordon Clark; based on 'Lost Hearts' by M. R. James) – p. 180
6. *Stigma* (1977, dir. Lawrence Gordon Clark) – p. 190
7. *The Ice House* (1978, dir. Derek Lister) – p. 203
8. *The Dead Room* (2018, dir. Mark Gatiss) – p. 159
9. *Woman of Stone* (2024, dir. Mark Gatiss; based on 'Man-Size in Marble' by Edith Nesbit) – p. 41
10. *Number 13* (2006, dir. Pier Wilkie; based on 'Number 13' by M. R. James) – p. 112